A Cure for Deceit

by

Margie Miklas

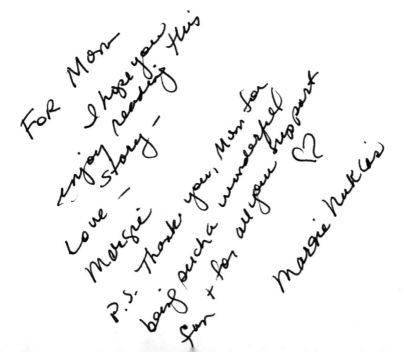

For Mom —
I hope you
enjoy reading this
story —
Love —
Margie

P.S. Thank you, Mom for
being such a wonderful
for + for all your support ♡

Margie Miklas

Praise for *A Cure for Deceit* by Margie Miklas

"A saga of medical intrigue that had me deeply engaged from page one. Margie Miklas has the uncanny ability to put you in the "skin" of the main characters."
~ Paula Vetter RN, MSN, FNP

"Miklas proves her explicit knowledge of the inner workings of the hospital and the nurses and doctors behind the scenes. Well described and realistic...*A Cure for Deceit* will excite and entertain Miklas' fans."
~ Catie Costa, Author of *Love on the Rocks: A Positano Tale*

"Miklas pulls the reader in with her inside knowledge of hospitals, healthcare administration, and the power of teamwork in this delightful read. I loved this book."
~ Tina Clark ARNP

"Ms. Miklas has a knack for drawing the reader in with the first page! Suspense, life and death hospital drama, extortion, new takes on the battle between good and evil...I truly loved the book!"
~ Raleigh McDonald Hussung Italophile, @lovefromitalia

"A suspenseful thriller that kept me on the edge of my seat. As a CVICU nurse practitioner I was impressed with the accurate portrayal of the hospital setting, making the story even more enjoyable. I couldn't wait to finish the book."
~ Melonie Durkin APRN, MSN

"A real page turner...with major twists and turns. Between episodes of terror and love, this is an engaging, do-not-miss novel. You won't want to miss a word!"
~ Stephanie Alessandrini, Director of South Forty Ltd

Dedicated to the medical professionals

who focus on doing the right thing

every single day

A Cure for Deceit

A Medical Thriller

~ Chapter 1 ~

Two hours post-op, the bleeding had not slowed down. Allison Jamison's fears intensified as her open-heart patient's crimson chest tube drainage flowed in one continuous stream. Experience told her this could be fixed only one way. She grabbed her cell phone and texted Dr. Gary Tamarino. "Urgent. You need to come back in. Bleeding escalated to 600 cc this hour. Coag results normal. On 3rd unit blood."

Confident the surgeon trusted her judgment, she knew he would make the right decision.

Allison could barely keep up with replacing the lost blood. Ten minutes shot by with no response. She fumed, worried her patient's vital signs would deteriorate enough to force a Code Red situation. Her heart raced, and the sounds in her head pounded like an approaching locomotive. *Where is Tamarino? He should have replied by now. Damn.* She called his cell, relieved when he answered.

"Dr. Tamarino, did you get my text? The bleeding has gotten worse, and I can't keep up with products. When are you coming in?" Her frenzied voice revealed a level of concern impossible to misconstrue.

In a matter-of-fact tone, he said, "You read my mind, Allison. I knew she was a little juicy when we finished

1

the case, but I thought the bleeding would slow down. I'm on my way. Call in the OR team."

Thank God, Allison thought. *I need to keep her alive for another thirty minutes.* The working relationship between the seasoned CSU nurses at San Francisco Bay Hospital and the cardiothoracic surgeons is what made this whole situation work. She knew he believed her when she described the circumstance as critical. But make no mistake; this met the criteria for high stress.

Reassured, the proficient critical care RN called out to her charge nurse. "Rosa, Tamarino's on his way in. He wants the team called in. My patient needs to go back for bleeding. Can you make sure the blood bank has four units on hold?"

"I'm on it." Within two minutes, the efficient Rosa Perez had activated the on-call cardiac surgical team and ordered the blood. "Everyone's been called and responded. What else do you need?"

"There's another unit of blood in that cooler. Can you hang it for me? She's bleeding faster than I can pump this in." Allison worked at a fever pitch to maintain a minimal adequate blood pressure on her sixty-year-old female patient. "Make sure her family is still in the waiting room, so Tamarino can talk to them when he gets here. Thanks."

Suddenly, a shrill overhead announcement sounded and interrupted their concentration. "Code Silver Emergency Room. Code Silver Emergency Room." The two nurses stopped dead in their tracks.

"What the fuck?" Rosa shouted. "A shooter in the building? God help us."

~ **Chapter 2** ~

Stay cool, Allison. Don't panic. She couldn't afford to allow the peaked stress levels to interfere with her efforts to save this patient's life. All her thoughts focused on keeping Mrs. Brock alive right now.

"Shit. This means another delay before we can get her into surgery," Rosa announced. Hospital protocol dictated all perimeter doors to be secured during a silver alert. No one was allowed to enter or exit the building until the all-clear sounded. "Everyone, be on alert. You know the procedure," Rosa said. Then she directed another nurse to go to the blood bank. "Bring the remainder of the blood on hold for Mrs. Brock in Room 3, and tell them to set up four more units too. She is going back to surgery ASAP."

Allison heard the command and hoped to God she could maintain Mrs. Brock's vital signs with intravenous emergency drugs and blood products until Tamarino could get inside the hospital. The clock was ticking. The heightened tension levels stimulated the adrenaline flow Allison needed to keep going. The code cart appeared in her room, thanks to Rosa, who also instructed someone to bring in the open chest procedure cart, in case Dr. Tamarino would be forced to open the patient's chest at the bedside as an emergency.

Despite the expected heightened state of anxiety due to the Code Silver, the professional nursing staff involved worked together to accomplish the required tasks, without stopping to worry too much about the active shooter somewhere in the building.

Thirty minutes later, though it seemed like an eternity, the hospital operator issued the all-clear. The CSU nurses relaxed a bit, but no surgeon had materialized.

"What is taking him so long? Tamarino should have been here by now," Allison spouted in frustration. Two minutes later, the fatigued, forty-five-year-old chief of cardiothoracic surgery, dressed in teal scrubs and brown loafers with no socks, appeared at Mrs. Brock's bedside. *Lucky for him he's good-looking*, Allison thought.

"Of all the times to have a lockdown." Dr. Tamarino viewed the patient's cardiac monitor and then glanced down at the almost-full chest tube collection device. "Still bleeding, I see. She needs surgery. Good call, Allison," he said, laying on the charm and showing no outward signs of angst.

"I've been hanging blood ever since I spoke to you. I'm glad you're here," a thankful Allison replied. "Did you have to wait until they announced the all-clear to get in?" Without uttering another word, Dr. GQ left the room and headed to the family waiting room before going to the operating suite. The surgical team appeared at the bedside, and they assisted with last-minute procedures to bring the patient back to the operating room. Still anesthetized from the original surgery, Mrs. Brock required no additional pre-op medications, and the surgical staff wasted no time as they wheeled the patient on her hospital bed back to the OR. A frustrated but grateful Allison hoped Dr. Tamarino would find and fix the source of the bleeding.

Satisfied that she'd delivered her patient to a competent team, the thirty-eight-year-old assertive and well-liked critical care nurse thanked her coworkers for being there for her during the crisis. "You guys are great. I don't know what I would have done without all your help. Thanks, everyone."

"That's why we're the best frickin' unit in this hospital," Rosa said, beaming with pride. "We help each other and we're a team." For the past two years, the petite, dark-haired, thirty-something single mother had been a CSU charge nurse on the 7 p.m. to 7 a.m. shift. Most of the staff were travel nurses with years of cardiovascular critical care experience, and they respected Rosa for her expertise and calm demeanor. Not much ruffled her feathers. Camaraderie among the CSU nurses prevailed, as many had worked in this unit for a long time, renewing their travel contracts over and over. "Thank God that lockdown is over. I heard the ER cops got the guy before he could harm anyone."

Curiosity promoted questions from the nurses. "Did you hear anything more about the shooter or his motive?" one of them asked.

Rosa replied, "It's just hearsay, nothing confirmed, but the nursing supervisor mentioned something about a disgruntled pharmacy employee. The word is he was forced to resign a few days ago for stealing drugs. He showed up in his lab coat with a gun, and an ER nurse recognized him. The on-duty police officers were able to subdue him just in time. The entire situation could have been much worse. Allison, you've been going nonstop for close to three hours. Take a break, and then you can catch up on your charting in time to readmit your patient," Rosa added with a smile.

The never-ending documentation – in triplicate sometimes, Allison mused. She remembered what a challenge the computer charting had created for her two years before, when she first started in critical care. It seemed like a lifetime ago, and now she managed to complete everything on all the necessary screens with efficiency. "Yes, I can use some time to chill. With luck, Tamarino will fix everything, and my patient will be stable the rest of the night," Allison said. She knew she had at least an hour, and probably more, before her patient would return. Dr. Tamarino's ability to solve problems in the operating room compensated for his cavalier attitude and lack of punctuality at times. No wonder his patients referred to him as a god. Most of the nurses did too.

I need coffee. Allison headed toward the nurses' lounge, where she found Rosa, who had just poured a cup of java for herself. "That's the third takeback we've had in the last week, and they've all been Tamarino's patients," Rosa said. She paused and waited for a reaction from Allison. "What do you make of that?"

"I don't know. Maybe the patients were high-risk. But it does seem strange, doesn't it? Nothing about this lady sent up any red flags. Other than her heart disease, she exhibited healthy past medical history. Haven't Tamarino's stats always been the best?"

"Yeah, they were, but not anymore." The RNs stared at each other in silence.

~ Chapter 3 ~

Annette Brashton had already scrubbed in and waited for Dr. Tamarino to walk through the door into the operating room. Anesthetized and on the table, the draped patient occupied center stage. Sounds of Tamarino's favorite nineties music filled the air, and Annette hummed along to Hadaway's catchy "What is Love?"

More than familiar with emergency takeback situations, the knowledgeable and skilled nurse practitioner understood this surgeon's specific preferences and personality. Her daily experiences, side by side with Tamarino and his partner in the operating room, taught her the nuanced lessons unavailable in books.

Beneath the bulky, nondescript surgical gown, the striking, physically fit, tall, forty-year-old woman owned a strong sense of self. A true professional and extremely skilled in her cardiovascular specialty, Annette not only provided a stable balance but presented an even match for the narcissistic surgeon's unpredictable, explosive temperament. It was all part of her job as a cardiovascular surgery nurse practitioner, and she loved the work and knew she rocked it. Tamarino's charisma and proficient surgical flair provided the compelling argument as to why she put up with his darker side. But she had to admit these reoperations happened more often than necessary.

"Are we ready to go? How did all of you make it here before me today? I got held up with that damn lockdown." His rhetorical questions needed no answers. Tamarino wanted to get started. "Let's have the time-out, please." A time-out is a necessary protocol used in every surgical procedure before the operation begins.

Required by The Joint Commission for all hospital procedures, this is routine and serves as an independent verification check intended to prevent specific types of medical errors, including wrong-site surgeries.

Two minutes later, the re-exploration surgery began through the same incision, and the perfusionist placed the patient on the heart-lung machine, known as cardiopulmonary bypass. To the background sounds of the Dave Matthews Band, Tamarino worked to try to locate the source of the bleeding. As it turned out, the process was not a simple one. "She's bleeding from several areas. I thought her coags were normal."

No one replied, but from her vantage point opposite Tamarino, Annette discovered a bleeder. "She's bleeding near one of the pacing wires. I've got it." While she worked to correct it, another problem arose.

"Damn it, the mammary is leaking too," Tamarino announced in an angry tone. He observed the compromised mammary artery graft and knew the only solution involved a complete redo of the graft. Not good. "Change that music to something else," he growled. The circulating nurse switched to his classical playlist, and soft piano sounds shifted the tone in the room.

Additional arterial bleeding persisted on the upper chest wall in the vicinity of the mammary artery takedown. Tension filled the air, and Annette took care to inspect and cauterize the blood vessel, until she convinced herself the bleeding ceased. No additional sources of bleeding were apparent, although Tamarino spent extensive time inspecting the area behind the heart. "Annette, see if you can detect anything back here. I like to believe another set of eyes is worth the time." Annette complied, knowing this area occasionally got overlooked as the bleeding source. She concurred about the extra set of eyes, and she wanted this fixed once and for all. But her growing concerns about Tamarino's proficiency increased a degree.

With the extent of manipulation in the chest cavity, the swelling increased enough to create another problem, and they were unable to close the sternum, yet another obstacle. Annette knew the patient would have to be transferred back to CSU with an open chest, delaying sternal closure and increasing the risk of even further complications. A takeback carried a greater mortality risk; an open chest raised the stakes even higher. *What an awful week we've had*, Annette mused. Maybe in a day or two the swelling would decrease and allow the chest to be closed, necessitating another return to the OR for a third surgery.

Close to 2:00 a.m., the frustrated nurse practitioner watched Dr. Tamarino walk out of the OR, while she and the rest of the exhausted surgical team finished up and prepared to move the patient back to the cardiac surgical unit. *We do all the work, but he gets the glory.*

~ Chapter 4 ~

The double, electronic steel doors of the surgery department swung open, and Allison spotted Dr. Tamarino. He trudged into the unit with the appearance of an old man rather than the athletic, desirable, career surgeon she knew. He plopped down into a black swivel chair in front of a vacant computer at the empty nurses' station and proceeded to input his post-op orders in silence. Accustomed to this scene, Allison, like the other CSU nurses, had learned to leave him alone when he emerged from a late surgery. His persona, especially when tired, projected an ugly image. "Tamarino's out. I wonder what he found," Allison whispered to a coworker.

"The OR just called with a heads-up. Your patient's coming out with an open chest," Rosa announced. "They must have run into a lot more than they had anticipated. Maybe Annette will fill us in. I'll help you admit her, Allison. Good thing you had enough time for an extended break, because it's showtime soon."

Dr. Tamarino completed his computer orders, stood up, and stretched. "Is anyone from the family still here?" he asked in a monotone voice and with no outward signs of emotion.

"Yes, sir, they're in the family waiting room," Rosa announced. Without a word, Dr. Tamarino walked out of the unit. Allison retreated to the patient's room to access her computer and review the new post-op orders, although she could anticipate most of them. She knew the patient would arrive within minutes, and she had already prepared as much as she could. With an open chest, specific additional precautions and protocols needed to occur. She could recite them by heart. Her concern focused more on the increased complication rate and higher mortality risk her patient had just incurred.

Rosa came in to help. "As much as I respect him, he's so full of himself," she said. "He's probably going to tell them how he saved their mother's life, yada yada yada. I've heard him exaggerate many times when he talks to families, and then they are forever grateful."

"Yeah, he always comes out smelling like a rose, even when he screws up. And lately it seems to be happening more and more. I'm really interested in how he'll explain this bleeding. What is it about him that makes everyone fawn all over him, even when he treats them like shit? All of us do it, too, and we put up with his bullshit." Allison had to admit to herself that even she got caught up in his charisma. It seemed that no matter what he did, a part of her liked him anyway.

"I think it's just that he is great most of the time," Rosa reasoned. "He's got that God complex. After enough times of him hearing just how brilliant he is from his patients, or doctors and nurses, he believes it. He really thinks of himself as a god."

Loud beeping from the equipment and the noisy entourage of surgery personnel transporting Mrs. Brock from the operating room alerted Allison to pick up the pace. Along with the anesthesiologist, Annette and two other members from the surgical team accompanied the patient to Room 3. Allison and Rosa, along with another CSU nurse, worked to readmit her, since all the equipment needed to be plugged in or hooked up to the monitors. Roughly two minutes into the hectic but organized process, the anesthesiologist gave Allison a brief verbal report. After they exchanged the initial information, she inquired about the source of the bleeding, but he referred her to Annette.

The nurse practitioner's pained expression hinted not to expect a comprehensive answer. "I saw a bleeder near the pacing wires. And we did have to redo the mammary graft. She had a little chest wall bleeding too. Maybe Dr. T can expand on it." Annette shrugged as if to say, "Don't count on it." She knew he didn't like to be too specific in answering such queries.

Just then Dr. Tamarino entered the room and observed the orderly post-op readmission process for a minute without saying a thing. The patient's blood pressure and EKG seemed to be maintaining normal numbers, and the chest tube drainage was now minimal. It appeared that he had fixed the problem, which pleased Allison. But the vague concerns about the source of the bleeding still haunted her.

"She should be okay now," Dr. Tamarino said. "I spoke to the family. Let them in as soon as you can, Allison. I'm going home, and I don't expect any more calls tonight." He had this not-so-subtle habit of manipulating the situation, almost like a threat. She knew he expected her to take care of things without bothering him.

"Okay, Dr. T. She does appear to be improving, and I'm optimistic. But you know me, and if I need you, I'll text you. I'm curious, did you pinpoint the source of the bleeding?"

"Mainly chest wall stuff. Oh, and we redid the mammary." With that, he turned and disappeared for the night.

After twenty minutes, Mrs. Brock's condition stabilized, and her chest tube drainage maintained in the normal range. She would remain anesthetized all night since her chest remained open. Before Annette left for home, she checked in one last time. "Everything going okay? If you need Tamarino and can't get him, you know to call me, right, Allison?"

"Yes, thanks, Annette. I appreciate it. You know he can be such an asshole."

"Don't think I don't know that. I have to work with him every day in that OR. Listen, between you and me, I think he's got a personal issue he's not telling us. He's missing things and isn't as sharp in the OR. I'm more than a little worried."

"Is that why we've had all these takebacks lately?"

"If I had to guess, I'd say yes, but I don't know for sure, and he'd never admit to any problems. He's too vain. I'd say he's hiding a deeper issue. I'm leaving now."

"Okay, thanks. Be careful driving home." *What is going on with Dr. T?*

~ Chapter 5 ~

Light traffic at three in the morning allowed Gary Tamarino to navigate his red Maserati Gran Turismo Sport up Masonic Avenue at lightning speed. He should be tired, but his mind raced as he pondered the past hours' events. He slammed his left hand on the steering wheel and swerved around a sharp corner, cursing out loud to an audience of one. "Fuck it. I should have known I'd have to come back in tonight. I noticed the bleeding when I closed. Damn." He knew he dodged another bullet with Mrs. Brock. How many more times would he get this lucky?

This can't be happening to me. I'm too young for anything to be wrong. I just need sleep. Justifying his worst fears through denial, he had calmed himself down by the time he reached the driveway of his Pacific Heights home. Once inside his empty house, Tamarino contemplated his upcoming early surgery schedule and knew he couldn't afford to stay up any later. He ripped off his clothes, jumped into the shower, dried off, brushed his teeth, and flopped into bed. For once, sleeping alone provided a much-needed respite.

***

Stress because of the divorce. Ego. Lack of focus. God complex. Stock market losses. Transient vision loss. Smoking too much pot. Too young to retire. Like a tornado out of control, these thoughts bombarded Gary's mind during his early morning drive to the hospital. The piercing siren of an ambulance jolted him to attention. He slowed down and glanced at the analog clock on his dash. 7:10 a.m. *Thank God that ambulance is going the other way.* With luck he might make it in time. If not, they'd simply have to wait for him. It wouldn't be the first time, and besides, he had his junior partner today. *Pull yourself together, Tamarino.*

At seven thirty on the dot, he drove into his designated parking spot and emerged inside the doctors' lounge by seven thirty-five. Ten minutes later he showed up in the OR, dressed and scrubbed, ready to begin his day. The other members of the surgical team busied themselves with the draped and anesthetized patient on the table.

Tossing all negative thoughts out of his mind, he greeted his team. "Good morning, girls and boys. I hope you're ready to roll. How's Mrs. Brock this morning, Kumar?"

"She's holding her own. The bleeding is under control. Not sure if we can close the chest today. She still has a lot of swelling, but her vitals are stable. And labs are okay. No major problems through the night. We may have to wait another day or two."

Dr. Tamarino liked Dr. Kumar Chanrami, his junior partner, who had exceeded all expectations from his glowing resume. Talented, reliable, efficient, and quiet, he'd also maintained an excellent rapport with the nursing staff in the two years he'd been at San Francisco Bay Hospital.

Good. I don't need any bad news today after last night. "Great. Glad you were able to see her on early rounds. I'll check on her after this case. Thanks."

Surgery today consisted of a CABG (coronary artery bypass graft) on a seventy-two-year-old male patient in fairly good health. An uncomplicated case, the team finished in two hours. Simple. "Okay, that's a wrap. Thank you all. Good job." This is how it always used to be for Dr. Tamarino, and he hoped his luck had turned. No case too difficult, he managed to save lives despite the worst circumstances. He prided himself on his impressive reputation — until now. His life had gotten too complicated and stressful, a situation he loathed. "I'll talk to the family, Kumar." Tamarino disappeared through the OR door without any further conversation.

Dr. Tamarino commanded attention the moment he walked into the crowded CSU family waiting room. "Mr. Fellner's family?"

"Yes, Doctor. How is he?" a timid woman of slight build inquired. Two younger people who were sitting with her focused their attention on the man they had entrusted with their father's life.

"I did three bypasses, and he made it through fine. He really needed the surgery. Without it, he could have dropped dead at any time. You'll be able to see him in CSU soon. The nurses will come out to get you when they're ready."

"Oh Dr. Tamarino, we can't thank you enough for saving his life," the relieved wife said. Tamarino smiled and walked down the hall toward CSU. He prided himself on creating just enough drama to force family members to be grateful that he saved the patient's life. *I'm a hero and a savior. That's what I'm meant to do.* Once again, he felt good about himself, and this delusion became his reality.

Tamarino wandered into the busy, sixteen-bed CSU with no fanfare. At ten in the morning, other surgeons, hospitalists, and nurse practitioners flitted about as they made rounds on their patients. The CSU nurses were either in the patient rooms or rushing down a hall, focused on agendas that did not include him. He recalled the days when everyone paid homage to him, the only cardiac surgeon at the time. Memories of those days made him smile, and today, as chief of cardiothoracic surgery, he still received a sufficient amount of respect and admiration from the experienced nurses here.

"Hi, Dr. T. Mrs. Brock is doing better. Stable and no bleeding," Jason said as Tamarino entered Room 3. "She wakes up and follows commands when we decrease the sedation."

"All good. Can you pull up her x-ray? And what are her latest labs?"

"Sure. I have it right here." Jason opened the computer screen to display a digital image of this morning's chest x-ray. As Tamarino reviewed it, Jason rattled off her lab results, in order of priority, and then handed a printout to Dr. T.

As the patient's primary nurse, Jason's responsibilities entailed providing minute-by-minute care to this critically ill patient, not even eight hours post-op. In addition, he stayed updated on the latest diagnostic developments. Dr. Tamarino appeared pleased. "Okay,

Jason. We'll leave her intubated one more day and then plan to take her back tomorrow to close her chest. Then we can focus on getting her to breathe on her own. Has the family been in?"

"Yes, sir. They just left to go home to sleep. They were here through the night."

"Okay. Keep me posted." Tamarino traipsed back to the desk and inputted the patient orders. A few minutes later, his CABG patient arrived in the unit with the surgical team in tow. He glanced at them, nodding to Annette and the anesthesiologist.

Kumar followed, but did not enter the patient's room. Instead, he pulled up a chair next to Tamarino and spoke in a low voice. "We need to talk."

~ **Chapter 6** ~

"Code Red CSU. Code Red CSU. Code Red CSU." The urgent alert sounded just as Allison punched in for her last of three nights in a row. Her time card stamp read 6:35 p.m. She doubled her pace as she made the trek down the long hall to her unit. *I wonder who coded,* she thought as she used her badge to open the electronic door to CSU. *Please don't let it be Mrs. Brock.*

The blinking red light identified the Code Red in Room 9. *Thank God it's not who I thought.* Plenty of activity flooded the room, as personnel raced to the site. A quick glance at the assignment board revealed this coding patient did not belong to Allison. Happy to see her name scribbled next to Mrs. Brock on the assignment board, she headed to Room 3 for shift report. Consistency of care, while not always feasible, continued as preferable. Despite the current emergency, the remainder of the unit would function as normally as possible during the transition from days to nights. CSU nurses were professionals and the best in the hospital, in Allison's opinion, biased as it might be. When pressed, she admitted those ER nurses rocked too, especially when it came to codes and starting IVs.

***

Gary Tamarino heard the overhead Code Red the same time his cell phone vibrated, alerting him to an incoming call from CSU. He answered it.

"Dr. Tamarino, Mr. Fellner, your patient in Room 9 is coding. We think he's tamponading."

"Damn. What happened there? Who is this? Aren't you people on top of things?"

"This is Jason, the charge nurse on days. The chest x-ray shows he has a widened mediastinum. We were getting ready to call you and he coded. We're doing CPR and everything's ready for you to open his chest at the bedside." Despite Tamarino's abusive outburst, the composed charge nurse painted a clear image of the emergency. "Are you in the hospital?"

"Christ, yes, I'm on the third floor. If you waited five minutes more, I would have left the hospital. But I'm coming down. Call the OR and tell them not to send the team home," he snapped.

Relieved to reach Dr. T, Jason updated the code team. "Dr. Tamarino should be here in a minute or two. He's probably going to open the chest to relieve the tamponade. A heads-up . . . he's in a foul mood. All of you better be ready to go."

"Everything's all set," one of the CSU nurses replied while others continued CPR. Cardiac tamponade is a life-threatening complication following cardiac surgery. Blood pools around the heart, compressing it to the point where there is not enough space to pump effectively. The quickest way to relieve the pressure is to open the incision and the chest at the patient's bedside. With a trained staff, this can be accomplished. Once the heart is freed from the compression and exposed, the tamponade can be resolved, and the heart pumps normally again.

The looming presence of Dr. Tamarino filled the room, with CPR still ongoing. His scowl shot daggers at anyone who made eye contact. "This guy should have been ready for transfer. I don't understand what happened here," he growled. "Let's get this chest opened." Without a word and under immense tension, the capable CSU nurses helped Dr. T into the sterile gown, after which he gave the order to stop compressions to allow him to access the patient's chest.

In less than a minute, he cut the stainless steel sternal wires. With the chest incision opened and the heart no longer constrained in a tight space, the situation improved. A nurse in sterile attire suctioned out the excess blood, which almost filled a canister on the wall. The heart started to pump effectively, and the cardiac monitor displayed a normal EKG. "His pressure's coming up," a nurse said as she cycled the blood pressure cuff. Emergency over, the patient would now return to the operating room.

The exasperated surgeon never uttered a thank you as he headed to the OR. Jason knew Dr. T needed to locate the origin of the bleeding that had caused the tamponade, fix it, and close the patient's chest in a sterile environment. From Dr. T's attitude, Jason assumed he hadn't visualized his workday to end in this manner.

***

Across the unit, Allison finished getting shift report on Mrs. Brock. To her surprise, her patient remained fairly stable. Alerted to the noise in the hall, Allison noticed a patient being wheeled out of the unit, accompanied by the surgical team. "What happened? The Code Red?" she asked Rosa.

"Can you believe it? Tamponade. Two days post-op, ready to transfer to Stepdown, and the patient coded. This makes the fourth takeback for Dr. T. He's really on a roll, and I'd say more of a downhill slide."

"Somebody's got to be scrutinizing his numbers by now. Why are his patients bleeding? He's bound to be questioned at the next M&M conference. Has anyone mentioned a Root Cause Analysis investigation?" Allison's suspicions about Gary Tamarino's disastrous week had reached a peak. The time to take action had arrived.

~ Chapter 7 ~

When Dr. Kumar Chanrami made evening rounds in CSU, he stopped in Room 3 last. "And how is our Mrs. Brock doing?"

"Hi, Dr. Kumar," an eager Allison replied. "She is much better. The swelling is way down, and her vitals have been stable. Is Dr. T thinking of closing her chest tomorrow?"

"If she stays stable through the night, we'll take her back as the first case tomorrow."

"Excellent. I hoped she'd do well after the initial bleeding and redo. Before you leave, Dr. Kumar, do you have a few minutes?" Allison had a knack for prompting physicians, especially surgeons, to talk with her, and she maintained good relationships with most of them.

"Yes, Allison. What is it?"

"This is confidential. I feel like I can talk to you. I'm concerned about Dr. Tamarino. He always managed his work, and his stats were impeccable, as you must know. But lately he's had four patients return for bleeding and provided vague answers as to any reasons. Annette and Rosa have also noticed. He seems to be aggravated all the time, like he's ticked off at the world. He's yelled at the nurses, almost like he's a different person."

Dr. Kumar hesitated to reply without more information. "What's your question?"

"All right, I know he's your business partner, and I understand you don't want to say anything negative about him. I feel like you might possess a little insight about what's going on with him. His patients' lives are being affected. And I can't sit here and not say anything."

He waited.

"Dr. Kumar, I'd like to confront him, but if he won't talk to me, I might refer the matter to my healthcare oversight company and have them investigate him."

Raising his eyebrows, Dr. Kumar leaned in as his jaw dropped. "What healthcare company? I don't understand."

"I'm the creator and owner of Critical Cover-Up. Have you heard of us?"

Dr. Kumar opened his mouth to speak, but it was a full five seconds before he uttered a word. "I remember now. I've heard about that company and how it took down a medical center in Florida two years ago. That's you?" He stared at her in disbelief.

Allison nodded. "Yes. And the company has taken off. I have capable people running it, because I prefer working at the bedside as a critical care nurse. I also published a best-selling book called *Critical Cover-Up* and do occasional speaking engagements on exposing corruption and cover-up in healthcare."

He smiled. "Wow. I had no idea. Congratulations." He quickly returned to business. "But I don't think it would be a good idea to expose Dr. Tamarino without knowing all the facts. You know he's pretty well-connected here with administration, and he golfs with the

CEO on a regular basis. Why don't you try to talk to him? I'll tell you this. I know stuff is going on in his personal life, but I don't feel right sharing it. I agree, he's been sloppy lately, but I think he'll straighten up. Maybe it would help if you tell him that others are aware."

Dr. Kumar's efforts to make excuses defined his unwillingness to involve himself in any negative talk. The subtle warning didn't go unheeded. Allison understood her job here could be on the line if she blew the whistle. But she'd reached her tolerance limit.

~ **Chapter 8** ~

Dr. Kumar answered a call from the cardiovascular operating room, CVOR. A frantic female spoke with urgency. "Dr. Kumar, we need you stat in CVOR. Dr. Tamarino and Annette have Mr. Fellner open and had to put him on bypass."

"I'll be right there. I'm by the CSU exit door." *What could have happened? All Tamarino had to do was find the bleeding source, repair the damage, and then close the chest.* Allison's recent remarks burned in his mind as he rushed toward the surgical suite. Inside the steel double doors, he rounded the corner and knocked on the window to alert them of his presence. Without wasting any time, he scrubbed in and entered the OR Room 2.

Annette and Kumar established eye contact, and she shook her head. The tension in the air hovered like a heavy cloud. Kumar could see Tamarino's hands deep inside the patient's chest, while the cardiopulmonary bypass machine maintained blood flow. No one spoke a word.

"Lucky I hadn't left for home yet. What's going on?"

"I need you here, Kumar." In a quieter voice, Tamarino admitted, "I can't catch a break this week. I found a bleeder on one of the grafts, the posterior descending artery. Nothing I did made it stop. We had to put him on pump for me to redo the graft. In the process, I nicked the marginal artery, and now we need to bypass that one too. I can use another pair of eyes and hands."

Kumar stayed silent and began working alongside Tamarino to repair the damage. Annette repositioned herself down by the patient's leg to help the surgical nurse retrieve more of the femoral vein to be used as the graft. Kumar focused on the surgical field in front of him but could not erase what seemed to be an indelible image seared into his memory. Anxiety crept in as he considered the possibility of Allison reporting his partner. Having their practice exposed in a negative light would be devastating.

Mr. Fellner's straightforward case now veered far from textbook, and the morbidity risk increased. Not a good thing at all. Kumar anticipated Tamarino would be under increased scrutiny at the next Mortality and Morbidity Committee meeting coming up this week.

All of a sudden, Dr. Tamarino shouted, "Shit! What happened here?" In an instant, massive bleeding filled the open chest cavity, and despite suctioning and clamping off bleeders, the never-ending blood flow escalated. "I can't see where this is coming from. Fuck!"

Without responding verbally, Kumar explored and prodded every way he could, as he hoped to determine the origin of the bloodbath. Trying to keep his gloved hands away from his partner's in that small space of a chest cavity, he strengthened his efforts. The perfusionist transfused copious amounts of products through the machine's circuit in an attempt to replace the massive blood loss. With the swirling pool of red in his visual field, finding the graft alone developed into a huge challenge. The intricacy of suturing a vein graft to the coronary artery and then the aorta was all but unachievable. Bathed in blood, the surgical field became almost inaccessible. Powerless to curtail the rapid blood loss, Tamarino and Kumar stared at each other. The inevitable outcome faced them head-on. An intraoperative nightmare, the hemorrhaging prevailed. Mr. Fellner became another statistic.

~ Chapter 9 ~

The death of their patient in the OR shook Dr. Kumar to his core. Not only did Gary's sloppiness contribute to and perhaps cause the patient's demise, but he'd jeopardized Kumar's reputation as well. He knew he had to talk to him.

He found Gary Tamarino alone in the surgeons' lounge. Hesitant to broach the delicate subject, Kumar reacted in surprise when his partner initiated the discussion. "Damn, I didn't need this today, especially after the week I've had."

Astonished to hear Gary accepting no blame for Mr. Fellner's death, he pulled up a chair, sat directly in front of him, and glared. "How can you say that, Gary? The poor man shouldn't have died."

Tamarino glared at his partner. His right jugular vein bulged, and his nostrils flared. "Are you blaming me? What are you trying to say? You know we did everything we could. You were right there." His narcissism didn't allow for any culpability. But Kumar didn't shrink from the confrontation.

"Listen, man, this is a patient's life we're talking about. I've cut you plenty of slack with all your personal problems, the divorce, and your financial losses. I know you haven't been fully focused at work."

"Goddamn you, Kumar. I gave you the opportunity of your career when I brought you here two years ago from that rinky-dink, nothing hospital across the state. And this is how you thank me?" His voice raised to fever pitch, Dr. Tamarino raged at his partner, berating him like a child.

Kumar had endured enough. He stood and walked out of the lounge without another word. Furious with Tamarino, his dignity precluded him from continuing to argue. He knew Tamarino would have the last say, true or not. With Gary, all problems were someone else's fault, and when anything good happened, he claimed all the credit. Narcissism at its finest—or worst, depending on one's perspective.

Upset and disheartened, he searched out Annette. "Are you able to talk?" he texted. Two minutes later, his phone pinged with her reply.

"Just finishing late rounds in CSU. Meet me in ten minutes in the cafeteria."

Divided into two sections, the hospital cafeteria provided a separate room for physicians. Nurse practitioners and physician assistants were included. Dr. Kumar found a table in the corner where he and Annette could speak in private. He stood up to greet her with a half smile when she approached. "Thanks for meeting me."

"Rough day, I know," she said. "A tough loss."

Dr. Kumar's grave expression set the stage for a serious dialogue. "You know we never should have lost Mr. Fellner, don't you?"

"Absolutely I do. Not only did Gary miss that graft that bled and caused the tamponade, but then he nicked the marginal and who knows what else. Before you knew it, we couldn't see much of anything. By the time you got there, the damage was next to impossible to reverse." Incensed, Annette continued. "Do you feel the same? This is exactly what Rosa, Allison, and I have been concerned about. At first it just seemed like sloppiness. But we realize a deeper, more serious, problem is going on here, and we can't sit by while more patients die."

"Exactly, Annette. Listen, we have to act. I'm his partner, but I'm not willing to go down with him. He's got most of the physicians here wrapped in the culture of a code of silence. Plus, the CEO is his golfing buddy."

"But really, how much can the hospital let him get away with by turning a blind eye? What do you propose?"

"Allison talked to me earlier. Did you know about her company, Critical Cover-Up?"

"I've heard about it, but I didn't know she had any connection to it."

"I say we should encourage her to have them investigate Tamarino's latest blunders. At first, I chalked these fiascos up to bad luck, but not anymore. He needs professional help before he kills more people. And out of obligation, I feel I have to talk to the CEO. Since Tamarino's the chief of cardiothoracic surgery, he can't police himself. And the chief of surgery is his good buddy too."

"We can report him to the ethics hotline, although I don't think that does any good," Annette said.

"Yeah, it's just an exercise in futility. This case will be addressed at the next M&M meeting, but the problem won't be solved. He'll still be operating and placing blame everywhere but where it really belongs. The death will get reported to JCAHO as an intraoperative complication. A Root Cause Analysis will occur, but rarely does a physician end up sanctioned to the point of having privileges suspended."

Kumar added. "I just tried to talk to him, and of course he ripped my head off. He won't listen to me or anyone else. I'm sure of one thing, Annette. The divorce launched a downhill run for him in the monetary department. And now he's gotten himself into deep financial trouble trading options. He's stressed to the max but won't admit it, and he's screwing up as a cardiothoracic surgeon."

Annette almost felt sorry for him, until she recalled the most recent abusive tirade he staged in surgery. "I agree. Talk to Allison and have her get Critical Cover-Up to investigate and expose his screwups. It seems like the only way."

Dr. Kumar walked out of the cafeteria and back to CSU to talk to Allison Jamison. *I'd give anything to find a better way.*

~ Chapter 10 ~

When Allison and the other CSU nurses learned that Mr. Fellner died in surgery, a sadness permeated the staff. To successfully resuscitate a patient at the bedside, only to lose him later in the operating room, devastated everyone involved. Expectations for this patient to transfer and go home in a few days had been high, but it wasn't going to happen now. The surgeon of record: Dr. Tamarino.

Allison's radar intensified, and her determination to act strengthened. Before she had the chance to broach any subject with Tamarino, Dr. Kumar appeared at the door of her patient's room. "I thought you had gone home. I'm so sorry about Mr. Fellner," Allison said.

In a low-pitched, steady voice, his tone somber, Kumar said, "Tonight turned out to be a disaster, Allison. Mr. Fellner is dead, and Tamarino won't listen to reason. Believe me, I tried, to no avail. Forget about talking to him. It will only be a colossal waste of time. I know you and Rosa have also been alarmed about his recent performance. I consulted with Annette, and I think this situation warrants a referral to your oversight company. Can you make that happen?"

"Annette agrees, even though both of you work closely with him?"

"Yes. I'm not afraid of him or any power he might yield here as chief of cardiothoracic surgery. If we don't intervene, more patients will surely die, and then we could also be liable for staying silent."

"Okay, I'll contact my people and have them get right on it. It may bring bad publicity to your practice and also the hospital. You could both be at risk of losing your jobs, you know. My investigators and reporters can be quite aggressive in exposing corruption and unethical practices."

"Allison, we have to do what's right. I'm telling you that Dr. T has been dealing with major financial stressors, and he has been frazzled to the point of lacking judgment and focus. Now it has affected his work in a dangerous way. He needs professional help but won't hear of it. When can you contact the Critical Cover-Up people? I'll be happy to help any way I can, give interviews or whatever."

"I'll notify them in the morning after I get home and instruct them to get the ball rolling. And then there's no turning back. Believe me, I know."

Dr. Kumar nodded and gave her a thumbs-up. "Take good care of Mrs. Brock. At least she seems stable. Have a good night. And thank you."

With mixed feelings, Allison finished her shift and left the hospital. With her patient in stable condition, she looked forward to having the next seventy-two hours off. The past two days had been labor-intensive, in addition to being filled with unbelievable tension and drama. She welcomed the break. Even though she had a speaking engagement in Berkeley, which technically qualified as work, she anticipated her dinner date with a friend. A 180-degree change of pace, to be sure.

During her twenty-minute drive home, she wished she could have spoken with Dr. T, that he might have been receptive enough to hear her, and that she didn't have to enlist her company for the next move. She no longer respected him as a surgeon. His recent actions and attitude unmasked the skilled and fun surgeon she had gotten to know. He could be arrogant and full of himself, but he'd never put patients at risk until now. She questioned whether he might be having a nervous breakdown of some sort. She assumed his personal life had impacted his professional career to the point where he had failed in a major way. She hoped her decision resulted in a solution, but she second-guessed the move.

~ Chapter 11 ~

Allison arrived home to her studio apartment in lower Nob Hill, where her kitty, Snowball, greeted her with a loud meow. After dedicating some attention and quality time to her furry friend, Allison checked her email. With nothing pressing from anyone at Critical Cover-Up, she composed the crucial message to Sherry Dolan, the administrator of her company and a woman she trusted to get things done.

The subject line read, "Urgent – Surgical Deaths – Sensitive." With mixed feelings, she typed,

Good morning, Sherry. A situation has come to my attention at San Francisco Bay Hospital, where I'm doing a travel assignment. It involves the chief of cardiothoracic surgery, Dr. Gary Tamarino, a reputable surgeon with high grades who has suddenly had an unacceptable number of cardiac surgery patients with complications. These have involved excessive bleeding, for the most part, and required a return to surgery. Last night, one of these patients died in surgery. Tamarino's abusive attitude toward the nurses and his partner has also become problematic, and he's in tight with the hospital CEO. I'll need an investigation into his personal finances and recent divorce, which may be contributing factors to his erratic and sloppy performance of late. I've always worked well with him, and I hate to have to initiate this, but what's happened isn't right, and patients are compromised. You can also contact his partner, Dr. Kumar Chanrami, and his nurse practitioner, Annette Brashton. Both are aware I'm referring this to you. Thank you, Sherry. I'll be speaking in Berkeley tomorrow, but you can contact me any time. Allison Jamison.

By nine o'clock, Allison craved sleep. After a quick shower, she headed to bed.

She awoke, refreshed, after six hours' sleep. She wanted to be sharp tomorrow. She still needed to pack and prepare for her presentation. Although Allison had given the talk to other groups in the past, this time she would address a large group of nurses as a featured speaker at the American Association of Critical-Care Nurses' National Teaching Institute, an annual conference. It was a true honor to be selected as a presenter, and Allison knew she needed to be on top of her game.

At eight in the evening, halfway into her preparation, her phone pinged. A text message from Rosa read, "I know you're off. Just wanted to update you that Mrs. Brock coded and died." An angry-face emoticon accompanied the words.

Allison gasped. *This can't be!* A lump formed in her throat as sadness gripped her entire being. Her first thoughts, once her brain could formulate anything that made sense, were questions. *Why? What could have happened? She had been doing so well.* Allison typed a reply. "I'm sad. What happened? Dr. T?" She waited for Rosa's response. None came, but she knew Rosa was probably busy. Deep sadness morphed into anger and exasperation. *A second death in less than twenty-four hours.* On hearing this latest bombshell, she assured herself she'd made the right decision in contacting her business to investigate Tamarino.

***

Tomorrow's events shifted into the foreground, and Allison finished packing. She phoned her friend before it got too late. "How great to hear your voice, Allison. And it will be even better to meet up in person tomorrow."

"Hi, Mark. I know. It's been a long time, and I'm really excited and looking forward to seeing you again." Mark Derning and Allison had remained friends after she'd assisted the homicide detective in solving two murder cases in Orlando two years ago. Since then, she'd hired him to work for her company as an investigator, but she rarely had any interaction with him, other than business-related email and occasional friendly phone calls.

No longer a detective, Derning's current job as a consultant to the Orlando PD offered more flexible hours, allowing him the opportunity to travel to California to see her while she was there for the conference. Allison acknowledged her feelings were mixed about getting involved, but she couldn't deny the attraction. Derning's role as homicide detective had first brought the two of them together when Sean, her first love and good friend, was murdered. She'd been devastated to the core, but now a part of her longed to find love again. Her heart told her to go for it, but her mind said to keep things businesslike.

With a smile on her face, she continued the conversation. She wanted to tell him about Tamarino but decided against it, at least for the time being. "I should be finished with my presentation in Berkeley around five tomorrow. As soon as I get out and am in an Uber, I'll text you, okay?"

"Perfect, Allison. I'm staying at the Grand Hyatt in Union Square. We can have a drink in their lounge off the lobby before we go out for dinner. I made reservations for eight o'clock."

"That sounds wonderful, Mark. See you then." She ended the call and smiled, filled with uncertainty but excited about what tomorrow might bring.

~ Chapter 12 ~

Inside his palatial home, Gary Tamarino found no solace in the luxurious surroundings. Alone, he mused about his life. He couldn't grasp how fast success and power had deteriorated to failure and misery. *I think the homeless people in Union Square might be happier, even though they have nothing to their name but a flattened cardboard box as a bed.*

He rolled a joint and hoped it would provide relief from his gloom. After two hits, his mood lifted a little, but he couldn't prevent the obsessive thoughts that bombarded him like the constant beat of a bass drum. Reminders of his huge losses in the stock market and visions of his bitchy ex-wife hounded him. What loomed bolder than anything else, though, were the images of his two post-op patients who'd died in the last twenty-four hours. The self-loathing engulfed him, but he didn't dare reveal this dark side to anyone.

Tomorrow he'd be back in surgery, saving lives just like he always did. He kept his persona in a bubble where accountability and shame didn't exist. His strong denial of reality allowed him to continue his life. Any situation or person that threatened his perception of reality had to go. And until now, he had succeeded in influencing most people in his life to see him as the hero and savior. He could not afford to have this illusion disintegrate.

***

Tamarino spent his commute to work calculating how he planned to defuse the disasters of the past week. The hospital would have to report the deaths to the Joint Commission, and Ed Manning, his friend and CEO, would require an in-person meeting to discuss what occurred. *Good thing we're golfing buddies. He knows it's just been a string of bad luck. After all, I'm Dr. Gary Tamarino, Chief of Cardiothoracic Surgery.* He knew he'd have to face the Mortality and Morbidity Committee soon too. And he never doubted his ability to schmooze those physicians. He'd be extra nice to Kumar and Annette in hopes that they'd cut him a little slack. *Everything will be all right.*

Gary couldn't deny the vital need to improve his statistics. Maybe he'd give his partner the more complicated cases, and he'd take the easier ones for now. He'd figure out a way.

A pleasant surprise greeted him when he arrived at the hospital—a lighter than normal surgery schedule for the day. The first case had been cancelled due to the patient's elevated platelet function assay, a screening test for platelet dysfunction. Operating on a patient with this specific abnormal lab value would be medical malpractice, since it ensured bleeding, and a legitimate case for a lawsuit. It was definitely a predicament he didn't need.

Gary knew Ed Manning would be in his office, since he was an early morning kind of guy. "Good morning,

Ed. Do you have a minute?" Gary said after a quick knock on Manning's slightly open office door. The hospital CEO raised his head from his computer screen. The fifty-four-year-old administrator dressed like a Wall Street executive and prided himself on his impeccable appearance. His short, chestnut-brown, gelled hairstyle complemented his hand-tailored, thousand-dollar, charcoal-gray suit.

"Hello, Gary. Come in. I expected to see you today." Encouraged by Ed's gracious demeanor, Dr. Tamarino sat down and wasted no time as he began to weave a narrative he presumed would get himself off the hook.

Using a low voice, he tried to appear sincere, but in no place in his DNA did empathy exist. "Listen, Ed. I feel awful about the deaths of Mrs. Brock and Mr. Fellner. I never expected that kind of outcome in either of those cases. A horrible situation, all the way around." He shook his head, attempting to appear sorrowful, but he was acting. His effort to express compassion lacked substance.

But Ed Manning no longer acted like the understanding ally Tamarino assumed him to be. The smile faded from his tanned face in an instant. He glared at Dr. Tamarino, and his reaction alarmed the overconfident surgeon. "Close the door, Gary," he ordered.

Tamarino stood up and followed his command. Unnerved in this noticeably strained atmosphere, he waited for Manning to speak before he took his seat.

"What on God's earth gave you the idea I'd be okay with what happened, Gary? Two patient deaths in twenty-four hours? One of them in the OR? This is far from okay. JCAHO will be all over us, not to mention the State of California."

Gary took a deep breath and said nothing, but inside he seethed. *Who does he think he is? He has no clue what kind of pressure I'm under every day in surgery.* Furious with the surgeon, Ed Manning continued. "Tomorrow is the M&M meeting, and you should expect to be grilled. Based on the outcome, it's possible your surgery privileges could be suspended."

His eyes narrowed as he stared at his cardiothoracic chief and then unleashed the remainder of his wrath. "This is about as critical as it gets, Gary. That's all. You can go now."

Rage bubbled just beneath the surface, and Gary almost snapped back at him in anger. Infuriated at the way Manning dismissed him, he stormed out of the office.

~ Chapter 13 ~

Overwhelmed by the thunderous applause of fifteen hundred critical care nurses, a gratified Allison Jamison beamed. She thanked them several times and then stepped away from the podium at UC Berkeley. Recognition by her peers at this venue validated Allison's choice to focus on exposing corruption in healthcare through her company, Critical Cover-Up. The successful RN and best-selling author hurried offstage, as she anticipated a pleasant evening with Mark Derning. Her fashion choice of a navy-blue suit over a cream-colored silk blouse would suffice for the evening as well. "The Grand Hyatt in Union Square, please," she instructed the Uber driver.

She then sent Mark a text. "Hi, Mark. I'm just leaving the university. Should arrive in an hour, give or take traffic on the expressway. Looking forward to tonight."

In less than a minute, Mark replied to her text message. "Good to hear, Allison. Can't wait to see you. Text me when you get close. I'll be in the lounge on the first floor."

"Okay. Also want to discuss a situation at work about a cardiothoracic surgeon. Just referred the case to Sherry Dolan this morning, but I wanted your take on it."

"We can talk about it later if you want, Allison. Hope to enjoy our time together first, away from business."

As much as she valued and needed his professional opinion on the problem, Mark's hint to share a relaxed evening rang clear. The prospect of a romantic evening sent a tingle down her spine, and she smiled as she imagined what might ensue. Flattered by his words, she closed her eyes, optimistic about the night ahead.

A voice jolted Allison back to the present. "We're almost there. The hotel is around this corner," the driver announced. Congestion at the intersection of Sutter and Stockton signaled she had arrived in the center of the city.

When the light changed to green, the driver made a left turn and stopped in front of the thirty-six-story, four-star hotel. She glanced at her phone and saw the time: six-fifteen. Allison hadn't expected to doze off during the ride, but she appreciated the extra rest. "Thank you. Have a good evening," she said as she departed the car and stepped onto the sidewalk. She took a moment to alert Mark of her arrival and then caught sight of two doormen, one of whom nodded in silence as he held the door open for her. Short and brawny, dressed all in black, including a wool, gangster-style fedora, the guy looked like he belonged in an Al Capone movie. *They're pretty serious about the security here*, Allison mused.

Once inside the spacious, modern lobby, she surveyed the sophisticated scene and noticed a sign for the lounge, past the bank of elevators. Allison entered the trendy OneUP Restaurant and Lounge and focused her attention on the bar area as she searched for Mark. She assumed he'd be waiting for her, but she didn't see him. For a second, a twinge of insecurity crept into her mind. Then, a woman with a pleasant smile asked, "May I help you?"

"Yes, thank you. I'm meeting a gentleman here. I'm not sure whether he arrived yet." As she resumed her scan of the room, a strong, familiar male voice prompted Allison to spin around. Totally unprepared for the person who presented himself, she found herself staring into the steely blue eyes of her trusted friend. Her facial reactions failed to conceal her shock. With her eyebrows raised and her mouth agape, she gasped, "Oh my God. Mark?"

"Hello, Allison. You are gorgeous." His grin triggered a response deep inside her, and a hint of a smile appeared. She snapped to attention, and the delight of this moment bolstered her prior expectations for an enjoyable evening.

"Mark, you look incredible." They hugged each other like two people who had been apart for a long time. Then Allison stepped back. "Let me look at you. I guess cutting back on the full-time detective work has agreed with you. It's wonderful to see you. I'm so pleased you're here."

As Allison recollected, this seasoned homicide officer had never been credited with a sense of fashion. It had been two years since they saw each other in person, and now she almost couldn't believe her own eyes. Mark Derning appeared to have lost at least twenty-five pounds, and his wardrobe seemed like an ad straight out of *GQ* magazine. *Damn, he looks hot. Allison, it's definitely been too long.* Any concerns about keeping the relationship strictly a business one vanished. She thought her heart fluttered — a weird experience for her.

"We'd like a table for two away from the main area of the bar, please," Mark told the hostess. Allison loved how he played the gentleman role and took charge. She had always found it easy to talk with Mark and experienced a certain level of comfort around him. After all, they had worked together in the most stressful of circumstances.

But tonight seemed different. Their phone calls, though few and far between, had strengthened the bond between them and added an undeniable dose of chemistry. *Could this lead to something more?* she wondered.

~ Chapter 14 ~

Gary Tamarino dreaded the M&M meeting today. Worries about his less-than-stellar performance in surgery chipped away at his consciousness. How would he explain this sudden sloppiness in his work that caused the deaths of two patients? It couldn't possibly be all his fault. After all, he was the chief of cardiothoracic surgery. But now he faced sharp scrutiny from a group of peers and other physicians who, in his mind, didn't come close to his level of competence. Arrogance prevailed and he assumed he'd get through this, but he needed to talk to his partner.

Mortality and morbidity conferences typically occurred in large teaching hospitals as an effective process for reviewing clinical performance in surgical cases involving adverse outcomes or death. With a goal to improve the quality of patient care, the focus pointed to education. Residents normally presented cases, and attending physicians weighed in.

Though not a teaching facility, San Francisco Bay Hospital adopted the practice of peer review anyway, at the suggestion of their administration. The facility held these monthly M&M meetings on Saturdays, and attending physicians, rather than residents, presented the cases. Discussions had been known to grow contentious and critical, and since surgeons typically didn't like being second-guessed, they tended to become defensive. These events were meant to be collaborative and not punitive, but when you're the surgeon under the microscope, you tended to see it in a different manner.

Tamarino just wanted to get this over with. He had arranged to speak with Kumar in the surgeons' lounge prior to the meeting. "Thanks for coming. I know you tried to talk to me the other night, but I couldn't deal with anything at that point." He made no apology for his crass behavior.

"Listen, man, I understand, but this affects both of us, and I'm concerned about you and the outlook for our practice going forward." Dr. Chanrami spoke with resolve. "You have to level with me if you want me on your side. It's not a good feeling to be in the middle."

"I know, Kumar. You're a good man. I value our partnership and the collaboration we have with Annette too. But I'm not taking all the blame for why those patients coded or died. And although I hate to admit it, I will say I've not been as focused in surgery as I needed to be. I do think maybe my personal problems have contributed to that. I've been obsessed with these financial losses."

Gary knew he'd exposed a vulnerability at that moment, and Kumar responded with empathy. "I'm listening. It seems like things have gotten worse for you. What happened?"

Gary peered into his partner's dark brown eyes which remained fixated on his. "Listen, Kumar, I'm leveling with you, and you're the only one I'm confiding in. I've lost a ton of money day-trading in the stock market. Sort of like a gambling addict, every time I lose another twenty thousand dollars, I think I can make it up on the next trade. So I risk even more, doubling down, and luck hasn't been with me. And now my debts are astronomical. It all started out with trying to make some extra cash to afford my ex-wife's alimony and expenses related to the divorce."

Startled at the brutal honesty that spewed out of his own mouth, the almighty chief of cardiothoracic surgery hoped Kumar believed his sincerity.

His answer confirmed that he did. "I had no idea things had become this serious. You mentioned financial troubles once in passing, and I assumed you were managing okay."

Tamarino lowered his head. He no longer sounded like the know-it-all surgeon. "Far from it. Some days I think I'd be better off dead. If it weren't for this job and my patients who think I'm their savior, I'd shoot myself. I don't see an end in sight here."

"Man, keep it together. You've built a great reputation and have an impressive practice. You're still a skilled surgeon. It's just that you may need some professional help to deal with this other stuff and get to a place where you can focus again." Gary knew the genuine sympathy Kumar expressed came from his heart.

"We have this M&M in twenty minutes, Kumar. Promise me you'll have my back. I'll think about what you're saying, okay, man? Maybe I should take some time off. You and Annette can manage the caseload, and we can even hire a locum tenens surgeon for a short contract." In the past few years, quite a few surgeons and other physicians had opted for these contract positions known as locum tenens. Translated from Latin, the words literally meant, "to hold a place," and hospitals hired these doctors to fill in on a temporary basis for other physicians when temporary staffing shortages existed. Contracts could be for a few weeks or six months or even longer.

Kumar gave him a reassuring slap on the back. "We've got this."

~ Chapter 15 ~

The chic surroundings in the trendy San Francisco bistro enhanced Allison's lighthearted mood. The elegant dark woods, contemporary ceiling lights, and mammoth glass wall behind the bar created an air of sophistication. "This place is beautiful, Mark. So classy."

Mark's smile widened. "I'm happy you like it. I thought it would be convenient. We have so much to catch up on. But you must be hungry. Shall we order some drinks and maybe an appetizer or two? Our dinner reservation isn't until eight."

Away from the worries and pressures of the CSU, Allison realized how long it had been since she even entertained the idea of romance. Mark charmed her in a way she hadn't imagined possible. "That sounds great. I haven't had anything to eat since lunch, so a little something now is perfect."

Mark ordered a vodka martini, and Allison opted for a glass of pinot grigio. With a limited menu to peruse, they made their choices in short order. "I think I'll have the San Marzano tomato soup," Allison told the eager young waitress.

Mark ordered the Napa Sesame Chicken Salad and handed the waitress their menus. "So, Allison, how has it been going here? You've become a successful author, public speaker, entrepreneur, and still work in critical care. You certainly stay busy."

Allison shrugged. "Yes, a little too busy sometimes. My social life has been almost nonexistent. I love what I'm doing, but sometimes I wonder what's ahead for me. It's a good feeling to just relax and enjoy some time with you, Mark. I'm glad you decided to come out here for a vacation."

"I am too. I've been considering what's ahead for me as well. I like the consulting and, of course, the work I'm doing with Critical Cover-Up. By not working full-time as a detective, I have much more free time."

Mark and Allison caught up on each other's lives, and before either of them realized it, an hour had passed. "I don't think I've laughed so much in a long time," Mark told her. "This is fun."

"I know what you mean and feel the same." At the risk of ruining the mood, Allison switched gears and broached the topic of Tamarino. "I did want to talk to you about something more serious though." She noticed the smile disappear from Mark's face, but continued. "I mentioned this cardiothoracic surgeon situation earlier and wanted your opinion, Mark. In fact, I hoped you might work the case. Some things at work just don't add up, and I think he's hiding something. The case needs a good investigator, and a detective like you would be perfect for the job. I can put you in touch with a nurse practitioner and a CSU charge nurse who are familiar with this surgeon's latest disasters."

She hoped the offer appealed to his ego, but he steered the conversation in a different direction. "The case does sound intriguing, and I'll check in with Sherry and see about it. But right now, Allison, I'd much rather talk about us. In fact, I wonder if you could get enough time away to consider going to Italy with me."

Stunned by this surprise offer, Allison paused before she responded, a little uncertain. After the initial shock wore off, she wanted to accept the attractive invitation, yet she wavered. "I don't know what to say, Mark. I've dreamed about Italy, but I have to admit your generous proposal comes as a surprise. I'm not sure what to say."

"No pressure, Allison. Take some time to think about it." He winked at her. "But I know we'd have a wonderful time. There is so much I'd love to show you in Italy." Changing the subject, Mark called for the check. "I think we'd better get going so we aren't late for our restaurant reservation. With Saturday night traffic, it's probably wise to leave now. It's only about a fifteen-minute walk, but we'll take an Uber," Mark explained.

Relieved to escape further discussion, yet enticed by the idea of a trip to Italy, Allison appreciated the opportunity to take some time to mull it over.

Outside on this early November evening, the weather had changed, and a brisk wind made for an even cooler night. Allison wore a lightweight jacket, but the strong breeze seemed to penetrate through the fabric. She was glad Mark decided to call an Uber.

Without wasting any time, Mark opened the right rear passenger door and let Allison get in first. *Always the gentleman*, Allison noted. "È Tutto Qua, on Columbus, right?" the driver verified.

"That's it," Mark confirmed. "Allison, I hope you're hungry tonight. This place is known for having the most authentic Italian food in San Francisco and the best pasta in North Beach."

"You had me at the name, È Tutto Qua. In Italian it means, 'And that's all.' I already love it." Her eyes flashed, and she smiled with contentment. "And how did you know I love Italian food more than any other?"

As Mark predicted, the streets were busy. Once they turned onto Kearny Street, cars were bumper-to-bumper. Unconcerned, Allison enjoyed the time with Mark, and all thoughts of work disappeared. When he reached for her hand, she didn't demur. Instead, she squeezed his in return and gazed into his eyes. With the stream of traffic at a standstill, a light shone on his face at just the right angle, and she could see a hint of a smile. As his piercing blue eyes met hers, she felt something deep within her heart. For the moment, time stood still. No words were exchanged between them, but Allison sensed this instant would be etched into her memory forever.

As they approached Columbus Avenue, the gridlock lessened, and traffic began to flow at the usual speed. Since the restaurant loomed ahead, they might get lucky and make their reservation time.

Less than a minute later and without warning, Allison's svelte body slammed sideways against the left door, and her head collided with the window. Mark's body, restrained by his seatbelt, slid against hers and almost smothered the shocked Allison. Horns blared, tires screeched, sirens rang in the distance, and lightning flashed in the sky.

Careening out of control, the Toyota crashed into another vehicle with a loud boom, before it lurched to a sudden stop. Allison, unable to move and too weak to grasp what happened, spiraled down a black hole into the depths of unconscious oblivion.

~ Chapter 16 ~

Dressed in his street clothes, Gary Tamarino sauntered down the corridor that led to the hospital's parking garage. His emotions spent after the humbling experience at the M&M review, along with an exhausting surgery in the afternoon, he headed for home. Just before he reached the exit doors, he noticed a flat-screen television mounted on the wall near the door. Flashing red letters announcing Breaking News on the LCD TV monitor stopped him in his tracks. With the sound muted, closed captioning alerted him of the disastrous bulletin.

"We have breaking news. Just moments ago, a 6.1 magnitude earthquake rocked the San Francisco Bay Area along the Hayward Fault, with the epicenter believed to be near Oakland. Extensive damage has occurred, and reports are coming in live. Accidents are blocking major highways, and Bay Area hospitals have instituted disaster alerts. Mass casualties are expected."

Horrified, Gary attempted to process the information. He remembered feeling a bit of rocking while he showered earlier but had dismissed it, attributing the occurrence to low blood sugar.

As more images flashed on the screen, he focused his attention on the news story and then wondered about damages to this facility. Hospital protocol dictated the disaster plan to be initiated and that he'd be needed. At least San Francisco Bay Hospital maintained compliance with the 2020 deadline set by the statewide Seismic Safety Act of 1983, so he knew the building didn't risk a collapse.

Stunned by the gravity of the tragedy, Gary hurried back toward CSU.

He found business as usual in the unit, though the staff seemed on edge, as he expected. His cell phone pinged with a text from the CEO. "Earthquake 6.1. Disaster Plan in effect. Come to the hospital stat."

Before he left the unit, he inquired about his patients. "Rosa, any problems I need to know about? Are my patients stable?" Her response relieved any worries he harbored, and he walked toward the OR without another word. He found Annette and Kumar in the surgeons' lounge, along with some of the other surgeons and anesthesiologists. They gathered around the TV, watching for updates.

"Did you feel the earthquake?" Annette said. "I heard Oakland got hit pretty bad. And I know the ER has already been alerted to expect multiple victims. I suppose we'll be up all night again."

"I was at home and definitely felt a lot of shaking," Dr. Kumar said. "I've been through earthquakes before, and after a minute, everything stopped. I had to reassure my family that we were okay. We didn't have any damage. I heard the power is out in quite a few places."

Tamarino decided this would be the ideal opportunity for him to try and redeem himself. He'd be able to be the savior once more as he treated the earthquake casualties. He hoped to smooth over the previous tensions between himself, Kumar, and Annette. In a quiet voice and out of earshot of the other physicians, he spoke to his nurse practitioner. "Annette, we should talk before things get crazy here. We had the M&M this morning, and I know my patient stats have been terrible. All that's going to change, I promise you. I need you on my side."

***

What could Annette say? She had to work with Dr. T. Until the past few weeks, things had been good. Maybe he deserved another chance. She found it hard to disregard his charisma. "I'm listening. You know my main priority is always the patient."

"I understand, and that's all I care about too. I know my head messed with me for a time, and I couldn't concentrate because of all the shit at home. My personal circumstances just overwhelmed me. I think I have a handle on it now." He smiled that thousand-dollar smile and winked at Annette.

She recalled the conversation with Allison regarding her oversight company and wondered how that would pan out. *Were we premature in initiating the process?* Her only reply to Gary was, "Let's hope so."

***

Kumar listened in silence. His eyes held a puzzled look as he remembered the suggestion Gary had made about taking time off and letting Annette and himself handle things. Maybe even bring on a traveling surgeon. What happened to that? Uncertain about Gary's credibility, he decided not to confront him now. They had work to do.

~ Chapter 17 ~

Dazed and in pain, Mark Derning's level of consciousness vacillated. Unaware of his surroundings, he lost all sense of time. His thought processes slowed. His body adhered to Allison's motionless form in what felt like a tight space, and he couldn't move. Loud noises jolted him from his state of lethargy but only for a few seconds at a time. A bright light flashed, and a man's voice roused him. "EMS. We're here to help. There's been an earthquake. Can you hear me, sir?"

Mark heard the question, but everything seemed blurred, and he couldn't reply with words. He managed a weak nod and detected someone's hands on his body. "We're going to get you out of here, sir. Can you move your legs? Squeeze my hand."

Disoriented, Mark only caught certain words. At some point he saw other people and vehicles and ascertained that he was no longer inside the car. His body was strapped onto a stretcher, and lights flashed all around him. The cold night air stimulated his altered state, and his cognition improved a bit. He vaguely remembered Allison sitting next to him in a vehicle.

"Allison . . . is she okay?" he asked in a weak voice, relieved to finally have the ability to form a few words.

Nobody answered him. Unable to turn his head due to a cervical collar placed by the first responders, Mark's concern intensified.

By now he lay inside a moving emergency vehicle. He repeated the query. "I remember another person in the back seat with me. Do you know what happened to her?" At last, the female paramedic who had started his IV replied, "The other passenger is being treated, sir. Her injuries were severe, and the emergency personnel are doing everything they can for her. She's in another ambulance on her way to the hospital."

Alarmed, he feared the worst. "How bad is she? Is she conscious?"

"We're taking you to the same hospital. You'll be able to find out more information once we arrive. We don't know anything else now. I'm sorry. How does your head feel?"

Mark wondered how the crash had occurred and what had happened to the driver. *Too many questions.* His head throbbed, and everything started to swirl out of control in his mind. Someone applied an oxygen mask to his face. He closed his eyes and surrendered to the darkness.

***

Groggy and disoriented, Allison heard someone talking. "Can you hear me? Move your toes. Squeeze my hand." Nothing made sense. She tried to talk and couldn't. *What's happening to me?*

"Allison, you're in the emergency room. My name is Veronica. I'm a nurse, and you were in a bad accident.

Can you understand me?" Allison heard the words but didn't comprehend them. "You're at San Francisco Bay Hospital, and we're going to take good care of you. You have a tube in your throat to help you breathe, so you won't be able to talk right now."

Allison comprehended just enough of those words to grasp that she couldn't speak. Her throat hurt and fear engulfed her. Her eyes darted back and forth as she attempted to make sense of her surroundings. Her mouth tasted like cotton, and an overwhelming sensation of choking overpowered her. *If I could only get their attention,* she thought. *Please don't leave me alone here.* Terrified of the unknown, she feared the worst. *Am I going to die?*

As a nurse attempted to remove the ring from Allison's right hand, an authoritative male voice commanded attention. "She's losing blood, and we're wasting time. We need to move her now. Let's go, people."

In a fog and slow to fathom the gravity of her condition, Allison closed her eyes. Her traumatized body, numbed by narcotics for pain, no longer functioned as a conduit to alert her to the danger she faced.

Out of nowhere, a familiar voice materialized. A vision of Rosa's sweet face appeared, but Allison didn't understand why her night shift charge nurse showed up. "It's me. Rosa. You have a ruptured spleen, Allison, and they're taking you to surgery. You're going to come to CSU afterward." Rosa touched Allison's bruised hand and reassured her. "When you wake up, I'll be there to take care of you." Allison nodded before she closed her eyes.

~ Chapter 18 ~

"Mr. Derning, I'm Dr. Breshan, one of the hospitalists here. I have some good news. You've suffered some minor injuries, but you're going to be okay. As a cautionary measure, we'd like to keep you overnight, since you did sustain a concussion. They can repeat the CT scan tomorrow, and if that looks good, your doctor will probably clear you for discharge." A temporary wave of relief swept over Mark. "They'll work on getting you a room, but it may be a while. With the earthquake and all, it's been nothing but chaos here. We're lucky our hospital suffered minimal effects and is running almost at full speed."

"Okay, thanks, Doc." As Mark's ability to process information returned to normal, his concern about Allison increased. He needed answers—and fast.

"Listen, I don't mean to be a pain in the ass, Doctor, but I have to find out what happened to the woman in the car with me. Her name is Allison Jamison. I was told that she came here by ambulance, in critical condition. I don't know if she's even alive." His eyes filled with tears as he begged the young doctor to help him.

"I'll see what I can find out. You say you were both in the car?"

"Yes, we were in the rear seat when the car crashed. I wondered about the Uber driver too."

The ER physician disappeared, and Mark hoped he'd return with some answers. Not used to being in a position of helplessness, he focused on the last conversation he'd had with Allison. He recalled how intent she had been on filling him in about a cardiothoracic surgeon who messed up. Now he wished he had given her the chance to tell the story. He made a mental note to contact Sherry Dolan as soon as he had a chance.

Mark had his share of dealing with stressful circumstances, but the unknown heightened his anxiety. In his long career, he'd faced threats and danger numerous times, but as a law enforcement officer, he'd always managed to handle that type of pressure. Being left in the dark about Allison's condition created an exponentially worse situation for him. *Where is that doctor? I know they're busy, but it's been at least half an hour.*

"Excuse me," Mark said as someone in black scrubs breezed past his cubicle.

"Did you need something, sir?"

Surprised when the tall, forty-something female actually stopped and addressed him, he perked up. "Yes, ma'am. Thank you. I asked one of the doctors to check on a patient who came in just ahead of me. He must have gotten busy, because he never came back."

"Who is the patient? Do you have a name?"

"I'm beside myself not knowing how she is. Her name is Allison Jamison."

The moment Mark mentioned the name, the astute healthcare professional replied, "My name is Cheryl, and

I'm the charge nurse tonight. Yes, I know about Allison. She's pretty banged up, with internal injuries as well, and on a ventilator. She had a ruptured spleen and proceeded straight to surgery. She'll be in one of the ICUs afterward."

Grateful for the information and reassured by the fact that Allison was alive, Mark heaved a sigh of relief and thanked the nurse. *"I've got to get out of here,"* he mumbled as she pulled the curtain around his cubicle and walked away. *Hang on, Allison. Please hang on.*

~ Chapter 19 ~

Muffled voices competed with the constant noise of shrill beeps as the patient ascended to a higher realm of consciousness. Vaguely aware of her surroundings, Allison wondered why she couldn't move. Through glazed eyes, she perceived an indistinct image that soon morphed into the shape of a person dressed in ceil-blue surgical scrubs.

A pleasant, soft, female voice caught her attention. "Allison, everything is okay. It's me. Rosa. You're just waking up from surgery, and you're in CSU." As a courtesy to one of their own nurses, CSU admitted Allison straight from the operating room, bypassing the surgical recovery room. Her reality clouded, Allison stared up at the stark white ceiling. She listened as Rosa continued her assessment. "Can you wiggle your toes?" Allison heard the request and followed the instruction, but nothing happened. "Allison, squeeze my hand." After a short pause, Rosa leaned in closer. "It's okay, Allison. You're just starting to wake up. I'm here with you," she added in a reassuring tone. "You still have a breathing tube in your throat, so you won't be able to talk until we can take it out. It's temporary. Can you understand what I'm telling you?" Allison blinked her eyes and attempted to nod.

Twenty minutes later, the nurse anesthetist who had put Allison to sleep in surgery stopped at the bedside to check on her status. "I see she's starting to wake up. Let's give her a little more time and then start to wean her off the ventilator. I'm hopeful she'll be able to breathe on her own, and we can get her extubated."

She's talking about me, Allison thought. But nothing seemed real.

"Her vital signs are stable, and she's not doing too bad, considering all her injuries. Ruptured spleen, fractured rib, pneumothorax, and concussion. Lucky she's young," Rosa said.

Not quite alert enough to be alarmed, Allison absorbed Rosa's words but faded in and out of anesthesia-induced sleep. The next time she woke, she experienced an inordinate sensation of dry mouth. Her tongue thick and her throat on fire, she craved something wet but was unable to ask for it. As if Rosa could read her patient's mind, she refreshed Allison's dried, cracked lips with a wet cloth and swabbed her mouth. Instant relief.

"Allison, you're much more awake now. I see you can move. Are you having any pain?"

Allison grimaced and nodded, aware of severe pain all over her battered body. Rosa responded, "I'll give you something for your pain soon. I want to get you off this vent and get the tube out so you can talk to me. I don't want to give you any medicine that will make you go back to sleep. Hang in there with me a little longer, okay?" Allison squeezed Rosa's hands and wiggled her toes as instructed.

Rosa called over to the respiratory therapist. "Eva, she's quite a bit more awake now. The sedation is off, and she has spontaneous respirations on CPAP. Let's get some weaning parameters and a blood gas, okay?"

"That's what I like to hear. I'll be right there." As long as a patient maintained hemodynamic stability and met the criteria to breathe with adequate volumes, weaning became a realistic goal.

When the therapist returned, Rosa asked, "Do you know Allison? She's one of our travel nurses in CSU."

"I haven't been assigned to that unit much, so I don't know her."

"She's a little more alert, but she incurred some serious injuries during the earthquake."

"Yeah, I've seen plenty of those in the ER."

Wide-eyed and puzzled, Allison listened and wanted to know more. Rosa turned to look at her and asked, "Allison, can you hear what I'm saying? I'm talking about you."

Allison nodded and tried to turn her head. With the collar no longer around her neck, she could move a little. Her eyes searched for answers. Rosa continued to explain. "You have a chest tube and probably feel some pain at the insertion site here." She gently patted Allison's hospital gown in the area of her upper-left chest. "The emergency room physician put it in so your collapsed lung would reinflate."

Her memory jogged by these details, transient images flashed in front of her as she relived parts of the horrific disaster. A man accompanied her, but she didn't know who. She didn't remember the circumstances of the car travel. Her last clear memory reverted back to a time prior to getting hurt. She stood alone on a stage in

Berkeley, an exuberant crowd cheering and applauding before her.

~ Chapter 20 ~

Gary Tamarino was in his element. In the midst of a disaster, he rose up to save the day. Casualties from the earthquake poured into the emergency room, and trauma surgeons occupied every operating room. As chief of cardiothoracic surgery, Gary responded to emergency consults for any cardiac or thoracic traumas. His partner and their nurse practitioner also remained on call for the same purpose. He excelled at the role of savior, especially in intense circumstances like the current Bay Area calamity. He knew he could reclaim his reputation with this opportune event. Staying up all night only fueled the natural high he relished. At times like this, he required no chemicals or drugs.

At 4:00 a.m., Dr. T and his surgical team were close to completing their second emergency trauma case. The hospital had implemented the disaster code a little over eight hours ago. Tamarino left Annette and Kumar to close the wound and finish the case. "Fantastic job, team. We saved another life. Thank you."

Before he left the room, the circulating surgery nurse alerted him to a stat consult. "CSU is calling. They need you to see a trauma patient."

"Okay, I'm headed there now," he said as he gave a nod to his partner. Assured of his own importance, he strode into the hectic environment of the cardiovascular surgical unit, or CSU. With the nurses' station vacant, he walked down the hall and sought out Rosa to discover the need for the emergency consult. The usual protocol would be for the trauma surgeon to handle whatever situation arose, so he assumed this must be related to a cardiac emergency.

Dr. Tamarino found Rosa in a room near the end of the unit. Hovered over her patient's bedside, her back to the door, she turned her head as he approached. "I heard you have an emergency consult here on a trauma patient."

"Yes, Dr. T. This is the patient. Allison Jamison. You might not recognize her as one of the CSU night shift nurses. She came in last evening as a trauma from the earthquake. Dr. Iammetti did an emergency splenectomy. She looked good, ready to extubate, when she became hemodynamically unstable and her respiratory rate increased. Iammetti suspected a pericardial effusion and ordered a stat ultrasound and cardiothoracic consult. The ultrasound tech is on his way."

Traumatic effusions can develop fast and, if large enough, cause a cardiac tamponade, a life-threatening circumstance. Tamarino evaluated Allison's current vital signs displayed on the cardiac monitor. After reviewing her chest x-ray, he asked if she was awake.

"She's in and out of it. I don't think she grasps what's going on."

Tamarino welcomed Allison's decreased level of consciousness, especially after his last encounter with her. The ultrasound tech arrived, and Tamarino stayed to observe. Five minutes later he confirmed the diagnosis of a significant pericardial effusion and knew it needed to be drained as soon as possible. He didn't plan to waste time doing the less invasive pericardiocentesis at the bedside. In his experience, these procedures acted as temporary fixes and necessitated repeated procedures. Peering down at the motionless form in the bed, he spoke to his patient. "Allison, it's Dr. Tamarino. I'm going to take you to surgery to repair a pericardial effusion. We can't wait on this. Can you understand me?" Allison's eyes opened and her brows drew closer together.

"She's not alert enough for informed consent, Dr. T, and there's no family here. You feel this requires emergent action?" Rosa inquired.

"I have no choice. Alert the OR." Before Rosa could utter another word, he turned and disappeared.

~ Chapter 21 ~

Mark Derning received his official discharge papers from the hospital the afternoon following the accident. Fortunate to have escaped with only a mild concussion and some superficial bruising, his primary focus was on Allison. The last he knew, she had gone to surgery late last night.

He smiled at the volunteer who sat at the patient information desk. "I'd like the room number of Allison Jamison, please."

After searching her computer, the pleasant woman returned the smile and replied, "She's in CSU Room 7. Take the elevator to the second floor and turn left." She handed him a name badge, and he thanked her.

Mark's mind flashed back to the last time he and Allison were in an ICU together. The circumstances were so different, yet he remembered it as if it had happened last week. They'd both been on duty in their professional capacities that day, when he gave her the news that they had officially charged her boyfriend's killer with murder.

He rang the bell to be admitted to the cardiovascular surgical unit. A scratchy voice responded. "May I help you?"

How could he have foreseen that two years later he'd be in San Francisco worried sick about her? "I'm here to see Allison Jamison."

After a brief pause, a buzzer sounded, allowing entry for visitor Mark Derning. Not sure what to expect, he walked through the unit until he reached Room 7. Drab beige curtains inside the window obscured his view into the room.

He was still in his clothes from the night before and could use a shower, but leaving the hospital without first checking on Allison was never an option. He paced back and forth as he waited for permission to see her.

Soon, a nurse emerged from her room. After Mark identified himself, she provided him with an update. "She's a lot better now, considering she's had two surgeries. She had her spleen removed and then went back as an emergency to remove fluid building up around her heart. Recovery will take time, but she's tough, and she's going to be okay."

Mark entered the private room to find a small figure in a bed surrounded by IV pumps and a heart monitor. With her head elevated and her body propped slightly to one side with a large pillow, Allison looked so vulnerable and fragile. Derning noticed the nasal oxygen, another tube from inside her nose draining brown fluid into a suction canister, and two other tubes hanging off the side of the bed. All color had drained from Allison's cheeks, her eyes were closed, and her youthful face appeared worn. *Poor Allison*, he thought. His heart ached, seeing her like this. Tears welled in his eyes, and a sharp pain developed in his throat as he fought back the urge to cry.

He crept quietly toward her and held her bruised and swollen right hand. Gazing at her, he spoke in the softest tone possible. "Allison?" The constant high-pitched beeping of her cardiac monitor clanged like a car alarm in the otherwise silent environment. With a gentle touch, he brushed his hand across her cheek and called her name again in an attempt to rouse her. "Allison, it's me. Mark. Are you awake?" When she didn't respond, he pulled a chair closer to her bed so he could sit by her side.

So many thoughts reeled in his head as he relived last night's tragedy. Had he gotten into the car first, Allison wouldn't have been the one sitting near the door that got rammed, and she would be okay now. In his mind he knew playing the what-if game was a pointless exercise, but he couldn't help it. His feelings for her had grown from friendship to much more. He hadn't yet found an opportune time to share what his heart wanted to say. She had to wake up.

~ Chapter 22 ~

Where am I? Allison opened her eyes to a blur of muted colors and unrecognizable objects. Struggling to discern a familiar face, she thought she distinguished the shape of a person but lacked the concentration to complete an identification. With no success for her effort, she attempted to sit up.

The sound woke Derning from a light sleep, and he jumped to his feet. "It's Mark, Allison. You're awake. I'm right here." She recognized the man in front of her now. Her expressive blue eyes met his, and he picked up her hand and held it tight.

She stared at him. In a fragile voice, she asked, "Where am I?"

At the sound of her voice, Mark closed his eyes and whispered, "Thank you, God." Then he swallowed hard against the lump in his throat before addressing her. "You're in the hospital, Allison. You're waking up from surgery."

"How did I get here?" she muttered. Without going into too much detail, Mark recounted the events from the night before and told Allison he'd be there for her. She still didn't comprehend everything and wondered why they were together in a car. Mark Derning worked for her, but she hadn't seen him for a long time. *What is he doing in San Francisco?* Her furrowed brow begged him for an explanation.

"Allison, I'm glad you're awake, and I'm sure everything seems fuzzy right now. Maybe the accident or the anesthesia affected your memory. What is the last thing you recall?"

Allison closed her eyes and concentrated while Mark waited. Half a minute later, she looked at him and answered the question. "I remember speaking to an audience of critical care nurses in Berkeley. The crowd clapped for a long time, and I felt good."

"What about after that?"

She scrunched her eyebrows and did her best to remember. "Nothing. That's the last thing I know."

"You don't remember taking an Uber to the city? Or meeting me at the Grand Hyatt for a drink and appetizers?"

Perplexed by these questions, Allison shook her head. "Are you kidding me? What are you talking about?" Alarmed about the confusing circumstances that made no sense to her, she asked him to explain.

"I don't know all the details, Allison, but you had two surgeries. Your nurse said you're going to be okay, but it will take some time. Are you in pain?"

"A little, but it's not bad, at least for now. Tell me about the accident again. And how you ended up here with me. It's all so confusing."

"I know you said you don't remember, but I came to San Francisco to see you. After your presentation in Berkeley, you met me at the Hyatt in Union Square. We had a nice time catching up. You looked fantastic, by the way." He smiled.

"It sounds nice. I wish I could remember, though," she said, surprised to hear all of this. "Then what happened?"

"After dinner we got into an Uber headed for North Beach. We had reservations at a wonderful Italian restaurant." He paused, and she noticed he began to tear up. "Then, all of a sudden, we were involved in a huge accident. I can't even tell you how it happened, except the crash occurred as a result of an earthquake. Everything's a little blurry for me from that point on too. I had a concussion but no other serious injuries. You got the brunt of it, Allison."

She listened like a bystander hearing about an incident that involved someone else.

"I worried until I could see you," he said.

Mark's words made no sense to her. She found it curious that he expressed this degree of concern for her. *What else don't I remember?*

~ Chapter 23 ~

By the end of the weekend, Gary Tamarino's self-confidence soared. Despite sleeping only a few hours in his own bed, his energy level skyrocketed. He'd redeemed himself and restored his reputation as the best cardiothoracic surgeon at San Francisco Bay Hospital. Everyone viewed him as the rescuer who saved the day, and he was on top of the world. His affluent neighborhood had received minimal damage from the earthquake, and power had not been lost.

Getting stoned didn't even appeal to him this evening. He flipped on the TV, unable to pull away from the horrific images and video of complete devastation across the Bay Area. Luck had played a huge role in sparing his home from the destructive forces of the catastrophic earthquake. By eight o'clock, boredom set in, and he decided to return to the hospital. He wanted to check on his patients, and his call lasted through the weekend.

Still dressed in street clothes, he waltzed into CSU. Rose greeted him, wide-eyed. "Dr. Tamarino, I didn't expect to see you tonight. I hope you at least had a chance to catch up on some rest."

"I did, thank you. How's everything going here?"

Blunt and to the point, Rosa replied, "Busy. Two of our nurses called out because they had damage at their homes, so we're a little short tonight. At least most of the patients are fairly stable, and the OR isn't going nonstop anymore."

Not commenting on Rosa's words, Tamarino asked for an update on Allison. "She wasn't awake when I left early this morning, so I wanted to check on her."

"She's in Room 7, Dr. T."

When Gary entered Allison's room, he found her asleep. The vital signs displayed on her cardiac monitor looked good. He noted two chest tubes and was happy to see she was no longer on the vent. "Allison?" he called out.

Her eyes opened, and Dr. T walked toward her bed. "Good to see you doing so well, Allison. How are you feeling?"

Allison gasped. "Dr. T? What are you doing here?"

"Didn't someone tell you I saved your life last night?" he said with a smirk, happy for the opportunity to brag about his lifesaving skills.

Without pausing to give her a chance to answer, he continued. "They called me in the middle of the night, suspecting a pericardial effusion. Luckily, I was just finishing up a late case. You were getting ready to tamponade, so I took you to surgery and did a pericardial window."

He examined the dressing and glanced at the drainage containers connected to her chest tubes. Maintaining a businesslike persona, he ended with a professional statement. "From my standpoint, you're going to be okay. Dr. Iammetti, the trauma surgeon, will handle the rest of your case. Do you have any questions for me?"

Allison eked out a quiet thank you and said nothing else. Gary Tamarino left the room.

***

What the fuck just happened? How did I end up in a position to have to thank the Almighty God Tamarino for my life? Allison's memory demonstrated no signs of impairment when it came to Dr. Tamarino. Images of her night with Mrs. Brock flashed before her. Without a doubt, she remembered the email she sent to Sherry Dolan when she referred him to her Critical Cover-Up company. Now she wondered whether they'd started the investigation.

Wait a minute. I wanted Mark Derning on that case too. Select details began to emerge in her mind as she tried to stir her memory. A fleeting thought about a conversation with Mark. *Yes, in a hotel bar or restaurant. What did that entail?*

More alert now, she sought to take stock of her present circumstances. She understood she'd had surgery due to injuries from an accident. The acute pain she experienced each time she moved convinced her of that. She vaguely remembered Rosa explaining the circumstances that preceded her admission to the hospital. Mark had been here too, and he'd told her the same thing. Now that her grogginess had disappeared, she wanted more information.

As if on cue, Rosa walked into her room before she had a chance to press the call bell. "So great to see you smiling, Allison. You were really out of it last night."

"So I hear. Do you have a few minutes? I don't even know who my nurse is tonight."

"Your nurse is Marie, but I do have a few minutes. Do you remember anything from last night? I took care of you myself."

Shaking her head, Allison said, "No. I wish I did. I'm glad you were there. Rosa, I need some answers. Tamarino just came in here and told me he saved my life. Is that true, or is he just being an asshole?"

"Actually, it's sort of true, although he may be exaggerating a little. You came here straight from surgery, and I took care of you. A few hours post-op, you developed a huge effusion and were hypotensive. Dr. Iammetti consulted Cardio, and Dr. T evaluated you. He thought a needle pericardiocentesis wasn't the best option and took you to surgery to do an emergency pericardial window instead."

Still unable to absorb all the details of what she'd been through in the past twenty-four hours, Allison appreciated her friend Rosa more than ever. "Thank you for being here for me. I'm still confused. There's a lot more I want to talk to you about, but I'm having too much pain and I'm tired now. Promise me you'll come back?"

"I'll have Marie bring you some pain medication." Rosa squeezed Allison's hand. "And don't worry, I'm not going anywhere. I'll be here all night."

Helpless, vulnerable, and weak, Allison wished she could go to sleep. *Maybe when I wake up, I'll realize this was all just a bad dream.*

~ Chapter 24 ~

A sliver of light streamed through a narrow opening between the wall and the edge of the window shade. Mark Derning rolled over in his luxurious, king-size, hotel bed and wondered what time it was. Using the remote-control button on the wall, he raised the roller shade just enough to be almost blinded by the bright, early morning sun. The sudden realization that he had slept through the night became clear in an instant. Raising the shade higher, he admired the panoramic view of San Francisco, recognizing famous landmarks like the Transamerica Pyramid and Coit Tower. Two days ago, he had hoped to share this experience with Allison. As he wiped away a tear, the image of her traumatized body in that hospital bed jerked him back to reality.

Shifting gears, he ordered room service and checked his phone. No texts and nothing important via email. He had no idea whether Allison had access to her phone, but since it was still early, he decided to wait a bit before trying to text her. Instead, he composed an email to Sherry Dolan. On the subject line he typed, "Urgent — Allison Jamison — Earthquake." In the body of the email he filled her in on the situation. He then referenced the case Allison had mentioned, the one about a cardiothoracic surgeon at San Francisco Bay Hospital. He told Sherry that he was currently in San Francisco and that Allison had requested for him to be assigned as investigator on the case. Mark asked Sherry to contact him by phone as soon as possible, adding the caveat of urgency.

A knock on the door announced the arrival of his much-needed coffee and a full breakfast of sausage and eggs with a serving of fresh fruit. After filling his stomach with fuel for the day, he showered and dressed in a hurry. By nine o'clock his Uber ride transported him to the hospital.

As he entered the front door of the medical facility, Mark received a call from Sherry Dolan. He took a seat in the well-appointed, spacious lobby and answered in businesslike fashion.

The low, hoarse voice of Sherry was one he recognized at once. "Mark, I'm so glad you contacted me. I haven't heard from Allison since she referred that case to me on Friday morning. I had no idea she was involved in an accident. It's been chaotic around here since the earthquake. How is she?"

Mark told her he was on his way to visit Allison and would know more later. Then he inquired about the specific case Allison had mentioned. Sherry replied, "We have already opened the case and started working on it, but we certainly welcome your expertise. We'll get you up to speed in short order, and you can start immediately. I'm going to send you an email with all the information we have. You'll be working with Christy Newsell."

"Okay, Sherry. Thank you. I'll be on the lookout for the email and will be in touch with Christy."

"Be sure to tell Allison not to worry about a thing. She just needs to concentrate on getting better. We have everything covered here."

"Good. I'll let her know. I'm on my way to check in on her now. Thanks again."

Pleased at his success in making contact with Sherry, he focused on his prime agenda, seeing Allison. He registered at the information desk and took the elevator to the second floor. By now he knew the drill.

When Mark walked into her room, Allison was sitting in a chair. Delighted at the progress she'd made since he last saw her, he made his way toward her and gave her a kiss on the cheek. His face revealed the joy in his heart, and she returned the smile. "Mark, it's good to see you."

"You look a hundred percent better than when I left. I'm happy you're able to be out of that hospital bed." He noted she still had some tubes connected, but the oxygen had been removed.

"They tell me I'm progressing, and I'm a lot more alert, now that I'm not so drugged up with anesthesia and pain meds."

"That's all good news, Allison. Do you have more of an understanding of what happened and everything you've been through?"

"Yes. I know about my injuries and surgeries. What I'm still not too clear about is what happened just before the accident. I know you told me we were on our way to dinner, but I still don't have any memory of that." He interpreted the look in her eyes as apologetic. He would have given anything for her memory of that evening to be as clear as his.

In an attempt to elicit some recall, Mark Derning stepped it up a notch. "Allison, I wonder if you recollect anything about a new case you just referred to Critical Cover-Up. You said something about a surgeon who was messing up, and you wanted me to investigate. Things weren't adding up, and I believe you told me of your suspicions he might be hiding something."

"Yes, I did refer a case to Sherry, and I wanted you on it. How did you know?"

Without answering directly, and hiding the disappointment he felt over her inability to remember their previous discussion about the case, he told her he had spoken with Sherry and was waiting for a corresponding email with details of the case. "I'll be working with Christy Newsell. Sherry said they've already started looking into it. By the way, I told her about the accident and that you're in the hospital. She said to get better and not to concern yourself with anything at the company. They're handling things fine."

"Thanks, Mark. That's a relief. I've been so out of it that I didn't even think about calling anyone. Can I ask a favor of you? See if my bag is in one of those drawers. My phone should be in it."

Happy to be of help, Mark opened all three drawers of the bedside table and pulled out her black-leather Michael Kors handbag. Allison opened it and found her cell phone intact, its battery depleted. Mark attached the charging cord and connected it to the wall outlet for her.

"Are you feeling good enough for me to visit for a while? I don't want to be a burden."

"Oh no. You're not a burden at all. I'm glad you're here. I wanted to tell you more about this doctor."

For the next twenty minutes, Allison described the incidents that had alarmed her enough to report Dr. Gary Tamarino. "And are you ready for this? I woke up from surgery to find out he's my doctor."

Derning raised his eyebrows. "What? How did that happen?"

"I guess I wasn't conscious enough to give informed consent, and he operated on me under emergency conditions. Then he came in here all high and mighty and told me he saved my life. He forced me into a position of gratitude."

Mark detected no love lost between the two. His concern for her escalated as he pondered how this surgeon might react once he became aware of the investigation by an oversight company owned by his patient. The sooner Mark got on board, the better. "Allison, I'm going to leave so you can rest. I'll get to work on the assignment, but I'll be back. Now that you have your cell phone, don't hesitate to text me. I can be here in less than half an hour if you need anything."

"Thank you, Mark. Listen, I did want to say one thing. A good contact for you is a nurse practitioner who works with this surgeon. Her name is Annette Brashton. She's on our side and knows I referred the case."

Mark took out his smartphone and created a file for the case. He added Annette 's name and her title. "Do you have a contact number for her?"

Allison checked her phone and gave him Annette's cell phone number. "Thank you, again, Mark. I feel better knowing you're here and working on the case. What are your plans for staying in San Francisco?"

"I'm not sure," Mark said as he winked at Allison. "That depends."

~ Chapter 25 ~

The euphoria Gary Tamarino had been enjoying for the past thirty-six hours, as he worked almost nonstop to save lives, reached an abrupt end late Monday morning when he received the dreaded margin call from his brokerage firm. Over the past month, despite heavy losses in his options trading, he'd believed in a sure-fire solution to generate quick cash in the stock market; in the process, he overextended himself.

Throughout the years, Apple stock had paid off for him, so he decided to triple his investment into the tech giant. Soon after, Apple's price began to drop, and he saw his investment profit disappear. In an attempt to compensate for the losses, he started to double down and purchased more stock at the lower price. He repeated the stock buys three times, but Apple continued to plummet. Certain it would recover in time, he ignored the red flags in front of him and didn't sell any of his stock.

Impatient and cocky, he began to trade on margin, at a huge risk. Margin trading is, in effect, borrowing money from the broker. This dangerous type of investment took a toll when Apple stock tanked, and the value of his equity fell below the specified percentage requirement, or margin. He was expected to replace the funds in cash by the end of the trading day or face the prospect of the remainder of his portfolio being sold off to make up what he owed. He had over $100,000 of his own money invested and now risked losing that amount, as well as another $100,000 from the margin account plus interest he was charged. He knew he was screwed, since most of his exposure was in the tech sector and predominantly in Apple. He didn't have enough money in his portfolio, and he realized he was about to lose it all. The brokerage firm would liquidate his account and send him a bill for the remaining money he owed. His net loss was substantial—close to a quarter of a million dollars.

Time had run out, and he had squandered most of his disposable funds in these perilous investments. He wished he had free time to make calls between surgeries to try and engineer some way to pay off his debt.

***

"Well, Gary's good mood is already a thing of the past," announced Kumar. Annette looked up to see him standing next to her with a lunch tray in hand. He sat down beside her at a corner table in the physicians' cafeteria and shook his head, exasperated with his partner. "Just when I wanted to give him the benefit of the doubt. What's the story with him?"

"A leopard doesn't change his spots. Something's been going on with him for a while. He got lucky this weekend," Annette replied. "He's unpredictable. This morning during the first case he seemed fine, singing and joking. And he hasn't had any bad outcomes since Friday. With the trauma cases this weekend, he was in high spirits. I know it's only been three days, but that's a new record."

"I can't take much more of his Dr. Jekyll and Mr. Hyde personality. He needs to straighten out his life, whatever's wrong with it. I wonder if Allison had a chance to report him before the earthquake."

"Maybe she did and that's why he's acting like a child whose candy was taken away. When I make rounds I'll talk with her about it and let you know. She may have mixed feelings, since he's her surgeon now. But make no mistake, Kumar. I'm sick of Gary's mood swings too. And I'm not going to put up with him much longer."

His dark eyes focused on hers. "I'm glad we're on the same page, Annette."

~ Chapter 26 ~

The hospital's expansive, well-appointed, open, lobby resembled a stylish boutique hotel more than a healthcare facility. With its high ceilings, a media wall decorated with changing nature scenes, and soft sounds of New Age music, the beautiful space met its goal of providing an ambience of tranquility. The serenity appealed to Mark Derning, and he decided the soft swivel chairs afforded enough comfort for him to work there. He pulled a laptop out of his briefcase and settled in.

Reassured of Allison's progress, he directed his efforts toward his work. An email from Sherry Dolan caught his attention. The subject line read, "Critical Cover-Up Case 267 – Intake." A duplicate copy had been sent to Christy Newsell.

As Allison had mentioned to him, the subject of the probe involved a cardiothoracic surgeon at this hospital. He noted the list of allegations regarding Dr. Gary Tamarino, chief of cardiothoracic surgery. The email referenced contact numbers for Christy Newsell, ARNP Annette Brashton, Dr. Kumar Chanrami, and Rosa Perez, RN.

Reviewing the email a second time, Mark drafted his reply to Sherry and Christy. On the subject line, he typed,

"From Mark Derning - Case 267." He wanted to touch base and let them know his availability, effective immediately. He told Christy he would text her to schedule a phone call later today.

His next order of business at the hospital centered on a meeting with Annette Brashton. Allison had emphasized the importance of getting in touch with her, so he wasted no further time. Assuming she might be at work and hoping he'd catch her between surgeries, he sent a text. "From Mark Derning, friend of Allison Jamison. She asked me to contact you. I'm in the hospital lobby and would like to meet with you today if possible. Awaiting your reply. Thank you."

***

Annette strolled into Allison's room, delighted to see the smile on her patient's face. She embraced her friend and stepped back to have a better look at her.

"It's wonderful to see you sitting in a chair. I see Dr. Iammetti removed your chest tube. And you're eating now, too?" she said, pleased at Allison's speedy progress.

"Yes, I'm coming along. It feels good to finally be out of that bed. I guess you guys knocked me out good for a day or two. My mind is working like it should again, or close to it, anyway, so I was hoping you'd stop by for a visit."

Annette used her stethoscope to listen to Allison's heart and lungs and glanced at the vital signs on her monitor. She reviewed the morning's digital chest image and lab values on her iPad. "You're good to go, from a cardiac standpoint," she said with a smile, giving Allison a thumbs-up. "Perhaps Dr. Iammetti will transfer you to Stepdown tomorrow."

"That sounds good. I don't want to spend any more time as a patient than I need to. Annette, do you have a few minutes? I'd like to discuss an unrelated issue with you."

"Sure, I needed to talk to you too. You go first."

"Okay. Rosa filled me in on what happened . . . the earthquake and accident and all. I was too out of it to know that I had to go back to surgery for a pericardial effusion and that Tamarino took me. He came in here later and bragged about how he saved my life."

"Well, it may be a bit dramatic, but yes, he did take you for emergency surgery. That's why I'm making rounds on you. You're our patient."

"I guess I should be grateful, but I haven't changed my mind about his actions and attitude these last weeks."

"Interesting you should mention all that, Allison. It's the exact reason I wanted to talk with you. Did the referral you told me about go through yet? To Critical Cover-Up?"

"I contacted them Friday, so I assume they've started looking into it by now. And there's another detail you need to know. Mark Derning is a friend of mine and works for my company. He's a homicide detective and an excellent investigator, and he's here in San Francisco working this case. He visited me this morning, and I asked him to contact you for information about Tamarino, from your perspective."

Annette nodded. "Okay, now it all makes sense. Just before I walked in here, I received a text message from him. He asked to meet today. I waited to talk with you before I replied. Anything else I need to know?"

"Well, it's weird. We've been friends for over two years. He came out here to see me this weekend. We had a dinner date Saturday night, and he told me we were in a car crash together. Annette, it seems like there's more to the story and the relationship, but I have a blank slate about it. I don't remember an iota of what he related." Allison furrowed her brow in frustration. Annette thought she detected some sadness in her eyes.

~ Chapter 27 ~

Mark Derning's phone pinged with his answer from Annette. "Just finished rounds. Can meet you in the lobby at 4 pm. Is that good?"

A minute later, he replied, "Okay. See you then."

He spotted Annette the moment she appeared in the lobby in her teal-green scrubs and white lab coat, her cell phone in hand. He stood beside a chair at a round table near the wall and watched as she glanced around the spacious room and then approached him. His eyes met hers, and he extended his hand. "I'm Detective Mark Derning. And you're Annette—"

"Yes, Annette Brashton," she said, shaking his hand. "It's a pleasure to meet you, Detective."

"Just call me Mark. Thank you for meeting me. Please sit down." He waited for her to be seated before he followed suit.

"I just came from Allison's room. She's still in CSU but is doing well, sitting up in a chair. I understand you were involved in the accident, in the same vehicle?"

"That's right, but I only had a concussion. Nothing serious. When I didn't know where they took her, I didn't know what to do. I visualized the worst."

"She said you've known each other quite a while and that you're working on the case about our surgeon."

"Correct. I'm just getting started. Anything you can tell me will help me with the investigation. How well do you know this Dr. Gary Tamarino?"

Annette adopted a businesslike tone and summarized her work relationship with Gary. "The three of us are a team. Dr. Tamarino, his partner, Dr. Kumar Chanrami, and me. I work with them in the operating room and make rounds in the hospital, and I also see patients in their office. I'm actually an employee of the hospital."

Mark took notes as Annette continued with the story. "I work beside him every day in surgery, and I can see how he's missed things over the past month." She paused and then said, "It's difficult for me to go against him. He used to be at the top of his game, but something has changed. I've tried to talk to him. He doesn't want to hear about it from Dr. Kumar or me." Her eyes glassy, she wiped away a tear with her left hand. "I'm siding with Allison for his own good, but I still feel like I'm betraying him."

The camaraderie between the surgeon and Annette must have been strong. "I can see this isn't easy for you, Miss Brashton. I just have a couple more questions. Are you aware of situations outside the hospital that might have impacted these changes with Dr. Tamarino? I understand he went through a recent divorce."

Annette composed herself and answered. "It's true. The divorce upset him in a big way. They had been married about fifteen years, I think. No children. I don't know the details about it, but his wife filed. Rumors about an affair flew around."

"And what about his financial problems?"

"He never discussed his personal finances with me. I've overheard him make references to the stock market and his broker, so I assume he had investments. Kumar mentioned to me that Dr. T's been upset about losing money in the market, but that's all I know. You might want to talk to Dr. Chanrami. I think he probably knows more, and he might be open with you. He's just as worried about Dr. T as I am, and any negative outcomes affect the entire practice."

Annette's phone buzzed. "Excuse me." A short text message triggered an immediate end to the conversation. "I need to go." The alarm in Annette's voice was obvious. She was halfway across the lobby before Mark uttered a thank you.

~ Chapter 28 ~

"Kumar, what happened? What's the emergency? I got here as fast as I could." By the time she met Kumar in the back of the cafeteria, Annette needed to catch her breath.

"Gary's one step from going over the edge, and I can't deal with him myself. He left the hospital in a fit of rage. He told me I'd have to take all the calls tonight and said he wouldn't be available." His faster-than-normal speech pattern signaled his intensified distress level. "I had to listen to his nonstop rant before he took off. Annette, he isn't stable."

"What triggered all of this? Do you know why he got agitated?"

"He started to whine about his investments, something about losing his shirt to Apple stock. Then he lit into me like his financial losses were my fault."

"His poor investment strategies aren't our problem, Kumar. He's losing it. How could he possibly accuse you?"

"Does that narcissist need a reason? Any time I disagree with him or tell him something he doesn't want to hear, I get the blame."

"You know he only thinks of himself. But we have to work with him," Annette said. "Before I forget, Allison got the process going last Friday, and they're already on his case. I met with one of the investigators just now, a man named Mark Derning. He's a friend of Allison's and also happens to be an experienced homicide detective."

Kumar relaxed a bit. "Good to know. That may come in handy." He laughed. "But seriously, Annette, if I had any second thoughts about reporting him, they've gone out the window. We're together on this, right?"

"Absolutely, and if you're really in doubt as to whether he'll show up tomorrow or not, we'll need a plan B."

"Exactly what I thought. If he doesn't show tomorrow, we'll just go forward without him. If necessary, you and I can do the surgeries alone. It wouldn't be the first time."

"You're right, Kumar. And I have a hunch things will get worse before they get better."

"Do you know what he had the gall to say to me? His last words as he walked out were, 'You'd better have my back, after all I've done for you.' All he's done for me? Who knows, I may leave the practice and go solo. It's not something I haven't considered."

Annette shook her head in disbelief. "More evidence he's lost his mind."

"Nothing surprises me anymore. He'll probably be here first thing in the morning and act like nothing happened."

"Oh, one more thing. Before I forget to tell you, that investigator will probably contact you. I gave him your name."

"Fine by me. I have nothing to hide and plenty to say. You know, once they start checking up on Gary, they'll find out about the M&M review too. He won't be able to deny what's been documented. And I doubt that wimp of a CEO, Manning, will be able to keep protecting him either."

***

Incensed over the brutal reality of his catastrophic investment loss, Gary Tamarino had sunk to a new low. He blamed his ex-wife, as he rationalized his need to generate large sums of money in a short time frame. If she hadn't divorced him, he wouldn't be in this godforsaken hole. How else was he supposed to cover the alimony and debt he had accrued thanks to that bitch?

He didn't remember a single sight on his way home. As if his car operated on autopilot, the ride turned into one big blur. He didn't even know why he came home. He stood still inside the mammoth living room and looked around. An empty space with nobody inside. If he owned a pet, he could expect the animal might look up at him with loving eyes. Didn't pets possess a sixth sense that allowed them to know when their owners needed a friend? Was this what despair felt like? Despite all his education, he had no clue. An overwhelming void enveloped him, and he lacked any means of control. He shuffled into his bathroom and stared at the mirror. He didn't recognize the face that stared back at him.

~ Chapter 29 ~

Derning wasted no time beginning his portion of the investigation. A personal favor to Allison, this one carried special significance. He had already spoken to Christy Newsell, his counterpart. A short phone conversation delineated their roles, and she confirmed that he controlled full authority over the review. Christy elaborated on the date of Tamarino's divorce but had uncovered nothing regarding financial records. He knew gaining access to fiscal documents required search warrants for cause, so for now, he focused on interviews with hospital personnel familiar with the surgeon. Since the posh lobby provided him with such a comfortable work space, he had not left the hospital. He focused his radar on Dr. Kumar Chanrami and Rosa Perez now.

Experienced with how certain processes work at major healthcare facilities like San Francisco Bay Hospital, Mark googled the phone number for the hospital and called from his cell phone. After listening to a litany of department choices, he asked for the operator.

"San Francisco Bay Hospital. This is Helen. How may I direct your call?"

"Hi, Helen. This is Jose from CSU. Do you know if Dr. Kumar Chanrami is still in the hospital?"

"Let me check for you. One moment, please." After a brief pause, Helen provided the information Derning needed. "Yes, he's still here."

Mark thanked her and then texted Annette. "It's Mark Derning. Still in hospital. I'd like to talk to Dr. Chanrami. Do you know where he is?"

Annette texted back in less than a minute. "He's on the Stepdown unit. 3rd floor."

Mark rode the elevator up two flights, and when the door opened, a man wearing a white lab coat stepped inside. On a hunch, Derning asked, "Dr. Chanrami?"

The doctor met his eyes and responded, "Yes, I am." Mark stayed in the elevator and rode back down after Dr. Chanrami pushed the button for the first floor. Introducing himself, Mark handed him his business card and asked the surgeon if he had a few moments to discuss a sensitive issue.

Kumar nodded. "I heard you'd be getting in touch with me. I know a place we can talk." As Kumar led the way toward the front of the hospital, Mark smiled and correctly assumed their destination to be the lobby.

"I appreciate you taking the time, Doctor. Are you familiar with our organization, Critical Cover-Up?"

Making himself comfortable in one of the taupe swivel chairs, the surgeon paused a moment before answering. "It feels good to just sit down. Yes, I know of the company and only recently discovered that one of our nurses is its owner and founder."

"You're talking about Allison Jamison, a great person and personal friend. She asked me to investigate a case involving your partner, Dr. Gary Tamarino."

"You say you're a personal friend of Allison's?"

Mark not only explained how he worked for Allison but detailed the situation related to the earthquake and car accident. "Allison told me she worked closely with Dr. Tamarino, and you as well, as a CSU nurse. Among other things, she became particularly concerned about two recent patient deaths. Can we talk about those?"

"Mrs. Brock and Mr. Fellner. Yes, a disastrous state of affairs." Kumar began the story of the cardiac arrest and takeback and complicating factors in the operating room. Mark took notes, and Kumar continued talking. What struck the investigator most was the willingness of one surgeon to reveal the vulnerabilities of another— uncommon in the medical community, where a code of silence reigned supreme. Mark wondered if this Dr. Kumar might be a little too eager to expose a partner. Did he have anything to gain from doing so?

Twenty minutes elapsed. "I appreciate your willingness to talk with me, Doctor. I'm sure you're tired. I have a few more questions related to another matter. Can you stay a little longer? I'll try and be brief."

"I'm happy to help, Detective. If I could figure out another way, I'd be all for it. But lately, he won't listen to anyone, and I'm worried about my own reputation as a surgeon, since I'm a partner in his practice."

"I understand he's had substantial financial problems after his divorce, which happened about six months ago. Correct?"

"Yes, the divorce created a nightmare for him. You're right about the time frame of the final decree, although the whole thing dragged on for a year prior to that. And you're definitely correct about the financial losses. He confided in me over a month ago about losing money in the stock market. After a while, I thought things improved, but this morning when he flew off the handle, he yelled about squandering everything on a bad investment with Apple stock."

"Tell me something, Dr. Chanrami. Do you have any reason to believe he borrowed money from the practice? Are you involved in the accounting aspects at all?" Mark stared back at Kumar's penetrating brown eyes as the full implication of this concept took hold.

Kumar averted his gaze and replied in a quieter tone, "I don't know. I hadn't thought about it." The detective knew the interview had ended.

~ Chapter 30 ~

"Okay, my friend, you're cleared to go to Stepdown, and your room is ready. I've already called report, and they'll be transferring you soon. That's great, isn't it?"

Rosa's news pleased Allison and excited her beyond expectations. "Yes, that's terrific. I'd hoped to hear those words from you. Rosa, I can't thank you enough. You were wonderful, and I'll never forget it. I shouldn't be out too long, I don't think. Once I recover and am cleared to work, I plan to return to the trenches and work side by side with you."

An understanding Rosa smiled. "One day at a time, kiddo. Your doctor will let you know when it's time. And more important than that, your body will tell you when you're ready."

"Before I leave, Rosa, I need to update you. Beside the fact that Dr. T saved my life," — Allison paused and rolled her eyes — "he's the subject of a probe by my company, Critical Cover-Up. I referred him just before the earthquake."

From the expression on the charge nurse's face, Allison concluded that this information did not meet with Rosa's approval. "Allison, what the hell are you talking about? What company?"

"We spoke about this, remember? Rosa, I could swear that Annette, you, and I talked about Dr. T and how his patients were going south. Didn't you tell me that you were concerned too?"

Exasperated, Rosa replied, "Yes, we did talk, and I'll admit I've been concerned and upset about his attitude and slacking performance. But after the past few days, in light of the disaster and all, I think he deserves a break. You, of all people, should think so too." She frowned at Allison. "Would you care to explain about this company? It's the first I'm hearing about it." A hint of disbelief crept into Rosa's voice.

Allison feared her memory issues affected her in more ways than she realized. The idea that she never talked about Critical Cover-Up with Rosa became a distinct possibility.

"Yes, I guess I need to clarify. I apologize, Rosa. Since the accident, my memory on certain situations has been erased. It's been more than a little freaky." She paused and inhaled as deeply as possible and let it out slowly. "I'll start from the beginning. Do you remember when a big medical center in Florida was exposed for corrupt practices a couple of years ago?" Allison's eyes stayed fixed on Rosa's face.

"Yes, I saw it on the news. A big place in Orlando, I believe."

"Well, when I worked there, I saw firsthand all the corruption going on, and I just couldn't close my eyes to it. I strategized with two other critical care nurses, and we exposed the hospital wrongdoers for who they were. In the process, I created Critical Cover-Up as an oversight business to uncover unsafe practices and corruption in the healthcare field."

Rosa glared at her. "Are you telling me you went ahead and reported Dr. T?" she snapped. "I don't understand how you could do this."

Allison tried to smooth things over with her. "Rosa, I thought we were all on the same page. Kumar even encouraged me to do it. And Annette got on board too. Honestly, I thought you knew all about this."

"Listen, Allison, I have my job to think about. I'm not willing to go out on a limb on this like you. You're a travel nurse and can go anywhere and find a nursing job. I've worked hard to build my reputation. Besides, I have children and a house here and can't risk getting involved and possibly losing my job."

"I understand, Rosa. But you're probably going to be contacted by the main investigator, Mark Derning, anyway. I gave him your name."

"Great," Rosa snorted. "What am I supposed to say?"

"Just tell him the truth. It's Dr. T who caused this problem, not you."

Rosa ended the conversation without committing any support. The scowl on her face summed up her feelings. "I need to get back to work. Take care of yourself. I'm sure we'll talk soon." She turned around and vanished, leaving Allison to mull over what just occurred. If Rosa intended to shame her, she'd succeeded.

Did I do the right thing? I hope this doesn't end up biting me in the ass. It was too late to turn back.

~ Chapter 31 ~

Mark Derning thanked Annette once more before he left the hospital. Without her help, he would not have been able to obtain printed copies of the electronic patient medical records he needed. Unlike the homicide cases he'd led, no charges had been filed regarding the deaths of two of Tamarino's patients. "I'm happy to help, but I don't know that you're going to find much, since the surgeon who dictates the operative report does not typically admit to errors. You might consider asking Dr. Chanrami to get you a copy of the M&M meeting minutes. I think it will include information that may be a more accurate version of the truth."

Reviewing the records would be the focus of the evening later in his hotel room. He texted Allison to check on her again. "I've been working on the case and getting ready to leave the hospital. I can stop in for a short visit, if you like."

When no return text message appeared, he walked out the front lobby door, a little disappointed. Just as he opened the app to order an Uber ride, Allison replied. "Okay. I was transferred. I'm in room 302."

Encouraged, he backtracked into the hospital, found his way to the elevator, and pushed the button to the third floor. Delighted to find Allison in fresh surroundings, sitting up in a chair and looking much more like herself, he greeted her with a smile. "You look amazing."

Her cheery face told him she welcomed his visit. "How is everything going so far?"

Mark pulled a chair close to where Allison sat. "So far, so good. I met with Annette and Dr. Chanrami. They both extended a warm welcome."

"Kumar is wonderful to work with, and Annette is too. I'm sure they can fill in the blanks for you during your investigation." She then told him about her encounter with Rosa Perez. "I want to give you a heads-up. She may not be as cooperative."

"Okay, that's good to know. I didn't make contact with her yet."

"She works the night shift like I do, seven to seven."

"I'll catch up with her. I have enough to do for tonight. I'm so glad you're making progress, Allison."

"Thank you, Mark. And thank you for everything. I always feel better when you're on a case, and this one is personal."

Mark heard the last word and thought about how personal it was for him, but in a different way. *God, I hope her memory comes back.* "I'm going to let you rest for now, but I'll be back tomorrow. Good night, Allison."

***

On the ride back to his hotel, Derning noticed the damage along the way. Parts of streets were cordoned off, and businesses were boarded up. "Is all this from the earthquake?" he asked the driver.

"Yeah, man. It's been a mess down here. The trolley isn't running, and only some of the buses are in service. We had a lot of damage downtown. Oakland had it a lot worse, but it affected the city pretty bad too."

Half an hour later, Derning arrived at his hotel and was grateful to find it open. From all appearances, it looked like business as usual. He decided to grab dinner in the OneUP Restaurant, the same place where he and Allison had spent such a pleasurable Saturday evening, before the shit hit the fan.

Was it only forty-eight hours ago? It seemed like a week ago, after everything that had happened. Grateful to be seated in a different section of the restaurant, Mark ordered a drink and perused the menu for something appetizing. Hospital food didn't do a thing for him, and he craved some real food. The Dungeness crab cake with a side of coleslaw and sourdough bread sounded perfect. While he waited for his order, he reflected on his day. One thing in particular gnawed at him. Dr. Kumar's reaction when questioned about the finances of the practice raised a red flag. Something didn't seem quite right to him.

~ Chapter 32 ~

Kumar and Annette scrubbed in for the first surgery of the day. "Not a word from Gary?" Annette asked.

"Nope, nada. I messaged him this morning and no answer."

"You know, Kumar, I'm worried about him. Do you think we should send the police to his house?"

He paused before he answered. "Probably . . . just to be on the safe side. I'd feel awful if something happened to him and nobody even checked. I guess the responsibility lies with me, as much as my feelings are all over the place about him. I'll call someone after we finish the case. Maybe he'll even check in with us by then," he said, attempting to remain optimistic.

Surgery proceeded without any problems. The case was a straightforward aortic valve replacement on a sixty-five-year-old female. The competing cardiothoracic surgical group occupied the second OR, so life moved along at its normal pace despite the absence of Dr. T. Kumar appreciated one thing: the drama scale registered on the low end today.

As he promised Annette, Kumar called the San Francisco police department and requested them to check on Gary at his home. He conveyed just enough information for them to determine that he called as a concerned business partner.

***

Gary Tamarino was inside his Pacific Heights home in the early afternoon when his doorbell chimed. He wondered who it could be, since he seldom stayed home during the day. A sudden apprehension surrounded him at the sight of two uniformed men standing at his front entrance.

Gary opened the door to two San Francisco police officers. "Good afternoon, officers. Is everything okay?"

"Dr. Gary Tamarino?" one of them asked.

Unnerved, Gary answered with a simple, "Yes."

The second officer spoke up. "We are here as a courtesy to your partner, Dr. Kumar Chanrami. He's been trying to reach you and was worried something may have happened to you."

Gary reassured the officers that he was fine. "I didn't feel well yesterday and came home. I told him not to expect me today. But I'm feeling better now, and I'll get in touch with him."

"Okay, Doctor. If you need anything, please give us a call. We know you doctors aren't always too eager to ask for help, but we're here if you need us."

"Thank you. I appreciate that. Have a nice day."

A good night's rest generated an attitude adjustment, and Gary calculated a plan to turn things around for himself. *Damn Kumar. I'd better call him.*

He glanced at his watch. It was almost twelve thirty, and he assumed Kumar might be between surgeries. He didn't feel a bit guilty for shirking his surgery responsibilities and leaving the bulk of the work for his junior partner. He deserved the break after the years he put in building up his prestigious Bay Area cardiothoracic practice. He knew Kumar could handle the cases with Annette's help.

He scrolled the favorites in his iPhone and placed the call. As expected, his partner answered on the first ring. "Gary, you're all right?"

"Yes, Kumar. You didn't have to send the big guns to check on me."

"The police came? I'm glad. Annette and I were worried about you. As long as you're okay, then that's fine. We have it covered here. Do you have any idea when you'll be back?"

"I'm taking today and tomorrow off and will be back at work Thursday morning. I plan on talking to Ed Manning after this call with you."

"Good move. I was going to suggest you touch base with him."

"You and Annette should be good without me for another day or so, right?"

Kumar reassured him that they would manage the workload. "Take whatever time you need, Gary. I know you were pretty stressed out."

"Getting it together, Kumar. Everything is going to be okay. See you Thursday." He ended the call. *One down, one to go.*

~ Chapter 33 ~

By Wednesday afternoon, Allison wanted to go home. Not fond of her role as a patient, she sought to convince her surgeon that she could take just as good care of herself at home. After all, she was a critical care nurse. She'd achieved the expected goals of walking unassisted, eating a regular diet, and maintaining control of her pain with Tylenol in less than seventy-two hours. Oh yes, and the mandatory bowel movement. What more could anyone want?

"You've been cleared by Cardio, and I agree we've done our job here, so I'll write discharge orders and you can get out of here."

Successful in making her case to Dr. Iammetti, Allison beamed with joy. "I appreciate everything you did. You don't know what this means to me." He left her room, and she knew her nurse would be in soon to update her about the discharge. She texted Mark and gave him the good news. "

Two minutes later, he called her. "That's fantastic, Allison. I can come to the hospital and help you get your things and get you home."

"Are you sure it won't be too much trouble, Mark?"

"Nonsense. I planned to visit you today anyhow. When do you think you'll be ready to leave?"

"I don't know, but discharges usually take a couple of hours, with all the paperwork. How about if I text you just before I'm ready to go?"

"Perfect. I'm not that far away."

"Thank you, Mark. You've been great. I'll keep you posted."

***

Mark Derning meant it when he said he wasn't that far away. He had been in the CSU waiting room for the past hour, working on his computer while he anticipated the opportunity to speak to Dr. Kumar. According to the patient tracking board on the wall, Dr. Chanrami was still in surgery. A convenient way to update families with patients in the operating room, the board provided Mark with the exact information he needed. The hospital volunteer assigned to the waiting room had instructed him how he could determine which room the surgeon occupied by his initials. She further explained that once the status changed from surgery to recovery, the surgeon would then go to CSU to dictate a post-op note and see the patient.

After ten minutes passed, he moved to the CSU door to wait for Dr. Kumar. His sense of timing resulted from years of stakeouts and surveillance experience, and he didn't have to wait too long to be rewarded. Surprising the surgeon, Mark greeted him as he exited the unit. "Dr. Chanrami, can I speak with you for a moment?"

The detective perceived mild annoyance in Dr. Kumar's response. "Yes, Detective, but don't count on more than a minute. I have another surgery."

"I understand, Doctor. I promise, just one minute. Is there a way you can get me the minutes from the most recent M&M meeting?"

"You mean the one from Saturday?"

"Yes. They would facilitate me in my investigation."

Dr. Chanrami told him it would not be a problem. "Everything is recorded electronically, so I can print out a copy for you. Follow me."

The appreciative detective walked beside the surgeon in silence. Kumar busied himself on his phone until they reached the surgeons' lounge. "Wait here," he told Derning as he entered the locked room. In less than a minute, he returned with a sheaf of eight-by-eleven papers and handed it to Derning. "Don't you just love technology? You couldn't have done this ten years ago." Kumar retrieved a card from his lab coat pocket and handed it to the detective. "My personal cell number is here. You can text me if you need anything else. I'm glad to be of assistance." Derning thanked him and concluded that he may have misjudged the doctor.

Allison had not yet texted him, so he returned to his corner in the lobby and began to read the document Kumar gave him. While he didn't anticipate anything specific, the revelation on the second page grabbed his attention.

~ Chapter 34 ~

Tamarino's call to Ed Manning didn't connect until the fourth ring.

"Ed Manning."

Gary considered the CEO's peculiarity of always answering in such a businesslike manner downright annoying, since every cell phone featured caller ID. But he decided not to allow this idiosyncrasy to interfere with his carefully thought-out agenda.

"Gary Tamarino. I wondered if we could talk. It's important." He made a point to sound almost as impersonal as Manning. Three seconds went by with no reply. "Ed, can you hear me? It's Gary Tamarino."

Manning responded curtly. "I heard you, Gary. I have a meeting coming up. I can see you in my office at 3:00 p.m."

"Yes, that works for me. I'll be there." Tamarino thanked him and ended the call, satisfied with the outcome of the brief conversation. *Manning thinks he has the upper hand here, but he has no idea what's coming.* The anticipation of his afternoon appointment with the CEO fueled Tamarino's heightened state of excitement.

Ten minutes prior to his appointment, Dr. Tamarino arrived near the CEO's office. Not wishing to be too visible, he stepped into a stall in the nearby men's room to kill time. Twenty seconds later, he heard two people enter the room. One person's voice resonated with a vague familiarity, but he couldn't quite identify it. The men's candid conversation caught Gary by total surprise, and he assumed they had no idea of his presence. His curiosity was piqued when one man mentioned the CEO by name. On a whim, Gary opened the voice recorder app on his phone and began recording them.

"Have you heard the news about Manning?"

"No, what's going on?"

"This is huge. Once it gets out, it'll spread through the hospital at warp speed. I honestly can't figure out how someone in his position could be so stupid. I don't get it. If you're going to screw around, don't do it at work, and especially not with an ICU nurse. I heard he got the chick pregnant and then bullied her into getting an abortion, intimidating her with risk of losing her job. Now she's talking to a lawyer."

"Fuck me dead. How did you find out about this?"

"You won't believe it, but my wife sat next to the nurse at the nail salon, and she told her all about it."

"You mean the nurse he was involved with?"

"Yes. How's that for timing?"

"What a loser. I guess we can expect some administrative changes soon. They'll have to get rid of him to cut down on any negative publicity backlash to the hospital."

"Can you imagine? It'll be all over social media pretty soon."

The duo left, and Gary ended the voice recording. Uncertain how he might leverage this salacious evidence, he smiled and nodded, his mind working overtime. The time had come for his one-on-one with Ed Manning. *How life changes.*

The office door was half open, and Gary's watch indicated 3:00 p.m. on the dot. He stood at the entrance and knocked. Manning waved him in, and Gary closed the door behind him. He assumed Manning would create a formal atmosphere, as he did before the M&M conference.

"Have a seat, Gary. We need to resolve our differences and get back to business. Are you aware your partner, Dr. Chanrami, had a chat with me?"

"I figured as much. And the M&M was a humbling experience, to say the least. I hope I've redeemed myself after all the traumas I operated on this weekend. I needed to take a day or two to regroup."

"Well, I'm glad to hear it. I don't know what issues you had. We still may have a lawsuit or two on those patients who died. We'll just have to deal with them."

"Ed, I need to come clean with you. I have no clue how much Kumar told you. I have some major financial problems, and they came to a head yesterday. I could use a favor from you, as a friend."

"Interesting . . . but what exactly do you need from me?" Manning said, his brow furrowed.

"Two hundred thousand dollars."

Ed's jaw dropped as he glared at Tamarino.

"What the fuck? What do you need so much money for?"

"I overextended myself in the market. I bought on margin, and the stock took a nosedive so fast I couldn't recover. I didn't have enough to cover my margin, and they closed out my positions and sold the rest of the stock I had at a huge loss."

"Geez, Gary. That's a ton of money. When do you need it?"

"Today. You're the only person I could ask. I figured you could cover it."

Manning shifted in his chair. "It's not that easy, Gary. I can't just access a couple hundred thousand that fast. It takes time to clear, you know?"

Gary wasn't playing games. His tone darkened, and he relied on his manipulative skills to pressure Manning to meet his demands. "I assumed our long friendship meant something, Ed. I hate to put you in this position, but I have to have that money before 5:00 p.m. today. I'm sure you don't want me to be forced to reveal the role you played in the cover-up scheme of that Medicare fraud lawsuit from a few years ago."

The not-so-subtle threat produced the exact response Gary intended. He'd succeeded in regaining the advantage in his orchestrated power play.

After an uncomfortable silence, Manning spoke up, his voice subdued. "I'll shift some things around and send you the money electronically. You'll have it by the end of the business day."

Tamarino stood up and thanked him, as if life had normalized. "Thank you, man. You know I'm good for it. I'll be able to repay it before too long." Elated, he sauntered from the office as if he'd just won the lottery. Once again, he claimed the title of big cheese.

~ Chapter 35 ~

When Mark entered Allison's hospital room, she no longer wore a hospital gown. Instead, her clothing consisted of the same navy-blue suit she'd worn last Saturday when they met at the Grand Hyatt. The noticeable rip in her skirt and bloodstains on the left sleeve of her jacket didn't deter Mark from complimenting her appearance. "I'd say you look amazing, a far cry from the person I saw in an oversized green hospital gown yesterday." He walked toward her and kissed her cheek.

She enjoyed the attention. "I didn't have much choice. It's not like I packed to come here, you know." She laughed and continued. "But you're right. Anything's better than hospital clothes. I'm eager to get out of here."

Mark glanced around the room. "Is everything packed and ready to go?"

"Yes, and my discharge papers are almost completed. I'll call for the tech. They have to take me out by wheelchair. It's protocol."

"I'll walk with you and carry your bag. It won't take long to get an Uber once we're outside the hospital."

Ten minutes later, Allison and Mark slid into the back seat of an Uber and headed toward Nob Hill. "I can't believe everything that's happened in just a few days.

Not something I'd like to repeat," Allison said. As they approached her neighborhood, she observed random damage to some of the buildings. "Oh my God! I hadn't even considered the earthquake damage. I hope my apartment is okay inside." She didn't need any more surprises, especially when all she wanted was to return to her comfortable bed. Then, without warning, a vision of Snowball appeared in her mind. Panic set in as reality confronted her. Her chest tightened and she gasped. "Mark, I forgot all about the cat. She's been without food and water all this time."

"Let's see how she's doing when we get inside. I've heard cats can manage on their own for days," he said, doing his best to reassure her. "They're resourceful animals." With more than a tinge of guilt, Allison hoped he was right.

They arrived in front of her apartment on Jones Street. The centrally located, four-story Victorian brick building was within walking distance of Union Square. "I hope there's an elevator, Allison."

"Don't worry. I made sure of that before I rented a third-floor unit." Mark accompanied Allison inside the building and she led the way to the elevator. As soon as the elevator door opened on her floor, they heard a loud, continuous meow from behind her apartment door. With a sigh of relief, Allison wasted no time unlocking her apartment, and Snowball didn't stop meowing. "Oh, you poor thing! You must have missed me. I'm so sorry I left you alone, Snowball." The cat's food and water bowls were empty and flipped over, but her white furry pet didn't look too bad. Handing a bowl to Mark, Allison asked him to fill it with water while she opened a can of

Fancy Feast and dumped it into Snowball's food dish. She topped it off with half a cup of dry kibble.

"Allison, you lucked out. The electricity works, and nothing looks damaged here," Mark said after a quick assessment of the small apartment.

"I'm going to change my clothes and will be back in a few minutes," Allison said as she disappeared into her bedroom. "Make yourself at home, Mark."

After finding everything intact in her bedroom and bathroom, she let out a deep breath. When she returned to the living room, she sat down on the sofa next to Mark.

As if all the strain and worry were over, she allowed herself to be still. Allison closed her eyes and said a silent prayer. *Thank you, God, for everything. I'm grateful to be alive.*

~ Chapter 36 ~

As Allison leaned back on the sofa with her eyes closed, Mark contemplated the moment. He didn't take his eyes off her, and a sense of comfort seemed to permeate the space. He couldn't deny his feelings for her and hoped to show her one day exactly how much she meant to him. Uncertain whether his feelings might be reciprocated, he sat in silent reflection.

When Allison opened her eyes, she said, "I don't know what to say, except thank you, Mark. I'm glad you're here."

"Allison, you know I'm here for you. There's a lot we need to talk about but probably not this minute. First things first. Why don't I order some takeout and have it delivered? What are you hungry for?"

"Anything will taste good after the hospital. There's a great little pizza place right around the corner. Gusto Pinsa Romana."

Mark placed an order for pizza and salad from his phone. "Do you have any bottled water, or should I order some?" Allison indicated it wasn't necessary. "Okay. Delivery time thirty minutes."

"That sounds great, Mark. I must admit I'm getting hungry."

"I didn't realize your apartment was so close to where I'm staying. I knew you lived near Union Square. The hotel is less than a ten-minute walk from here, so it's really convenient."

Allison wasn't sure what he meant but continued to listen. "If you're not too wiped out, I'd like to talk about something."

"I am a little tired, but I'm interested. Tell me what's going on with the Tamarino investigation."

"Okay, where to begin?" Mark detailed the progress he'd made so far, the interviews he'd had, and the documents he'd obtained. "Did you hear anything about the M&M meeting?"

Allison stared at Mark and shook her head. "The last I heard anything was Friday, when Rosa called me at home and left a message that Mrs. Brock died. When was the M&M?"

"They had it on Saturday, and Dr. Kumar gave me a copy of the minutes today. While I expected a dull account, an interesting detail emerged."

"Really? What did you find out?" Allison asked, eager to know more. Mark obliged her.

He paraphrased the report rather than reading every line. "They listed who attended, and the only name I recognized among the physicians was Dr. Chanrami. Then they stipulated that the emphasis should be on patient safety issues and the reduction of preventable errors. They discussed how the focus of these peer review meetings has shifted to education, rather than blame." Mark summarized the major problems of both patients' surgical complications which resulted in their deaths.

Since Allison worked in CSU when these patients deteriorated, the information revealed nothing new.

Then Mark zeroed in on the crucial admission, the one point that stood out like a giant red flag to him. "One of the general surgeons not involved in either case introduced the possibility that Dr. Tamarino might have experienced visual impairment during the surgeries under review. He grilled Dr. Tamarino and asked him point-blank whether a shred of truth existed in this speculation. He wondered why the surgeon missed a bleeder behind the heart. He wanted to know if a temporary vision loss may have caused Dr. Tamarino to not see an oozing blood vessel."

Allison perked up at this last statement, because nothing remotely like this idea had ever been mentioned. "Did Dr. Tamarino respond? What did he say?"

"Yes. Get this. He actually acknowledged that this might have been the problem. When asked to elaborate, Dr. Tamarino conceded that he'd experienced some intermittent blurred vision in the past month."

Allison gaped at him, her blue eyes as wide as saucers. "It makes no sense. Why wouldn't a brilliant surgeon seek medical attention for himself as soon as he recognized a problem? Why didn't he just explain, instead of risking his patients' lives?"

"They questioned him about that. Listen to this." Mark read her the next few paragraphs from the minutes.

"So, when asked whether he had addressed this problem with an ophthalmologist, Tamarino stated he hadn't. He assumed the problem to be temporary, and said, 'It doesn't happen all the time.' Based on these findings, the committee's recommendation requires him to schedule an ophthalmology appointment immediately to determine the cause of his visual problems."

"That's all? No suspension of surgery privileges or requirement that a second surgeon operates with him?"

"Nothing. They're not playing the blame game."

"But two patients died. That's so frustrating. I'm interested in what Kumar and Annette think. One of them should be able to find out when he sees the ophthalmologist. And I'd still like you to continue the investigation of the other aspects—the money and the divorce stuff."

Mark agreed and reassured her that they were on the same page. "I plan on touching base with Sherry and Christy, the other investigator. She may have some of this information by now."

The doorbell buzzed, ending the work conversation. "It must be the pizza delivery," Allison said. "Perfect timing."

Mark answered the door and arranged their salads and pizza on Allison's coffee table. "It's not exactly an elegant Italian dinner with wine in North Beach, but it's not bad," he said.

~ Chapter 37 ~

D r. Tamarino strolled into CSU at just after eight in the evening to make final rounds on his post-op patients before leaving for home. The unit stayed busy almost all the time, and the vacant nurses' station validated that fact tonight. His presence didn't attract the usual fanfare and gushing by the younger nurses, since they were in their patients' rooms. No big deal. Nothing could ruin his good mood tonight. Ever since Ed Manning transferred the money to his account, he'd maintained a perpetual natural high.

After he reviewed significant labs on his phone, he made rounds and obtained the latest updates from the nurses. Pleased that all his patients remained stable and were progressing as expected, he walked toward the door. For once, he welcomed a low-key encounter in the usually busy ICU. But he heard his name a moment too soon. The unmistakable voice belonged to Rosa Perez.

Tamarino's rapport with the diminutive charge nurse prompted him to walk toward her. She stood in the hall near the last patient room, close to the emergency exit door. He valued her critical-care expertise and respected her nursing leadership. A mutual respect governed their relationship. "You've got the unit under control, Rosa."

"Yes, so far so good. We could use a less hectic night after this weekend."

"Keep it that way. Good night, Rosa." Eager to go home and get some dinner, he turned and sauntered back toward the center of the unit.

"Dr. T, don't leave yet. I wanted to talk with you about something. It won't take long." *That voice again.* He retraced his steps and stood next to Rosa. She lowered her voice and peered deep into Gary Tamarino's eyes. "I want to give you a heads-up, because I think you deserve to know." The seriousness of her tone emphasized the gravity of her revelation. "I'm telling you this in confidence." Tamarino remained silent and attentive. "I have mixed feelings about even saying anything, but I couldn't live with myself if I didn't warn you."

Tamarino's strong points didn't include patience, especially in a conversation. "You're killing me, Rosa. Just tell me already," he snapped.

"Okay, but don't shoot the messenger. You're being investigated. An outside organization is looking into your stats and recent surgical complications and patient deaths."

"Investigated? What the hell, Rosa? How do you know this?"

She hesitated and then told him what she knew. "Allison told me."

"Allison Jamison? When did this happen? I just saved her life. Isn't she still in the hospital?"

"Dr. Iammetti discharged her."

"So, who's investigating me? I don't understand. I just did the M&M Saturday."

He waited while Rosa took a deep breath. "I know that once I tell you this, I'm permanently jeopardizing a relationship. But you need to know. There's a company that specializes in exposing corruption in the healthcare field. They focus on medical errors, unethical practices, patient safety issues, and corrupt policies in hospitals."

"So how did they get involved? Did someone report me to them?" Tamarino said, still confused.

Rosa closed her eyes. Torn between loyalties, she sided with the surgeon. She told him the story about Critical Cover-Up and Allison's position as founder and executive officer. "Look, I know it's been rough lately. Your performance problems bothered me, too, with all the complications your patients had this past month. There must be a reason for it, and I hope things improve. The cases from this weekend did great," Rosa said, doing her best to believe in Tamarino, despite her qualms.

"You did the right thing in telling me, Rosa. At least now I'll be prepared when someone starts snooping around. Thank you. If you hear anything more, keep me posted." He exited the unit, not giving a second thought to the relationship she just put at risk.

~ Chapter 38 ~

Gary Tamarino didn't need a fucking M&M committee to tell him to see an ophthalmologist. He knew he had an issue, but he wasn't ready to admit it yet. Anticipating his fiftieth birthday later this year, he abhorred the notion that he might be getting old.

When he first noticed symptoms of a visual disturbance, he freaked out. A surgeon's eyes are just as important as his hands. And a cardiothoracic surgeon's eyes are vital to his ability to suture miniscule edges of blood vessels when creating an anastomosis in a coronary artery bypass graft operation. Better than anybody, Tamarino grasped the possible impact of any impairment of his vision. He remembered a colleague who had disclosed his eye issues to the hospital administration, certain he was doing the right thing in the interest of transparency. They forced him to resign prior to his retirement date. Under no circumstances would he put up with that — especially now, at the peak of his medical career.

His vision changes were subtle and the onset insidious. First, he saw small flashes of light on rare occasions. It seemed to occur in his left eye only. He ignored the problem and blew it off as stress. Sometimes his field of vision flickered for a few seconds; other times, it lasted longer, but always less than a minute. The episodes when everything went dark were sporadic and, again, for seconds at a time. He couldn't ignore this recent vision situation, and he did worry, but most of the time he tried to brush it off as an irritating symptom of getting older.

Gary first detected the aberrancy while reading at home. The initial occurrence during surgery, though, created anxiety, and he'd lashed out at his surgical team. Since he hadn't disclosed his suspicions, they were at the mercy of his wrath. He'd blamed Annette for the patient's excessive bleeding inside the chest, accusing her of improper technique with the surgical instruments.

Days passed without incident. Without warning, again in the OR, he experienced brief scintillations of light that almost looked like glitter. A weird but alarming vision.

After the M&M committee's recommendation, he scheduled an ophthalmology evaluation as soon as he could in order to appease the hospital bigwigs. Prior to meeting the eye doctor, Gary poured over medical journals online as he researched his symptoms. Self-diagnosis had long been an occupational hazard in the healthcare profession. Nurses did it too. Gary diagnosed himself and came to the conclusion that his vision disturbances were the result of an illness known as transient vision loss. Defined as an abrupt temporary loss of vision in one eye that lasts from seconds to hours, this affliction results from reduced blood flow to the affected eye.

From what he read, he decided he fell into the category of transient monocular vision loss. In all cases, discovering the cause served to determine the recommended treatment. He assumed he met the criteria for the most benign cause of vasospasm, which can trigger a temporary reduction in blood flow. After evaluating the other possible underlying factors, he dismissed them all. Based on his age, and by eliminating other options, he knew the cause had to be primary vasospasm, a sudden constriction of a blood vessel, narrowing its diameter and rate of flow. He liked the idea, since the recommended treatment for retinal vasospasm involved medication, either an aspirin or a calcium channel blocker.

In sharp contrast to his own habits, whenever patients came into his office for a consultation and they told him they googled their symptoms, he hated to hear what they said. They were so sure of their own diagnoses and told him how they thought they should be treated. And he did the same thing, with one difference: he was the chief of cardiothoracic surgery, and he knew a thing or two.

And just as he anticipated, when he met with the ophthalmologist, Gary hit the nail on the head with the diagnosis. But the vision specialist declined to make it official until Gary completed a plethora of tests to the satisfaction of the by-the-book eye doctor. Afterward, he left the office with a prescription for nifedipine, a common calcium channel blocker known to the layperson as Procardia. He hoped this would rid him of the problem and get everyone at work off his back.

~ Chapter 39 ~

With no surgeries on the schedule this morning, Annette made hospital rounds and then took advantage of her free time and phoned her friend. "Just checking in with you to see how you're doing at home, Allison."

"Coming along. Getting home yesterday felt so good. I'm actually getting around and not having any pain, to speak of. I should be back to work before too long. Anything new going on at the hospital?"

"Things have settled down a bit. No more takebacks or surgery complications, thank God." Annette updated Allison about the M&M report and told her that Dr. T had an appointment with an eye doctor.

"I heard about the M&M. Mark told me about it. Dr. Kumar gave him a copy of the minutes. Do you know about Mark Derning, my investigator?"

"Yes, we met at the hospital, remember?"

"That's right. I'm sorry. Sometimes my recall isn't what it used to be. I hope it's not a permanent effect of the concussion. I've noticed a slight amount of improvement though.

"Annette, have you talked with Rosa lately? She caught me totally off guard yesterday before my discharge. I guess I never filled her in about referring Dr.

T's case to Critical Cover-Up, so when I mentioned it, she went ballistic. She's definitely not on board with this."

Annette's temporary silence hinted at unease. "She might be a problem. Tamarino likes her, and they've always had a special bond between them. He talked to her a lot during the divorce, because she offered a sympathetic ear, and he could count on her to maintain confidentiality."

"Interesting," Allison said. "We need to strategize and include Dr. Kumar too. What are the odds of Rosa saying anything to Tamarino?"

"I don't know, but if I had to guess, I'd say her loyalty leans more toward him, despite her complaints to us about his attitude."

"If Tamarino finds out I'm behind this, he'll make my life miserable," Allison said.

Annette agreed. "You don't know him as well as I do, but don't underestimate his potential for revenge. I'll talk with Kumar and get back to you. He may even have an update on the ophthalmology exam."

Annette's fears for Allison increased once she heard about Rosa's surprising response. She hadn't expected Rosa to react as she did. On multiple occasions they had spoken of Tamarino's outbursts and his recent operative complications. Like Allison, Annette assumed Rosa agreed with them on this. Perhaps she resented finding out after the fact, rather than learning about it firsthand from Allison. She made a note to talk to Rosa when she saw her next.

For now, Kumar took first priority. Hoping he hadn't left the hospital, she texted him, and discovered she'd missed him. He had gone to the office, located in a building next door to the hospital, just a short walk away, to see post-op patients. Annette headed there. Five minutes later she met up with her favorite cardiothoracic surgeon.

"I'm glad you're here, Annette," Kumar said. "It's a zoo today, and with Gary gone, we'll be lucky to get out of here by six o'clock."

"We'll get it done together. I need to talk with you sometime, though. Do you have a few minutes before you see your next patient?"

Kumar nodded, and they entered his office and closed the door. "Have a seat, Annette. What's up?"

"I just spoke to Allison. She's home and recovering as expected. But there's a snag in the Critical Cover-Up thing. I guess Rosa got furious when she learned that Allison reported Tamarino. She wanted no part of it and thought he deserved a break."

Kumar shook his head and gave Annette a perplexed look. "We discussed this, didn't we? I thought Rosa agreed with us."

"Apparently, Allison left Rosa in the dark about the referral. She maintains it wasn't intentional, and she actually thought she had filled her in. Allison's had some short-term memory difficulties since the accident. If Rosa talks to Tamarino about it, it's all over for Allison. Tamarino won't put up with anything that makes him look bad, despite the fact that he created his own problems. He'll place all the blame on Allison. There's no end to what he might do."

"I wouldn't worry too much about it, Annette. Gary's in enough hot water with Manning. His ability to influence him or anyone else in administration isn't as powerful as it may have been at one time."

"I hope you're right. Have you had a chance to talk with Gary yet? I know he had that eye appointment."

"Not yet, but I asked him to text me once he knows more."

"Okay, we'll see how it goes. I think I'll try to talk to Rosa tonight if she's working, just to get an idea where she stands and maybe learn if she's planning on talking to Tamarino."

As Annette got to her feet, the office manager knocked on the door, officially ending their conversation. "Dr. Tamarino's on line one for you, Dr. Kumar."

~ Chapter 40 ~

The early morning sun streamed through Allison's east-facing window, flooding her bedroom with light. She rolled over to find out the time. Ten o'clock. She could hardly believe she'd slept almost twelve hours, but decided she must have needed it. Once she got out of bed, she appreciated that her body didn't ache too much this morning. But make no mistake, it would be a long time before she got back to normal. Thanks to her good health prior to the accident, she managed at home without help. Four days after surgery, she did her best to return to a routine of some sort. She headed to the kitchen, fed Snowball, and gave her kitty some special loving time before she made her morning coffee.

Allison knew she needed to rest between activities, so she sat down and checked her phone. Later she'd attempt the labor-intensive task of showering and getting dressed. She had a text from Mark, saying he hoped she'd gotten some sleep, and he'd check in with her this afternoon. An email from Sherry Dolan offered her condolences for the accident and surgery.

Of all the people Allison hired for Critical Cover-Up, she trusted Sherry without reservation. Reliable, professional, and intelligent, the twenty-eight-year-old executive excelled in her role as administrator of Allison's company, despite her relatively young age. In the majority of the cases, Sherry handled everything and just summarized the situations for Allison in a report. In this instance, however, Allison took a more hands-on approach, preferring to be directly involved.

Rather than reply to the email, Allison located Sherry's number and called her.

"Allison, it's great to hear from you. I felt bad when I heard about your accident. How are you coming along?"

"Hi, Sherry. Not too bad. I had some good care and am recovering faster than anticipated. I just wanted to check in with you. Mark said he talked to you and planned on an update with Christy Newsell. Everything's going as expected?"

"Yes. In fact, Mark filled me in just before you called. He and Christy haven't come up with anything too earth-shattering yet on the Tamarino case, but they're working some leads. Actually, a surprise twist turned up as part of their probe, and we're following that as well. In fact, we opened a separate investigation."

Her curiosity aroused, Allison said, "Really? Something else about Dr. Tamarino?"

"Not that we know of. This involves the hospital's CEO, Ed Manning."

"What is it? I haven't heard any hospital gossip lately."

"What we found appears pretty serious. It involves sexual harassment. I know Mark wants to give you the details, so that's all I'll say for now."

Stunned by this news, Allison thanked Sherry and ended the call. Her heart told her to call Mark and find out the rest of the story right away. Instead, she made her way to the bathroom for a real shower and a change of clothes. An hour later, she felt like a new person, though she had to admit that the effort tired her out. Not wanting to cook anything, she remembered she had some meal replacement shakes in the fridge. She grabbed one and settled herself on the couch. Snowball curled up next to her, as if she knew Allison needed something warm and furry beside her. Cats are like that.

Before she had a chance to call Mark, he texted her. "Are you awake? I'll give you a call if this is a good time. I have news for you."

"Yes, this is a good time. Call me," she texted back. Ten seconds later her phone rang.

"Good morning. How are you today?"

"I'm good. Can you believe I slept ten hours?" she said, laughing.

"Good for you. I know you needed it. Are you ready for some news?"

"Yes. I already talked to Sherry, and she teased me with a few details. She said you wanted to fill me in on everything yourself."

"She's right. Here's the deal. First of all, Christy came up with the details of Tamarino's divorce agreement. I'm not sure how she got the information, but the glaring element of the whole thing pointed to spousal support. The laws in California give a lot of leeway and no clear-cut guidelines. In their divorce agreement, Tamarino was required to pay $150,000 a year in alimony."

"Wow! No wonder he had financial problems."

"And I'm still checking on the vision stuff and his eye appointment. But the big surprise centered on the hospital's CEO."

"Sherry told me it related to sexual harassment."

"I guess this guy Manning had an affair with a nurse from one of the critical care units over a year ago. When she confronted him about her pregnancy with his child, he insisted she undergo an abortion. He threatened her job if she didn't comply. That's illegal. She hired a lawyer and filed a charge of discrimination with the EEOC."

"Do we know anything more?"

"Indeed. The hospital was notified and given the usual period of time to respond. The EEOC spent months conducting a thorough investigation and concluded that discrimination occurred, but in the end, the hospital and the EEOC couldn't agree on a resolution. Not long ago, her attorney filed a lawsuit in federal court. As soon as the hospital got wind of that, they fired her for some minor reason. And now she has cause to file another charge with the EEOC, this time for retaliation."

"Mark, you are really good. You uncovered all this while you were looking into Tamarino's problems? How?"

"Tamarino and Manning have been good friends for years, and Manning's name came up in our searches. When we started looking into the relationship, all this information on Manning showed up. We're going to keep digging. There may be even more dirt. I already submitted a FOIA request to the EEOC, but that could take weeks. In the meantime, we have plenty of leads, and the more we probe, the deeper this investigation reaches."

~ Chapter 41 ~

"Hello, Gary. I can talk for a few minutes. The office is full of patients."

"Just checking in, Kumar. Everything going okay?"

"Yes, we're managing. I wondered how your eye appointment turned out."

"It's no big deal, just as I thought. He diagnosed me with transient monocular vision loss, and it's treatable with calcium channel blockers. So, I got a prescription, and hopefully that's all there is to it. I'll be back to work tomorrow."

"That's good news. Two cases are scheduled. By the way, I have a question. Are we okay financially? I mean the practice."

Not expecting this line of questioning from his junior partner, Tamarino exploded. "What kind of question is that, Kumar? Don't you think I'd tell you if we had a problem? The practice is fine, and you don't need to lose any sleep over it."

"It's just that it's been on my mind, you know, since you told me about your personal financial problems."

"I've resolved that issue too, so everything is good, understand? One more thing. Rosa Perez from CSU told me something disturbing. Do you know anything about an investigation by an oversight company called Critical

Cover-Up?" Tamarino got no response. "Kumar, are you listening?"

"Yes, I am. I've heard of the company."

"Rosa told me they opened an investigation of me for the patient deaths and complications over the past month. Can you imagine? Wait until you hear the rest. Allison Jamison owns the company." He waited for a reaction from Kumar, but none came.

"I've got to see these patients, Gary. We can talk tomorrow. I'll see you in surgery in the morning."

Tamarino wondered why Kumar blew him off. *And why did he want to know about the finances?* His suspicions caused paranoia to creep in. He no longer trusted anyone.

His focus shifted to other concerns, like the Ed Manning scandal those two guys talked about in the men's room. With that story circulating, he expected an announcement any time about a new CEO. But then his mind reverted back to his own problems. *Maybe the Critical Cover-Up thing was exaggerated. What do they have on me anyway?*

Gary's deep-seated need to prove himself to his colleagues gnawed at his soul. *Tomorrow, Dr. Gary Tamarino, chief of cardiovascular surgery, will turn into a superstar in the OR.* Since he began the prescribed medication for his eye problems, he had not experienced any loss of vision. He regretted not seeking medical attention sooner, but so be it. *Get ready, people. Tamarino is back.*

***

Thursday morning, Dr. Tamarino showed up at 6:15 a.m. to make rounds on his post-op patients in CSU. When a nurse noticed his presence, she reacted with surprise. "Dr. T, what are you doing here so early?"

"I work here," he said with a smile—an unusual reaction from him, especially so early in the day. Rosa Perez was at the nurses' desk preparing for shift report and didn't see him as he approached. "Good morning, Rosa. I hope you had a good night."

"Hello, Dr. T. I didn't expect to see you at this hour. Did you have an emergency consult in the ER?"

"No, I just decided to get an early start and see my patients before surgery begins." In a lowered tone, he asked Rosa if they could talk for a moment. "Remember when you told me about that investigation, the one from the company Allison owns?" Rosa nodded. "Do you know for certain that's true?"

Rosa's eyes met his. "All I know is what Allison told me, and she said Kumar and Annette knew about it too."

~ Chapter 42 ~

Tamarino rounded on all of his group's CSU patients, most of whom officially belonged to Kumar, as the surgeon of record. None exhibited any major problems, and Dr. T left the unit. With lots of time before he needed to scrub in for the first case, he took the stairs to the third floor, where both of today's surgery patients' rooms were located. The surgical staff had already transported his first patient to the pre-op area, so he searched for his second case patient. He entered Room 316, expecting to find Mrs. Guadalupe Manderos, his sixty-year-old patient, but instead noticed an empty bed. "Mrs. Manderos?"

A high-pitched voice emanated from the bathroom. "*Si. Estoy en el baño. Un minuto por favor.*"

Tamarino's Spanish skills ranked in the low percentiles, but he understood her response and waited for her to come out of the bathroom. He knew Kumar had already spoken with the patient, but as the primary surgeon, he thought it important that he visit her as well. Soon, he heard the sound of running water, and thirty seconds later, a petite Hispanic woman, who appeared the picture of good health, walked toward him. "Good morning, Doctor. I am pleased to meet you." She topped her cheery greeting with a magnetizing smile.

Charmed, and relieved that the woman spoke English, he shook her hand and waited until she sat down before he introduced himself. "I'm Doctor Tamarino, your surgeon. I'll be the one operating on your heart today." Mrs. Manderos, a baptized Jehovah's Witness, had severe mitral regurgitation, known to the layperson as a leaky mitral valve. To avoid irreversible heart damage, a mitral valve repair, prior to symptoms becoming severe, remains the recommended treatment option.

Mrs. Manderos met the criteria for minimally invasive mitral valve repair. Performed through a small incision between the ribs using specialized, handheld instruments, this technique eliminated the need for cutting through the sternum or ribs.

As a matter of principle and adherence to their faith, most Jehovah's Witnesses do not accept blood transfusions, even to save their lives. Because of the firm stand they've taken on blood, they've influenced surgeons to hone their skills enough to perform surgery with minimal blood loss. Much less blood is used in cardiac surgeries today, and the practice is known as bloodless surgery. A surgeon's operative technique and meticulous care to control bleeding are major factors in the success of these patients.

Dr. Tamarino explained the risks of the surgery in detail. Because of the special transfusion issues, he wanted to be clear that he understood her desires so he could accommodate her wishes. "Mrs. Manderos, I'm aware that your beliefs and values dictate that you not receive any blood, is that right?"

"Yes, that is true. Under no circumstances do I want you to give me blood. My family has a copy of my paperwork delegating my wishes and surrogate."

"I want to be sure you understand that without blood, there is a possibility you might die."

"Si. I understand."

"And you will not allow any blood, even if it is your own blood given back to you through a tubing, a technique known as cell-saver blood?"

"No blood at all. If I die, I die. I am at peace with God."

"Okay, we're clear, then. I will do my best to make sure any bleeding is minimal. I'll see you in recovery."

Satisfied, he left her room and proceeded toward the elevator. In ten minutes, he'd be in surgery with his first case, another of Kumar's patients. According to Annette's update, he expected an uncomplicated aortic valve repair. *Today is going to be a good day.*

~ Chapter 43 ~

Reassured that Allison was on the mend, Mark funneled all of his energy into the Critical Cover-Up case. He narrowed his focus toward uncovering the deeper connection he presumed existed between Tamarino and Manning. Due to his years of detective work, Derning had developed an intuition for these types of situations and now set a goal to find answers.

After three intense hours of combing through court filings and documents, he discovered the link that had eluded him. Five years ago, two San Francisco Bay Hospital executives were charged in a sophisticated Medicare fraud scheme that included illegal billing, physician kickbacks, and falsification of patient records. To resolve the allegations, the hospital agreed to pay $20 million to the federal government in exchange for no determination of liability. The accused executives included the former CEO and CFO. After their dismissal, the hospital promoted the Director of Patient Financial Services, Ed Manning, to CEO.

Derning checked on Tamarino's length of employment at the same hospital and discovered a correlation between his dates and those of Ed Manning. *Tamarino was here when all this fraud went down.* Derning wondered how much the surgeon knew at the time and whether Manning possessed any culpability. His gut told him the CEO did, and he somehow flew under the radar. Without concrete evidence, the speculation proved nothing, yet it didn't quite pass the smell test. He'd delve into the documents more, but he needed a break and something to eat.

At one thirty he phoned Allison. "I wonder if you feel like getting out of your apartment. Maybe have a bite to eat somewhere? I'm kind of hungry. How about you?"

Her reply pleased him. "Yes, I'm going stir-crazy here. And I don't have much to choose from in my pantry. Maybe you can meet me at my apartment, and we can walk somewhere. I could use the exercise."

"Okay. I'll see you in twenty minutes. Is that good?"

"Yes, I'll be ready."

Elated, Mark envisioned this impromptu lunch as a date with Allison. He still wanted to take her to È Tutto Qua, but that restaurant was open for dinner only. Another time. He had checked out local eateries near her apartment and already knew where he planned to take Allison today. It was a small, family-owned restaurant with a cozy atmosphere, specializing in authentic, homestyle Italian food. Not a long walk from her apartment, his choice worked out well.

He entered Allison's building and took the elevator to her apartment. When she opened the door, his jaw dropped. Overwhelmed by her natural beauty, he said, "Hello, beautiful. What a difference a day makes. You look rested and refreshed."

She laughed. "You can't keep a girl like me down for long. I have places to go and things to do." They rode the elevator to the first floor and stepped outside. "This fresh air feels so good on my skin," she said. The unusually warm November day seemed more like summer than late fall. When the subtle breeze brushed against Allison's face, Mark admired her as she tossed her black hair out of her eyes.

He hadn't been in a gym for a while, so the uphill walk from Jones Street toward California proved to be a real cardio workout. "We're getting our exercise, that's for sure," he said. "We're almost there, and not a moment too soon. I didn't realize San Francisco got this warm so late into the year."

Allison never asked where they were going, and when they reached their destination, she flashed an appreciative smile. "You know, I've seen this place and always thought about eating here but never made it. This is wonderful."

At this point, nothing else mattered to Mark. He was enamored by this woman, whom he'd known only in a business capacity until now. Romantic by nature, he embraced the hope that this moment proved to be the beginning of much more.

~ Chapter 44 ~

One of the OR nurses announced the presence of the surgeon in an enthusiastic, booming voice when Dr. Tamarino walked into the operating room. "Welcome back, sir. Dr. T is in the house."

Delighted to be the center of attention and the recipient of such adulation, he enacted the role he enjoyed more than any other. "It's good to be back. We all need a little R&R once in a while. Who's ready to rock and roll? Let's get this party started."

Despite the fact that the case belonged to Kumar, Tamarino took charge. Addressing no one in particular, he said, "My rock and pop playlist, please." As he gowned and gloved with the assistance of the scrub tech, the party music wafted from the subwoofer speaker system, and the atmosphere turned jovial. Tamarino even rewarded his "fans" by singing along to the catchy chorus of "I Gotta Feeling." Others chimed in and sang along to the hip beat. To continue the fun atmosphere, the anesthesiologist entertained the room by rapping the appropriate parts while he waited for the surgery to begin.

Annette and Kumar stood across the table from Tamarino as the patient lay draped, anesthetized, and ready to undergo an aortic valve replacement, a serious heart operation. This team had performed hundreds of these surgeries, and to Tamarino, it was a routine day at work. He put all his negative experiences from the past week behind him.

No tensions flared, and all was well in Tamarino's world once again. He worked in rhythm with Kumar and Annette, and he even surprised himself at how effortless the surgery seemed. No vision problems, no lack of focus, and in two hours they were ready to close. "He looks good. Would you mind closing?" Kumar said. "I'll go update the family and write orders."

"You got it, Kumar." Tamarino completed the surgery with no complications and thanked the team before they left the room. Taking a moment to unwind, Annette and Gary found themselves alone in the surgeons' lounge. It marked the first time they'd shared a private conversation since the weekend when they operated on the earthquake victims.

"Seems like the time away had its benefits, Dr. T. Today was like old times again. It was actually fun working without any conflict."

But Tamarino couldn't keep his mouth shut. He intended to make sure Annette understood he was aware of the secret betrayal. "Yeah, let's see how that works out, now that I'm supposedly being investigated, thanks to your friend Allison," he snarled. "Yeah, I've known all about it for a while, and I know you and Kumar were informed about it too. So far, nothing has happened, you know?" Annette didn't respond, and Tamarino got the last word, just as he liked.

***

It took one hour to turn over the surgical suite. Mrs. Manderos was already anesthetized when Dr. Tamarino entered the room. The same surgical team he'd worked with earlier scrubbed in and took their positions. The atmosphere differed, partly because this was the second case of the day and the energy level was not as elevated. The mood also reflected the seriousness of this surgery. Without the possibility of a transfusion, they'd have to take extra precautions to control bleeding from even the tiniest source.

Instead of fast-paced dance music or the rock and roll sounds of Queen, Tamarino opted for the quiet, more calming sounds of Dave Brubeck from his customized jazz playlist. The old days, when surgeons brought their own CDs into the operating room, are gone. Today the music emanates from playlists on surgeons' iPhones. For Gary Tamarino, music played a crucial role while he operated.

"Okay, everyone knows this lady is a Jehovah's Witness, and she's refused all blood products. That includes cell-saver. She wasn't typed and crossed, since she's not receiving any transfusions. Let's get started."

~ Chapter 45 ~

Allison couldn't believe two hours had passed. She and Mark had finished eating some time ago at Nob Hill Café but were deep in conversation when the server reminded them in a friendly way that the restaurant closed at three o'clock.

"They must close between lunch and dinner. Don't worry about the time. Enjoy your prosecco. We still have fifteen minutes," Mark said.

Allison looked around the quaint restaurant and appreciated the rustic, yet intimate, décor. Quite a few other guests still remained at the closely packed tables. She relaxed and took a sip of her drink. "This has been great, Mark. The food was delicious and the company more than welcome. Thank you for bringing me here."

Mark replied, "Allison, I'm so happy to spend the time together. You know, this isn't just about work. I've wanted to do this for a long time. That's why I came out here to San Francisco, so I could see you. I'm not sure, though, how much you remember because of the accident." He placed his left hand over hers, and Allison noticed the warmth of his gentle touch as she allowed it to remain. Her eyes met his, and she couldn't deny the connection between them. More than a work relationship existed here for her too.

Something stirred inside her, a spark she hadn't experienced for more than two years, since Sean was killed. The pain she suffered at the tragic loss of her one true love influenced her life in profound ways. She dove headfirst into her work and immersed herself in her new business. She made no time for a social life and told herself she wasn't interested in looking for another relationship. If the slightest hint of attraction from anyone surfaced, she squashed it before it started. She hadn't been ready to open herself up again, until now. Maybe.

Just before three, Mark and Allison left the restaurant and walked back toward her apartment. The bright sun warmed the air, and they almost didn't need their jackets. They strolled along, taking time to stop and admire the architecture on the older structures. Fifteen minutes later, they stood in the shade in front of her building.

A part of her didn't want this time to end, but the exertion so soon after surgery tired her, and she knew her body needed rest. As if he could read her mind, Mark spoke first. Holding her hand, he looked lovingly into her eyes. "I really wish this didn't have to end right now, but you probably could use some rest, and I need to get back to work." She nodded without saying anything. "Do you think you'd feel up to having dinner later and spending the evening with me?"

She smiled and her heart fluttered. "I'd love that."

"I'll pick you up at eight then, and we can take an Uber to the restaurant. I'm going to take you to È Tutto Qua, the place where we were supposed to go last Saturday, before the earthquake changed everything. It seems like a lifetime ago. Do you think you can stand another Italian meal? It will be worth it."

Allison laughed. "Me? You know Italian is my favorite food. I think I could eat it every day."

Mark leaned in closer and wrapped one arm behind Allison's tiny waist. He touched her face and gently cupped her cheek as he kissed her tender lips. With her eyes closed, she moved with him and savored the moment. *I don't know what's happening, but it feels real, and it feels good.* She looked up at him one last time before saying goodbye. "I'll see you at eight, Mark." She disappeared into the building.

~ Chapter 46 ~

Two hours into Mrs. Manderos's mitral valve repair, Dr. Tamarino began singing along to the music. Kumar noticed a more relaxed Tamarino, now that the surgery was nearing the end and no problems had ensued. As the perfusionist weaned the patient off cardiopulmonary bypass — the heart-lung machine — Mrs. Manderos's heart began to beat again on its own, and her blood pressure and other vital signs maintained within normal limits. All good signs.

A presurgical transesophageal echocardiogram had been performed by the cardiologist in the OR. Since the cath lab required his presence now, the anesthesiologist performed the post-repair echocardiogram of the mitral valve on the patient's fully beating heart by manipulating the specialized probe with the ultrasound transducer at its tip. An echo has become standard procedure in valve surgeries. In addition to examining the effectiveness of the repaired valve, the echo also assessed for any air bubbles left inside the heart, adequate heart wall muscle activity, and coronary artery functionality.

As the echo progressed, Dr. Kumar observed the heart muscle activity on the LCD screen. What he saw caused him grave concern. He noted the appearance of a new regional wall motion abnormality, which could be an indication of a problem known as myocardial compromise. He waited for Tamarino to notice the same thing and react.

"Turn the music off," yelled Dr. T as he stared at the real-time results of the echocardiogram. Like any good heart surgeon, Kumar 's keen awareness of the anatomy of heart structures guided his attention to the juxtaposition of the circumflex coronary artery to the mitral valve. Although a rare occurrence, the close anatomical configuration made this particular blood vessel especially susceptible to perioperative injury. "She had left coronary dominance, right?" Tamarino asked Kumar, who confirmed Gary's query with a nod.

Kumar added, "She's got some ST elevation now on the EKG." These specific changes indicated compromised blood flow to the inferior wall of the heart and raised a strong suspicion of damage to the circumflex artery.

Tamarino never questioned the necessity to go back in to explore the cause of the obstructed blood vessel and correct it, if possible. "Put her back on bypass," he directed the perfusionist. "We have to do a sternotomy."

Any time a cardiac surgical patient had to go back on bypass, the surgery and anesthesia time increased, and so did the morbidity. Because Kumar knew his partner like an open book, he assumed Tamarino's thoughts focused on the effect this complication might have on his future statistics. In contrast, Kumar's compassion led him to worry for the patient, who could not afford any type of operative complications that might cause her to lose more blood. He looked at Annette and rolled his eyes. The music remained off, and the tension in the room escalated.

The small incision they'd manipulated to execute the valve repair no longer allowed sufficient access to explore the problem. "Damn. After all this, and now we have to go in through the sternum," Tamarino grumbled, his frustration apparent. The minimally invasive operation now converted to an open procedure. This necessitated a full median sternotomy, where Tamarino needed to employ a much larger vertical incision down the center of the chest and chisel the middle of the breastbone with a bone saw. He'd then spread the chest wide open with retractors to gain a full view of the heart and area around it.

Kumar expected Tamarino to find a problem with the circumflex artery. The damage could be a laceration of the vessel or a suture wrapped around it. He prayed Tamarino hadn't accidentally nicked the artery. If so, localized hemorrhaging would potentially be an even bigger problem. Time became crucial, and the surgical team acted with efficiency and speed.

With blood flow redirected through the bypass machine, the heart ceased all movement and allowed for easy inspection of the coronary arteries. However, a massive amount of bleeding prevented Tamarino from determining the source. "More suction," he ordered, although Annette already anticipated the need and sucked blood out of the chest as fast as it pooled.

Kumar wondered if Tamarino's eyesight remained problematic after all. "Let me get in there and see if I can locate the bleeding," he said, and Tamarino acquiesced. Sixty seconds later, Kumar pinpointed its origin and clamped off the circumflex. The sterile field became easier to see without all the blood, and Kumar pointed to the damaged circumflex blood vessel. He breathed a sigh of relief, looked up at his partner, and nodded. *We got this.*

Tamarino took charge again and announced they'd do a single bypass graft using the mammary artery. While Kumar busied himself taking down the mammary, Tamarino explored the other coronary blood vessels and double-checked areas of possible concern.

The team completed the graft, and the patient came off the pump for the second time without incident. Tamarino spent another twenty minutes making sure all bleeding had been controlled before he told Kumar to close. "Good job, people. Thank you." Kumar thought he detected a tone of humility, but Tamarino's recent suspicious behaviors forced him to believe otherwise. *Let's see how this goes.*

~ Chapter 47 ~

Mark walked back to his hotel with a light heart, thoughts of a future with Allison swirling in his head. Few of his friends would peg him for a romantic, but deep inside, the hard-ass detective was a caring and sensitive man. He liked that about himself.

Back in his hotel room, Derning switched gears and got down to business. Four and a half hours from now he had to pick Allison up for dinner. He made a list of the loose ends he needed to address on the Tamarino case and its connection to the Ed Manning case, which seemed like it may be a bigger deal. He wanted to contact Rosa, but since she worked nights, that would have to wait until later, maybe tomorrow.

He needed the results of Dr. Tamarino's eye exam, and a simple text to either Kumar or Annette would take care of that. The most important task on his agenda aimed at a review of the court documents from the hospital's Medicare fraud case. He focused on determining any possible connections to Manning, Tamarino, or both. Also, the federal lawsuit that the ICU nurse's attorney filed against Manning loomed large in his mind. Those two issues became his priorities. If he stopped working by seven tonight, it would give him three and a half hours before he had to get ready for his dinner date with Allison. Good thing he had a tendency to be a little obsessive-compulsive, a trait that proved valuable in his work.

First things first. He picked up his phone to text Kumar. "It's Mark Derning. Just wondering if you found out anything regarding Dr. Tamarino's eye exam. Thanks."

Kumar was obviously not in surgery, because he replied in less than a minute. "Yes, but it's easier if I call you. Are you available now for a quick phone call?"

"Yes. This is a good time." Derning waited for his phone to ring, and Kumar did not disappoint.

"Hello, Dr. Kumar. Thanks for getting back to me so soon."

"Well, the timing just worked out. Yes, Gary saw the eye doctor and underwent a complete evaluation. He does have an issue with his vision, but it's able to be treated with medication. He told me he's taking it as prescribed."

"Okay, that's good to know. How are things going?"

"To be honest, not that bad, really. We had two cases today, and the second patient was touch and go for a while due to a complication. Dr. Tamarino nicked a coronary artery, but we fixed it and she's okay. I can't really fault him for something accidental that could have happened to any of us."

Derning listened as Dr. Kumar continued. "I think Gary's surgical problems, aside from his personal issues, were due to the vision loss and nothing else. Before this last month, his statistics were great. We may have jumped the gun on this. I don't think you're going to come up with substantive evidence in your inquiry. Maybe you should back off on it."

Derning wasn't surprised. While Christy had unearthed interesting details about Tamarino's finances and divorce, nothing pointed to malpractice or negligence.

"Thank you for your insights, Doctor. I'll take it under consideration. I have a few more leads I'm following, but so far I tend to agree. I appreciate all your help."

Now he turned his attention to the larger issues. Regarding the past hospital fraud settlement case, Derning had a strong hunch that Manning was secretly involved, and possibly Tamarino as well. He wanted to examine the physician kickback documentation. He perused every page, hunting for the hidden connection. He also ran a Google search for potential comments on news articles or social media. In the past, he'd found a gold mine of information on public cases with this method. After an hour and a half, he uncovered a clue. The witness list included the names of both Manning and Tamarino. But since the case had been settled without a trial, no transcripts of any testimony were available.

However, plenty of online articles were posted with reader comments. More than once, the remarks implicated Manning for falsifying patient records and billing for procedures that were never performed. When Derning did a search on Twitter, he found tweets related to the fraud. They placed blame on Manning as patient financial services director, since he had direct access to billing. But in the end, no charges were filed against him.

Derning's scrutiny of the documents found no signs of Tamarino's involvement. *Maybe we've been barking up the wrong tree, and Tamarino's only crime is his friendship with Manning.*

~ Chapter 48 ~

When Mrs. Manderos came off bypass, Gary Tamarino felt like a million dollars. A little dicey for a while, but he saved another life and believed he deserved all the credit. Hers became the first high-risk surgery since those fiascos from last week, and now, in his mind, he had redeemed himself and restored his reputation. Although she hadn't yet awakened in CSU, he expected no problems through the night, and he'd see her in the morning.

The nagging memory of his last conversation with Rosa emerged into the foreground once more and interfered with his good mood. Unable to erase the concept of himself as the subject of an investigation by some fly-by-night company created by a CSU nurse, he made a snap decision. A quick glance at his watch confirmed he had time for an impromptu meeting.

"Mind if I come in?" Tamarino asked as he strolled into Ed Manning's office with his head held high. The upper hand belonged to him today, and he relished the position of leverage. Manning didn't appear the self-assured chief executive to whom Tamarino had grown accustomed.

"Have a seat, Gary. It's been a busy day. I was just getting ready to leave." Then he smiled and asked, "Are you here to tell me when you plan on repaying the 200K?"

Tamarino sat down and shook his head. "Not yet, Ed, but it won't be long. I promise you that." Gary lowered his voice and looked Ed straight in the eye. "Listen, did you know rumors are flying about a lawsuit against you from that ICU nurse? The one who had the abortion."

Alarmed, Ed Manning leaned forward and scrunched his eyes. "The legal stuff just happened. You already heard about it?" he snarled. "How?"

"I overhead two people talking in the men's room, man. It's probably all over Facebook by now. Have you been approached by anyone from the board?"

Manning hung his head and answered in a barely audible tone. "Not yet, but it's coming. I'll be out of here in a day or two, I'm sure."

"Listen, I'm sorry it all caught up with you. I know it's a bad time all the way around." Then in true Tamarino style, he asked Manning for another favor. "I need something, though, while you're still CEO."

Manning looked up and stared at Gary with no sign of emotion. Gary witnessed a beaten man. "What is it?"

"There's a CSU nurse named Allison Jamison. She's been here for some time, but she's a travel nurse."

"Yes, most of the CSU staff are longtime travel nurses. What about her? Did you knock her up or something?"

Tamarino didn't find it funny. "Worse than that. She has an oversight company called Critical Cover-Up, and she reported me to them because of my recent string of bad luck with those cardiac surgery patients who died. She has some private detective snooping around here asking questions. I want her fired."

Manning listened and then replied, "Just so you know, the nurse managers contract the travel nurses through their agencies, and we can't fire them. All we can do is cancel their contracts or not renew them when they expire. And even then, without cause it's a messy situation. The hospital has to reimburse the travel nursing agency."

"Whatever it takes. I can't trust her, and I don't want to work with her ever again. To make matters worse, she came in as a trauma patient after the earthquake, and I had to perform surgery on her. I haven't seen her since then. She's probably on leave."

In a resigned voice, Manning said, "I'll talk with the chief nursing officer and make sure she cancels her travel contract . . . or at least doesn't renew it."

"Thanks, man." Gary stood and shook Ed's hand. "We'll stay in touch, don't worry." Without waiting for a reply, Tamarino left Ed Manning's office for the last time.

~ Chapter 49 ~

Five minutes before eight, Allison's phone pinged with a text from Mark. "I'm in front of your building. No rush." She liked punctuality and liked early even more.

"I'll be down soon," she texted back. Allison smiled as her heart pounded with happiness. For the past hour and a half, she had been getting ready for this night. She must have tried on half a dozen outfits and finally settled on her black, V-neck, linen dress with three-quarter-length sleeves. Simple, but sexy, the dress flattered her trim figure, and the black pointy-toe heels clinched the deal. The weather forecast predicted warmer than usual temperatures, so she decided against a jacket. One last check in the mirror and she approved her look.

Mark waited outside to greet her as their Uber ride idled on the street. "Don't you look gorgeous!" He kissed her and opened the rear passenger door for her. Allison loved a man who knew how to treat her like a lady, and Mark met all the criteria of a gentleman. For a split second, she experienced a strong sense of déjà vu.

Mark slid in beside her, and she looked up at him, resting her hand on the sleeve of his navy blazer. "I like this, Mark," she said, leaning close to him. "It's so stylish and classy." Allison still had no memory of that awful collision the two of them had endured not so long ago.

"I hope you had a chance to rest this afternoon," Mark said as the car pulled away from the curb.

"A little. I didn't fall asleep, but I did lie down for an hour or so. I intentionally didn't make any phone calls or write email. Just getting away from that stress helped."

"I'm glad to hear it. And to continue in that vein, we will have no talk of business tonight, agreed?"

She squeezed his hand and nodded. Mark kept his hand entwined with hers until they reached the restaurant on the southeast corner of Columbus and Broadway. The lively upscale Italian eatery occupied space in a two-story building with a lot of history. While it had been the home to È Tutto Qua for more than a decade, the gray stone structure with high arched windows provided the home for the first Bank of America. Its builder, Amadeo Giannini, founded the Bank of Italy and later changed the name, which still exists today. The oval BA logo can be seen just above the entrance door, and the basement is said to house the original bank vaults to this day.

Allison's energy level ratcheted up a notch as they got out of the car and heard the invigorating sounds that emanated from inside the crowded restaurant. "I'm thankful you made a reservation, Mark. This place is packed."

"Its reputation speaks for itself. Just wait till you taste the food."

Her enthusiasm increased as a pleasant, good-looking, Italian young man greeted them with a broad smile. In less than a minute, he ushered them to a cozy table for two near the window. In keeping with the authentic flair, the tables were situated close to each other, just like in

Italy, and the atmosphere exuded good times. "It's like one big happy family here," Allison said.

From Mark's expression, she could tell he liked this place. Four young waiters with a strong familial resemblance flitted about the restaurant like a well-choreographed dance scene. They worked as a team, engaging with all the guests as if they'd known them for years. Unlike the atmosphere at other eating establishments, the unmistakable camaraderie among the staff took center stage. Later Allison would learn that these friendly waiters were all nephews of the Italian-born owner and executive chef, Enzo Pellico. They ran the restaurant, and did it well.

Allison couldn't be any happier, and before she knew it, other waitstaff were filling water glasses for her and Mark. Customer service shined here. Soon their waiter introduced himself and handed them their menus.

"Let's celebrate your recovery with some wine and an appetizer to start," Mark said. They perused the wine list and selected a bottle of Italian merlot. For an appetizer, Mark ordered carpaccio of chilled octopus with lemon dressing, olives, capers, and onions to share.

The growing attraction between Allison and Mark became more apparent to her as they spent quality time in a social setting. Although she did nothing to foster this spontaneous, euphoric mood, she relished every part of it.

The entire evening took on the characteristics of a fairy tale. They laughed for hours while savoring their delicious meals of veal scallopine in a black truffle sauce and squid ink pasta with mixed seafood in a white wine and fresh tomato sauce. Allison threw all self-control out the window when the waiter presented the dessert menu. She and Mark shared a *tartuffo*—a chocolate truffle with a creamy center and hazelnuts.

"Oh my God! It was all so delicious. I don't think I'll be able to eat again for a week," she said as they left the restaurant at close to eleven o'clock. "It's a beautiful night. Maybe we should walk back," she suggested, in part to burn off some of the calories she'd consumed, but also to extend the evening a little longer. With a hint of flirtatiousness, she gazed up at Mark, and their eyes met. He held her in a gentle embrace, and as she melted into his arms, he reached down to kiss her.

"Only if we can order room service for breakfast."

~ Chapter 50 ~

Mark found it difficult to remain focused on work after his romantic evening with Allison. He kept replaying every detail over and over in his mind—the ride to the restaurant, followed by the delicious Italian dinner that lasted three hours, and the wonderful stroll back on a balmy California night.

Although he'd hoped the evening wouldn't end with dinner, he'd made no assumptions in advance. His hopes turned into reality as their romantic evening exceeded all expectations and continued all night long. In the morning, he awoke with Allison in his arms. He thought they shared the same wish, to experience love again after all these years, and longed for this moment without even realizing it. Mark wanted to pinch himself to make sure he wasn't imagining all of this. He couldn't stop thinking about Allison.

After room service delivered breakfast for two, they'd spent the rest of the morning in a state of bliss. But the euphoria had to end sometime, as much as he wished he could press Pause and resume in a few minutes. Mark had called an Uber driver to take Allison back to her apartment.

Able to compartmentalize his thoughts, he prepared to work, knowing he needed to continue with his investigation. He made a phone call and got dressed. At two o'clock in the afternoon, he arrived at San Francisco Bay Hospital for an appointment.

He knocked on the half-open office door of CEO Ed Manning and was invited in.

"Good afternoon, Mr. Manning. I'm Detective Mark Derning. Thank you for seeing me on such short notice. I promise not to take up too much of your time." He couldn't help but notice that the hospital executive fidgeted with a paperweight on his desk.

"Please sit down. What can I do for you, Detective?"

"As I mentioned on the phone, I'm investigating two cases which involved you. I just have a few questions."

"You and everybody else," Manning muttered under his breath. "Everyone seems to know all about it now, so I have nothing to hide. I probably won't even have a job after this week."

Derning first questioned him about the recent lawsuit brought by the lawyers for the ICU nurse. Manning's responses surprised the seasoned investigator. In a quiet, but serious, voice, the CEO told Mark Derning his version of the story. He admitted to intimidating the nurse into aborting the pregnancy. He made no excuses and appeared disheartened, as if the case was already settled and he had been found guilty.

Derning inquired whether Manning knew why this hadn't been resolved when the EEOC filed the discrimination charges. "The process continued for months," Manning explained, "and in the end, the hospital declined to comply with their requirements. I guess they hoped it would just go away, and so did I."

"And now the nurse has been fired. Were you involved in that?"

Manning hung his head and didn't answer. Derning waited before he asked another question. "You are aware, aren't you, that she now has a reason to file another case for retaliation?"

This time Manning replied without hesitation, but with a slight smirk. "That will be for the hospital to deal with, not me."

Derning moved on to the older investigation. "I wanted to ask you about the case against the hospital, the one related to Medicare fraud and illegal billing charges. Were you the patient financial services director at the time?"

Manning acknowledged in the affirmative. "They questioned me at length about all that. I wasn't involved. Two hospital executives got fired, and that's when I became CEO." Manning told Derning nothing new.

Then he went out on a limb and mentioned Dr. Tamarino. "Both you and Dr. Tamarino appeared on the witness list. Online social media posts suggested you falsified patient billing records. You and Dr. Tamarino are good friends, I understand. We have reason to believe he has knowledge about the case and can provide information to us."

Derning knew he'd struck a nerve, as a flush crept up Manning's neck and spread across his cheeks. The CEO shoved back his chair and jumped to his feet. "This interview is over," he barked. "I'll have to ask you to leave."

"Thank you for your time, Mr. Manning. I appreciate your help." Derning smiled and left the CEO's office.

~ Chapter 51 ~

Gary Tamarino's good mood ended the moment Dr. Kumar confronted him with the unwelcome news about a visitor named Mark Derning. "Damn it, Kumar. He's here? Christ."

Kumar ignored the attitude. "I told him to wait in the small family conference room." Tamarino didn't miss the significance, intentional or not. When surgeons had to give family members the news that their loved one had died, they delivered this unpleasant information inside this seldom-used room. Tamarino didn't need any morbid conversations today, but that didn't seem to be an option.

"He's there now? Okay, I'm going to meet him. Page me in ten minutes if I'm not back. I have no intention of talking to this yo-yo any longer than necessary." Kumar gave him a thumbs-up.

The closet-size, windowless room occupied an inconspicuous space at the end of the hall, just outside the doors to CSU. When Tamarino arrived, he noticed the door was closed.

He walked in to find his visitor seated in one of the three upholstered cream-colored chairs, looking at his phone. "I'm Dr. Tamarino," he announced, as he closed the door behind him. Detective Mark Derning stood to shake his hand and introduced himself. After Gary sat down, Mark followed suit.

Exerting control over the situation, Tamarino spoke first. "I don't have that much time, Detective. I have to be in surgery soon. I understand you're investigating me."

"This shouldn't take long, Doctor. I realize you're busy. I've already spoken with your partner, Dr. Chanrami, and also your nurse practitioner, Annette Brashton. I've been assigned to look into the recent patient deaths and bleeding complications of several of your patients."

"You're working for a third-party company, Critical Cover-Up or something?"

"Yes, sir. It's an oversight company that investigates medical errors, fraud, and corruption in healthcare facilities."

"And Allison Jamison owns that company, I understand?"

"That's right," Derning answered. Tamarino couldn't tell by Derning's reply and lack of emotion whether the question caught him by surprise or not.

"I wanted to ask you about something related to that, and then I'd like to discuss one other issue. Can you tell me about the vision problems you experienced in surgery? I understand you saw an eye doctor."

Tamarino wondered who'd told him about this but decided to answer truthfully. He explained about the diagnosis and the medication. "And there haven't been any other problems since I started taking the medication."

"That's good news, Doctor. The other thing I wanted to ask you has to do with Ed Manning, your CEO."

Stunned by this statement, Tamarino worried that Derning knew something about the Medicare fraud settlement that could implicate him. His radar shot up, and he wondered about Derning's intent with this line of questioning. Determined to appear calm, he shrugged and said, "Ask away."

For the next ten minutes, Derning posed numerous situations and questions regarding not only Manning's position in the hospital at that time, but also Tamarino's. He asked about their friendship, their golf outings and loyalties. *Where did he get all this stuff?* Tamarino pondered. *Haven't ten minutes gone by yet? Why hasn't Kumar called?* Uncomfortable with the interview, Tamarino repositioned himself in the chair and tapped his fingers against his leg. A few seconds later, he stood up and excused himself, setting an abrupt end to any further questioning. "Listen, I don't have any more time. I'm needed in the OR." He opened the door and walked out, leaving Derning alone in the room.

As Tamarino walked through the surgery doors, he seethed inside. He'd never allow any more of these unannounced inquisitions. His rage focused on Allison Jamison. He sought revenge and intended to make her life miserable. Having her fired wasn't enough.

~ Chapter 52 ~

The events of the past twenty-four hours ignited a spark within Allison like nothing she'd ever experienced. What happened between her and Mark forever altered the lens through which she saw her life. Call it an epiphany or a magic moment—albeit a moment that lasted a day—but suddenly, living took on a new perspective. A happiness enveloped her entire being, like a natural high that didn't end.

Her energy level skyrocketed, and she cleaned her entire apartment until it sparkled, a sight which would have put Merry Maids' professional services to shame. Her convalescent days behind her, she yearned to return to work, to her job as a CSU nurse where she gained so much satisfaction. Now she realized how much she missed it. All this investigation stuff, combined with an injured, recovering body, had taken its toll. But she emerged a stronger and more determined Allison.

Her life seemed balanced. Her work would no longer be the sole source of her fulfillment and happiness. She'd find the best way to prioritize the important aspects of her life, something she had never done before. Allison hadn't realized the power of a loving, personal relationship, and now all that had changed. Nothing could take away this exhilaration.

Today's mission centered on reinstating herself at work, back on the night-shift schedule. She knew she could call Rosa and ask her to plug her in on some dates, but protocol dictated she go through channels, so she called her travel nurse recruiter. Not too surprised to reach the voicemail, Allison left a message. "Hi. This is Allison Jamison. I've been on sick leave at San Francisco Bay Hospital since the earthquake, due to an accident and subsequent surgery. I'm ready to return to work. Please call me. Thanks."

She realized she'd need clearance from the trauma surgeon, but she had an appointment this week and expected no problems in his releasing her. If she confirmed a return sooner than later, she'd cross that goal off her to-do list.

Ten minutes later, her phone rang. Anticipating the recruiter, she was pleasantly surprised to see Mark's number on the caller ID. Priorities.

They spoke for twenty minutes, the joyful conversation filled with laughter and memories of the day before. "I hate to change the subject and switch to business, Allison, but I have some news I want to share about your friend Tamarino."

"I wouldn't exactly say he's my friend, but do tell."

Mark summarized the details of his research and interviews with Tamarino and Manning. "I can't find anything illegal or corrupt regarding Tamarino. He's annoying and arrogant, for sure, but that's about it. I think Manning is the one who's been flying under the radar."

Shocked at this news, Allison had mixed feelings. "What about the bleeding patients and the two deaths all in the last few weeks?"

Mark informed her of the diagnosis from the ophthalmologist and his treatment plan. "Since he's been taking the prescribed medication, his patients haven't developed any complications, as far as I know. That's based on his remarks, as well as those from Annette and Kumar. I never did get a chance to speak to Rosa Perez, but I had enough information." He paused and let his words sink in. "There's nothing that speaks to negligence or malpractice."

Allison listened, ambivalent about her decision to report Dr. T. *How could we get this so wrong?* Some guilt crept in as she worried that she'd betrayed someone with whom, up until recently, she had enjoyed working. She'd always respected his surgical abilities and overlooked his personality quirks. Now she'd be able to work with him again and reestablish the camaraderie they used to have. "So, what's next?"

"Nothing. I'll make my report and submit it. I already consulted with Christy, who updated Sherry. But I'm still following up on Manning, for sure. Something isn't right there. On a lighter note, dinner tonight?"

"I'd love that, Mark." Allison's worries dissipated, and that natural high reappeared.

"Great. You choose the restaurant this time. Text me later and we'll figure out the details. I can't wait to see you."

"Me too." Allison hung up and thought of calling Rosa but decided to look over her wardrobe for tonight's date with Mark first. Five minutes later, her nurse recruiter called. Just like that, her world turned upside down.

~ Chapter 53 ~

Shocked and confused, Allison tried to make sense of the recruiter's words. "I don't understand. I've been on leave and called to tell you I'm well enough to return to work, and you're telling me my contract's been cancelled?" She didn't attempt to conceal the frustration in her voice.

"I'm sorry, Allison. We just got the word from Human Resources this morning. They gave no explanation and said they'd reimburse the agency for the remainder of your time."

"Well, this sucks. I didn't think they could cancel a contract with the person on sick leave."

"That's probably the case with full-time employees, but hospitals can cancel contracts for travel nurses at will. With no stated cause and no negligence on the nurse's part, the hospital is obligated to pay the agency back. I know this comes as a disappointment, but we've seen this circumstance a lot during times when the census drops and they don't need so many nurses."

Allison had been a travel nurse long enough to know that the recruiter knew the way the system worked. She just didn't expect this to happen to her. What made matters worse is that she had no idea of the reason for the cancellation. The census had not been low, and she swore being out on a medical leave could not have triggered this decision.

"Allison, we can find another contract for you, if you like, in an ICU at a different hospital in the area. Do you want us to initiate that process?"

Not at all what Allison wanted to hear, she had to weigh her options before she could make any kind of decision. "Thank you, but I need some time. I can't even think straight right now. Can I get back to you in a week?"

"Certainly. I'll wait to hear from you. Take all the time you need. And again, I'm sorry this happened."

Tears blurred her vision as Allison hung up the phone. The upbeat, joyful mood she'd been certain was here to stay disappeared as quickly as it came. Nothing could have prepared her for this.

She wondered if Rosa knew about this or, worse yet, what role she may have played in it. The last conversation between them had occurred just before Allison's discharge from the hospital. *Oh my God.* Now, things started to make sense. She suddenly recalled Rosa's unhappy reaction when she'd learned that Allison had referred Dr. Tamarino to Critical Cover-Up. *No wonder I haven't heard from her since then.*

Allison's strong need to find out about any involvement on Rosa's part prompted her to make contact. She remembered Rosa didn't always reply to texts unless they occurred during work hours or related to work situations, so she called her.

Rosa answered her phone on the second ring. "Allison, it's so great to hear from you. How are you doing? We miss you at work." Gushing with friendliness,

Rosa sounded as though everything was cool. Allison remained wary but wanted to believe her coworker possessed no culpability in this.

"I'm doing good, Rosa, physically. I'm ready to come back to work. I—"

Rosa interrupted her before she could finish. "That's wonderful. I'll put you on the schedule."

"Rosa, wait a second. I'd like that more than anything, but I just spoke with my nurse recruiter, who informed me that my contract had been cancelled."

"What? Why? That's ridiculous. We're already short a few nurses."

"Believe me, the news came as a total shock to me. I wondered if you had heard anything?"

"Not a word. Everyone's been asking when you were expected back."

"I don't understand, Rosa. I can't figure out why the hospital would do this. By the way, how are things going? I heard that Tamarino straightened up his act, and he's back to his old, lovable self." She gave a half-hearted laugh.

"It's true. His cases have all done well. There must be a way to get you reinstated. The recruiter gave you no reason?"

"None, and that's what's so aggravating."

"Why don't you come in and try talking to someone in HR? It can't hurt."

"I'll think about it. I'm not sure they have any authority, though. Thanks, Rosa. It's good to talk to you again." Allison said goodbye and ended the call, confident that Rosa knew nothing about this awful turn of events.

~ Chapter 54 ~

His investigative intuition advised Derning to dig deeper, that everything seemed too easy. He didn't buy the story that painted Tamarino as an altar boy. And he would bet money on the surgeon's less-than-ethical connections to Manning. After four hours perusing social media, his efforts rewarded him—not in a huge way, but he'd take it.

From Christy's research, he knew the name of the ICU nurse who'd filed the lawsuit against Manning. He started following Nicole Santorum on social media, including Facebook and some groups she belonged to there. She was active in ICU Nurses – What Really Happens. He read all her posts, as well as the comments beneath them.

Some Facebook groups are private, but this one listed itself as public, so anyone on Facebook could join or access it. This nurse's latest posts were filled with bitter complaints about the hospital administration, including themes such as unfair workplace practices, disrespect for nurses from doctors, and abuse of power by physicians. Her accusatory comments in a public forum surprised Derning, especially the ones that called out physicians and administrators by title. One post in particular grabbed his attention.

"We're always told to do the right thing and stand up for our principles, but because the hospital and its cowardly CEO refused to follow ethical guidelines, I saw no option other than to file a lawsuit. After that filing, the hospital fired me. Thank you, E.M. for giving me another reason to contact EEOC."

And he found a comment posted by another individual, Angelina Rodrigues, even more astonishing. "Don't worry. His job is toast. Paybacks are hell. Remember the Medicare fraud case? I was there, and he's no angel. E.M. and Dr. T made a great dynamic duo. #Gotawaywithit."

Bingo. I need to know more about this person. Derning now identified another possible witness to interview, someone who was already talking. He searched for her Facebook profile. Her bio described Angelina Rodrigues as an ICU nurse who currently worked at UCSF Medical Center but was formerly employed at San Francisco Bay Hospital. Derning found her contact information without much trouble and called her.

"Miss Rodrigues, this is Detective Derning. Don't worry, you aren't in any trouble. I work for a company who exposes corruption and fraud in hospitals." He went on to explain how he came across her name before he asked her to meet. "I think you may be able to shed light on a case I'm investigating at San Francisco Bay Hospital."

Angelina responded by asking Derning some questions and then agreed to talk to him in person. "I can meet you for coffee before I go in to work. How about 5:00 p.m. at Starbucks in Union Square? The one on the corner of Sutter and Stockton."

Thrilled at her willingness to cooperate, Derning thanked her and confirmed the time. How lucky could he get? With the Starbucks conveniently located right across from his hotel, he'd still have plenty of time to change for his dinner date with Allison. Just thinking about it made him miss her, so he gave her a call.

"Hi there," he said when she answered quickly. It's so good to hear your voice. How's your day so far?"

"Terrible. I found out I no longer have a contract at the hospital. They cancelled it for no apparent reason. I've been trying to get myself in a better frame of mind, but I haven't been able to stop thinking about it. I've racked my brain trying to come up with a reason, and I think I might finally have the answer." She didn't sound any happier.

"I'm listening. Go on."

"I thought Rosa might have said something, but she acted surprised when I talked with her. Then I called Annette to give her the news and sound her out as to anything she may have heard. She told me Tamarino had it out for me once he learned about the investigation. Mark, you and I never had a chance to talk about it, but you met with him, didn't you?"

"I did, and I'll be honest, he brought up your name and your business. Before I even mentioned it, he wanted to make me aware that he knew who instigated this investigation."

"Annette said Tamarino could be ruthless, and his wrath knows no bounds. He probably used his friendship with the CEO to force the hospital to cancel my contract."

"You might be right, Allison. Although I uncovered no negligence yet, and he seems to be improving as of late, I'm not so quick to put an end to this. I'm sorry about your cancelled contract. We can talk more about it later, if you like. For now, I wanted to confirm our date tonight and ask you where you wanted to go for dinner. I also have more to discuss later regarding this case."

"Well, I can't promise I'll be very good company, but I do want to go to dinner with you. I'll try to get in a better mood between now and then. I haven't given much thought to a restaurant. Wait a minute. Do you like seafood? Maybe we can go down to the Embarcadero. I know a place not too far from here. I think it's near Pier 9. The food is fabulous, and the view at night is magical."

"What's the name of the restaurant? I'll make a reservation. Is eight thirty too late?"

"It's the Waterfront Restaurant. Appropriate name, right? That time is good for me."

"I'll pick you up a little after eight, okay?"

"See you then."

Mark had an hour before his meeting with Angelina Rodrigues. After what Allison told him regarding her contract, his instincts made him more determined than ever to uncover Tamarino's dirty little secrets.

~ Chapter 55 ~

Less than twenty-fours after he predicted he'd be out of a job, Ed Manning's words became a reality, and he no longer occupied an office at the hospital. Faced with a sexual discrimination lawsuit and possibly another for retaliation after the firing of the ICU nurse, the hospital's board of directors had no other recourse. In this age of the Me Too movement and the focus on sexual harassment claims, they didn't need to be scrutinized under that kind of microscope. The official hospital announcement stated Manning had been fired. This choice of words sent a strong message, taking a 180-degree turn from past sugarcoated press releases that mentioned an administrator's "resigning to follow other opportunities."

So now, whether they liked it or not, San Francisco Bay Hospital became front and center in the news. The story of Manning's firing spread quickly, with details of the scandal all over Facebook and Twitter. Even the the major cable new networks ran the story about the San Francisco hospital CEO who threatened an employee into having an abortion and later used his influence to have her fired.

"You heard the big news, I assume?" Annette asked Kumar as they walked down the hall near the surgeons' cafeteria. "I wonder where this will leave Tamarino, now that his partner in crime is gone."

Kumar shook his head. "You know Gary. He can do anything and still comes out a winner. Everyone falls for his bullshit charm, and it seems to be enough to absolve all of his indiscretions and bad behavior. Even we are guilty of that."

"Well, we do have to work with him, so I guess unless he's killed patients, we're still forced to be on his side."

Kumar's stare spoke volumes and forced Annette to think about her choice of words. *Maybe they're closer to the truth than I thought.* He changed the subject. "I bet Tamarino knew about that nurse when Manning had the affair. They golfed together every week. Don't you think it came up?"

"Probably so." Just then Annette's phone pinged. "Wait a second. It's a text from Allison. I can't believe this. Did you know they cancelled her contract? I'm sure Gary instigated her getting canned. He probably got his buddy Manning do it."

"Are you kidding me? She's one of the best CSU night nurses. It's just not right. Maybe with Manning gone and this big scandal about the other nurse that got fired, she can fight it. We'll catch up later. I have a few consults to see," Kumar said as he turned the corner and walked toward the elevator.

Annette hurried to a quiet corner at the end of the hall and placed a call to her friend. "Oh my God, Allison! I just read your text. How are you holding up?"

"Thanks. As good as can be expected. Big changes are coming at work, I see. I saw the story about Manning on the news and Facebook. What's the word at the hospital?"

"As you can imagine, everyone's talking about it. No mention of his replacement, but he's gone. Had you heard about any of this stuff before now?"

"Not really, but Mark uncovered some of it during his research into Tamarino's background. I guess since they were such good friends, Manning's name stayed associated with his."

"So, any news on your contract?"

"I'm still debating what to do. Rosa suggested going to HR at the hospital, but I don't think that's of any use. My contract as a travel nurse is between me and the agency, not a contract between me and the hospital. But I'm considering talking to my recruiter. I'm just not optimistic anything will change. Maybe exposing the situation through Critical Cover-Up is going to be the only way, but then for sure I won't be working at this hospital anymore."

"With the hoopla about the ICU nurse they fired in retaliation, this may be a good time to expose them."

"The more I thought about what you said, the more this whole stinking mess reeks of Tamarino's involvement. But he doesn't scare me, and Mark hasn't exonerated him yet. He's still looking into stuff."

"You ought to consider getting a lawyer too, Allison. Would the agency provide one or take your side?"

"That's a good question. I can check into it. I have mixed feelings about leaving my job here. It's not the money. I'm making plenty with my business and related activities. I love what I do, and I can't stomach the thought of bowing out due to a narcissistic bully like Tamarino."

"That's my girl, Allison. I'm on your side."

"Thanks. I know you're sort of caught in the middle. And Dr. Kumar too. I'll keep you posted though. I won't go down without a fight."

Allison had no idea just how close those last words came to the truth.

~ Chapter 56 ~

When Gary heard that the hospital got rid of Ed Manning, he knew their relationship would be scrutinized ad infinitum. His only concern was how Manning's problems would draw attention to himself — attention he didn't need.

He didn't need anyone, and especially that prick Derning, nosing around in Manning's financial affairs. Tamarino hoped he wouldn't connect the dots and find out about the $200,000 loan Manning gave him. It might look like a payoff for silence. God, he wished he could rely on Manning to keep his mouth shut, but he didn't know whether his ally could withstand the pressure. A threat from Tamarino might not be effective when Manning's career and entire life looked ready to implode.

Experiencing more paranoia now than he ever had when stoned, Gary weighed his options. He realized Derning had made a connection between them, but he wasn't sure how much he knew. Had he met with Manning, too, and questioned him?

It was imperative that he find out for himself. He strategized how to contact Manning. Worried the news organizations might be staking out Manning's home, he assumed meeting in person no longer existed as a viable option. Rather than waiting months, Tamarino decided to cash in just enough CDs to cover his loan. He texted Manning and asked if they could talk.

"Yes, I'll call you in five minutes."

Four minutes later, he answered a call from a nervous-sounding Ed Manning. "I'm glad you called, man. The shit's hit the fan. My life is a complete mess."

"I know, man. I saw the news. I hope you've got a sharp attorney."

"I do, but I don't know how much good it will do. I'm screwed."

"Ed, I want to repay the money you loaned me. I can send it to one of your accounts. I'll need your current bank information so I can send a wire transfer."

"That will come in handy, especially now. I'll text you the information when we're done here."

"By the way, were you able to take care of the situation with that CSU travel nurse I told you about?"

"I did, and the chief nursing officer told me she handled it."

"That's a relief. She turned out to be nothing but a pain in the ass with her investigation business."

"You know, that detective came to my office and asked a lot of questions about the Medicare fraud case from years ago."

Tamarino's fears escalated as soon as he heard this. He wanted details.

Manning continued. "Yeah, he asked about you too." At this point, Tamarino's heart raced, and the hairs on his neck bristled.

"What did he ask, specifically?"

"He mentioned falsified patient billing records, suggesting I had been involved. And then he mentioned he had reasons to believe you were too."

Tamarino found it difficult to control his ire. "We have to put a grinding halt to this now. He didn't bring up the lawsuit about the ICU nurse, did he?"

"He did, but made no mention of you," Manning said.

"Well, that's one positive anyway. Leave everything to me. Just don't answer any more questions without a lawyer, especially any that include me, understand?" Manning agreed and ended the call. Tamarino's resolve to terminate this fucking probe left him only one option.

~ Chapter 57 ~

Mark sat at one of the tables near the window in the Starbucks across the street from his hotel. At 5:00 p.m. he heard his phone ping with a text from Angelina Rodrigues. "I'm almost there. I'll be wearing green scrubs."

Derning texted back. "I'm at a table near the entrance." Two minutes later, a short, slightly overweight, dark-skinned woman wearing royal blue scrubs entered the coffeehouse. Her stern facial expression indicated a businesslike demeanor. Derning waved her over to his table and stood to shake hands as she approached him. They introduced themselves, and she took a seat. "Thank you for meeting me, Miss Rodrigues." Derning offered to buy her a coffee. "What would you like?"

"Thank you, Detective. I'll have an iced caramel macchiato grande." Five minutes later, he returned with Angelina's drink and an Americano coffee for himself.

Derning got right to the point. He questioned Angelina about the dates she worked at San Francisco Bay Hospital and whether she knew Ed Manning or Dr. Tamarino personally. She indicated that she'd worked with Dr. Tamarino at times when his patients were in her intensive care unit. "Most of his patients go to CSU, and only occasionally did our unit have his patients. But in the three years I worked there, I got to know him pretty well." She described him much like Derning expected: full of himself; arrogant, yet charming; good-looking; and an excellent surgeon. She added, "And everyone knew better than to cross him. He had a temper."

She told Derning that she didn't know Manning at all, because he hadn't taken the title of CEO until the last year she worked there. She had heard plenty, though, about the big Medicare fraud and his role in falsifying patient records. "We all thought he'd get fired, too, and were shocked when they promoted him to CEO."

"You mean it was common knowledge that Manning participated in illegal schemes related to Medicare patients' records?"

"Oh, sure. Everyone knew he did it. He ran the patient financial services, or whatever they called it. He handled the billing for the hospital, so he had access to change anything related to patient charges. I think it's called upcoding, when they charge for a higher level of service. In other words, say a physician sees a patient as a consult or even just a simple office visit. With electronic records now, the doctors need to input their procedures into the computer and include the amount of time spent, in fifteen-minute increments. I've seen the screens and have had to help some physicians learn how to do it. Well, if they spend five or ten minutes with a patient but document forty-five minutes, the hospital gets to charge three times as much."

"And this became a common practice?"

Angelina rolled her eyes, and Derning knew the answer. "Are you kidding me?"

"No. And they were encouraged to do it. I don't know if they received kickbacks related to those inflated charges, but if I had to guess, I'd say yes."

"To your knowledge, did Dr. Tamarino ever illegally document the amount of time he spent with the patients?"

"Tamarino didn't do it as much, as far as I know, but some of the doctors did, especially the neurologists who made late-night rounds, maybe around midnight or one in the morning. All they'd do is step inside their patients' rooms, and most of the time, the patients were either asleep or unconscious. Without even assessing them, these physicians asked the nurse for a thirty-second report, and then they documented their patient assessment and charged for a visit. Sometimes they wrote two notes, one with the previous day's date with an earlier time, and then the current day with a later time. That way it looked like they made rounds on two separate days when they didn't."

Derning listened intently and took notes. "You witnessed this yourself?"

"Yes, on many occasions," Angelina replied.

"And nobody said anything about this?"

"Who were we to say anything? We were plenty busy with all of our nursing duties. It wasn't up to us to babysit and monitor the physicians. They ruled the roost anyway."

"And then the patients were charged for all these visits, and sometimes double charged?"

"I assume so. What would the point be otherwise? At the time, there was talk about illegal kickbacks, but I don't think any of the doctors were charged. The hospital settled for a huge amount of money, and the two top executives ended up fired."

"Angelina, I want to ask you about a comment you made in the Facebook group, ICU Nurses – What Really Happens. You mentioned that E.M. and Dr. T were a dynamic duo that didn't get caught. Do you have any specific knowledge you'd care to share?"

"Once Manning became CEO, those two made no effort to hide the fact that they were best buddies. You'd see them walking in the halls side by side or coming out of the physicians' cafeteria together. Most of the staff knew that Tamarino had an in with the CEO. After the Medicare settlement, talk continued about how the hospital rewarded Manning with the position. Rumors circulated, identifying him as a whistleblower on the former CEO and COO, all the while deserving an equal share of the blame. So, to answer your question, I had no direct knowledge of collusion between him and Tamarino against the hospital. I just heard all the rumors. One message resonated loud and clear, though. Tamarino exerted a high degree of leverage with Manning. If you got into it with the almighty Tamarino, he could have you fired in an instant with a phone call to Manning. I'd say that Manning functioned as Tamarino's puppet."

Derning noted the time and thanked Angelina for her help. "Here's my card. If you think of anything else, contact me. Have a good night at work." He knew more now than he did before, but questions persisted.

~ Chapter 58 ~

"Damn it, Kumar. How in the hell did that happen?" Annette heard the loud, one-sided phone conversation as Dr. Tamarino walked into the surgery department on Friday morning. "Christ, couldn't you have been more careful? You're a goddamn surgeon, for crying out loud. I guess you'll be handling the office for the next month." Tamarino's scowl made clear his utter disgust.

She cringed at the total lack of empathy Tamarino demonstrated for his junior partner. She had spoken with Kumar an hour earlier, so she already knew what had happened. He told her he had cut his left thumb and index finger late last evening while preparing stir-fry vegetables for dinner. The unexpected injury required eleven sutures, so now he was out of commission to operate. Annette knew the inability to operate devastated Kumar, and facing the wrath of Dr. T made the situation ten times worse. Annette sympathized with Kumar, and today she'd be forced to endure two surgeries with Tamarino without an ally in the OR. She anticipated a long day.

"It's just you and me, Annette. I can't believe Kumar could be so careless," Tamarino grumbled, shaking his head.

"It's not like he did it intentionally, you know. Don't you think he feels bad enough? You ought to cut him some slack, Dr. T." Always the victim, Tamarino sneered, and they entered the surgery room to begin their first case.

The patient, a middle-aged man, needed a triple bypass. This should be a straightforward case, Annette figured. He didn't have any weird medical history or bleeding risks, so she expected an okay morning. She missed Kumar's presence in the OR, but for once Tamarino maintained a decent mood throughout the surgery, so she relaxed. Two and a half hours later, she closed for Tamarino, and the patient went to CSU to recover without incident.

After lunch, Annette and Tamarino scrubbed in for their second case, an eighty-year-old woman scheduled for an aortic valve replacement combined with a double coronary artery bypass. Aortic valve stenosis in the elderly occurs together with coronary artery disease, in many instances. This combined surgery significantly increases the in-hospital mortality risk, compared to an isolated aortic valve replacement alone.

Tamarino had performed hundreds of these surgeries, but usually two surgeons worked on such a case. Although Annette was a competent and skilled nurse practitioner who specialized in cardiothoracic surgery, policy dictated that another surgeon be available in-house. In a hospital this size, it never created a problem, and Annette had made sure she made the surgery manager aware.

Surgery lasted five hours, and the patient came off bypass without too many issues. Significant bleeding required the use of blood products and the need to wait and be watchful before closing the chest. Annette sensed Tamarino's fatigue and guessed that he wanted to leave her alone to close. "Oh no you don't," she said to him.

"What do you mean? You can close, and I'll talk to the family."

"Not in this case. I want to be absolutely sure there aren't any tiny bleeders, no matter how long it takes. And that means both of us stay until the end." One of Annette's greatest assets in the OR included her meticulous attention to detail, and she knew Tamarino couldn't argue that fact. So they both stayed another half hour and stood guard over the patient's open chest until the two of them had explored every nook and cranny around her heart. Then they closed her chest together, which satisfied the nurse practitioner. Even if Tamarino's personality fit the criteria for asshole, as long as he honed his skills in the OR, she could accept that. It had turned out to be a good day.

~ Chapter 59 ~

Surgeons live to operate. Having the knowledge and skill to perform an operation and improve the life of a patient provides them with indescribable satisfaction. Surgery is what they do best—most of them, anyway. If they never had to see patients in their offices, they would be fine with that.

Dr. Kumar Chanrami was one such surgeon. He cursed himself for that careless slip of a sharp vegetable knife in his kitchen, and now he had to pay the consequences. Sidelined from the operating room, he made his way to the office to see the post-op surgical patients. Annette did her turn there as well, but now Kumar would be handling most of the work.

He always prided himself on his organizational skills, so he decided to make the best of the situation and enjoy some one-on-one time with his patients. They looked so much different when they were wearing street clothes.

Surgeons typically didn't score high on communication skills, but Kumar emerged as an exception, so his office patients were thrilled to see him. He kept to a schedule, and the office staff loved it too. All in all, his first full day in the office scored a big hit. With the understanding that this gig was temporary, and that he'd be back in the OR soon, he knew he'd be able to manage this assignment as long as necessary.

When the last staff member left at the end of the day, Kumar locked the office door and closed the blinds. He recognized the opportunity to snoop around and see if he could discover anything about the practice's finances. A computer whiz, he searched the hard drive and quickly found a file named Finances. *Piece of cake*, he thought. When he opened the file, he noticed subfiles such as Payroll, Office Expenses, Insurance, Self Pay, Concierge Patients Pay, Miscellaneous, and Personal.

The Personal file caught his attention, and he clicked on it. An Excel spreadsheet appeared, with nothing identifiable except dates and amounts of money. The two columns were titled Week and Expenses. Intrigued, Kumar scrutinized the information and noticed that the most recent entries were dated this month, with the last entry only one week ago. The corresponding monetary amount read $10,000, with the same amount listed each week, going back six months. At the bottom of the page, a cumulative total listed $250,000. He also noted the file's last modification date and the user's name: Gary Tamarino.

Alarmed, Kumar could only assume that Tamarino had been skimming funds from their practice for his own personal use. Until now, he had given his partner the benefit of the doubt, cutting him more slack than he deserved. But this was the final straw. Furious with Tamarino, beads of sweat rolled down Kumar's neck. His body flushed with heat, and he reached for a wet paper towel to cool himself off. Able to control his emotions most of the time, Kumar possessed enough discipline to think and act with logic. He retrieved a flash drive from his bag, inserted it into the office computer's USB port, and copied the file to it. Then he deleted the history showing his search on Excel and the latest computer activity before he logged off and shut down the computer. Maybe this office assignment turned out to be more of a blessing than a curse.

Forty-five minutes later, Kumar arrived home and, as soon as he had a chance, transferred the information from the portable thumb drive to his own computer. Everything he copied appeared in black and white. He texted Mark Derning. "I have information for you. Can we meet somewhere?"

~ Chapter 60 ~

Allison could not shake the constant barrage of negative thoughts blasting off in her head. Less than two weeks had passed since she addressed the Association of Critical-Care Nurses as a keynote speaker. Nurses applauded her as a role model, and now her status had dropped to a travel nurse without a contract. To make a bad situation even worse, she'd learned that a lawsuit had been filed against Critical Cover-Up.

In one hour, Mark would be here to take her to dinner, and he did not deserve to find his date in a bad mood. She considered begging off but couldn't do that to him. Besides, she needed to be up-front with him. If she couldn't talk to Mark, who could she talk to? She had grown close to him and trusted him. The more she thought about it, going to dinner with Mark sounded pretty good.

To change her mood, Allison opted for music. She needed upbeat sounds, so she selected one of her playlists that included music from Bruno Mars, Queen, Maroon Five, Journey, and Foster the People. Guaranteed to make you want to dance, the high-energy music by these artists always put her in a good place. As she got dressed for dinner, she sang along to the songs she knew by heart, and the loud voices in her head faded away. By the time Mark arrived, she had transformed herself into a happy Allison, ready to go out in the city.

Allison liked these late fall San Francisco evenings, when the cool, dry air called for a jacket. When she lived in Florida, only on a rare occasion did she ever need anything heavier than a sweater, so she welcomed the change. "I checked Google Maps and didn't think you'd want to walk all the way to the restaurant," Mark said. "With the wind blowing as hard as it is, the air is quite cold tonight."

"Yeah, it's not exactly walking weather. Besides, I don't know about you, but I'm hungry."

"I didn't eat that much, since I spent most of the day working, so I'm hungry too. Seafood on the bay sounds so appetizing."

Once they were in their Uber, Allison broached the subject of work, at the risk of ruining the evening. "Mark, I'm so looking forward to dinner and a romantic evening with you. And the last thing I want to do is spoil anything, but I need to talk to you about something serious. It relates to work and the investigation. To be honest, I just don't know whether there will ever be a good time."

"Let's enjoy our dinner and then discuss it afterward while we're still at the restaurant, maybe over dessert." He winked at Allison. "We can figure out whatever we need to and go from there. We're not going to have a ruined evening, I promise."

His compassionate understanding and gentle reassurance warmed her heart. She stared into his eyes, and nothing else mattered in that instant. The moment seemed surreal, maybe magical—almost as if time stood still. Nothing made sense, and at the same time, everything did.

For the rest of the ride, neither of them said a word. None were needed. Mark held Allison's hand and she closed her eyes, wanting to remember the moment forever.

Despite the heavy traffic, they arrived at the Waterfront Restaurant just in time for their reservation. Allison hoped they'd be lucky enough to be seated at a table near a window. Although the restaurant appeared full, the hostess guided them to a vacant table with a Reserved sign. Mark pulled the chair out for Allison before he sat down, and his chivalry only enhanced her growing feelings toward him. "Thank you, Mark. You are the ultimate gentleman."

"It's the way I grew up. A lady like you deserves nothing less." The Bay Bridge sparkled in the moonlight, its lights creating a magical reflection in the water beneath it. "Allison, you were so right about this view. I think it's best at night. You made a great choice for this evening."

Allison gazed out the window. "It is beautiful, isn't it? I'm so glad you like it." She looked up at Mark, and her eyes gleamed as she stared into his.

The restaurant's ambience did not disappoint, and the impeccable service only enhanced the experience. After perusing their menus, they ordered drinks and seafood entrees. Mark opted for the Dungeness crab, and Allison chose the sea bass. Their two-hour dinner flew by before either of them realized the time. "Well, that seafood surpassed any I've ever had. Let's order some dessert, and then we can talk," Mark suggested.

"The apple, pear, and cranberry crisp with vanilla ice cream sounds delicious," Allison said. "If it tempts you too, maybe we can share?"

"I'm game. Would you like any coffee?"

"Decaf for me," Allison said. Mark gave the waiter their order and included an espresso for himself.

"As promised, I'm not going to allow anything to ruin this delightful evening. It's been so wonderful, Allison. But we should talk business before we get too tired. Do you want to go first?"

"I couldn't agree more. Tonight's been heavenly. Okay, here goes." She took a deep breath and began the serious part of the conversation. "Well, you know my contract's been cancelled. My recruiter offered to reassign me to another hospital in the Bay Area, but that's not my goal. I suspect Tamarino orchestrated it. And here's why, Mark. Sherry notified me earlier today that Critical Cover-Up is being sued. And guess who the plaintiff is."

"Gary Tamarino?"

"Bingo. He's claiming harassment. It probably has no legs, and our attorney is on it, but it's just enough to be aggravating."

"You're right, Allison. That lawsuit won't go far, but nothing surprises me, especially after my meeting with him. The man has no conscience," Mark said. "I also met with someone earlier today who revealed a lot about the relationship between him and the CEO."

"Really? I'm all ears. What did you find out?" Allison leaned in closer to absorb every detail.

"I knew something more lurked behind this guy's story," Mark told Allison. "Tamarino and Manning were connected long before Manning became CEO. I met with an ICU nurse today who works at UCSF Medical Center. She worked at San Francisco Bay Hospital quite a while ago, including the years leading up to the Medicare fraud scandal and when Manning became CEO."

Allison focused on every word, wondering what else Mark had learned. "How did you find this nurse?"

"She had posted some comments on social media that caught my attention. Anyway, she indicated that Manning had been a whistleblower, but in actuality, he falsified the records himself. Apparently, Tamarino knew about it and has used it as leverage ever since. Physicians falsified patient records by documenting longer times spent with the patient. Tamarino furnished the physicians' names to Manning so he could check their records and charge more. Some of the information lacked clarity, and maybe the evidence didn't meet the burden of proof, but I got the distinct impression that doctors were encouraged to do this and possibly received kickbacks for their cooperation."

"And neither of them got caught?"

"No. The hospital settled the case for $20 million, and the two executives were fired. They avoided a trial."

"No wonder Tamarino got away with everything. Whenever he snapped his fingers, Manning did his bidding, it seems."

"That about sums it up. I wouldn't trust him for anything."

"And to think he held my life in his hands when he performed surgery on me." Allison shook her head. "It's a good thing I didn't know enough then to care."

"I still think there's more to this whole thing," Derning said. "I'm not finished with him yet. But that's enough business talk for tonight, don't you think?"

"Yes, I'm in complete agreement with you on that. It's good we're up-to-date, but I'd rather enjoy the rest of the night without these distractions." Her eyes flirted with his, and she smiled. Mark took that as a sign to ask for the check so they could leave.

Once they left the restaurant, they strolled along the Embarcadero for a bit, breathing in the fresh night air and holding hands without saying a word. After they reached the entrance to the next pier, Mark stopped and turned to face Allison. Taking both of her hands in his, he broke the silence. "Allison, I don't want this night to end, and I think you feel the same way." He searched her soulful blue eyes for affirmation.

She returned his intense gaze. "I can't deny the connection I feel between us, Mark, and I don't want to say good night either. Why don't you stay with me tonight? I make a pretty good breakfast."

Just as he had promised, nothing could ruin this evening. Mark called for an Uber with Allison's address as the destination.

***

Allison and Mark stayed up half the night making love, talking, and laughing. The chemistry between them was undeniable, and the more time they spent together, the more they desired each other. They eventually fell asleep and woke up to the sun's blinding light at nine in the morning. Neither of them wanted to get out of bed, but

Allison couldn't ignore the persistent meows from Snowball, who needed her morning kibble.

"I'll make some coffee and get breakfast going," Allison announced. "How does an omelet sound?"

By now Mark had gotten out of bed and followed her into the kitchen. "Great. Can I help?"

"Thanks, but I'm good. My kitchen is only big enough for one person. I know you probably need to check your phone for email and messages anyway."

Mark thanked her and turned on his phone. "What did we do without cell phones? We've all become so dependent on them."

"I know. Before all of us carried some type of device, we didn't know what we were missing. Now we can't seem to live without instant communication."

"Oh, I forgot to tell you. Dr. Kumar texted me yesterday, just before I picked you up for dinner. We're meeting today at one o'clock," Mark said.

"Really? I set up a meeting for today too, with Sherry Dolan and Christy at twelve thirty. I guess we'll be leaving around the same time."

"Yes, we can catch up later this afternoon," he suggested.

While Allison prepared breakfast, Mark scanned his phone. No other text messages or missed phone calls. But a certain email caught his attention.

~ Chapter 61 ~

Mark and Allison walked out of her apartment building late Saturday morning. As Allison's Uber approached, they kissed each other goodbye before setting off in opposite directions. Mark's destination was only ten minutes away on foot, so he headed south on Jones Street, toward the Grand Hyatt. He had plenty of time to go to his room to change clothes before his meeting with Kumar.

At quarter to one, Derning found a seat at a table in the crowded Starbucks and waited for Kumar. He took out his phone to check his email, and a news notification captured his attention: "Medical negligence lawsuit filed against San Francisco hospital." The story was about Dr. Gary Tamarino's patient who died after surgery. The detective wondered whether Kumar knew about this.

As Mark continued to scroll through his phone, Kumar, dressed in jeans and a light blue polo shirt, walked in and headed for his table. "Detective Derning, thank you for meeting me."

"Dr. Kumar, please sit down. I almost didn't recognize you. You look more like a college student than a surgeon."

Kumar smiled. "Yeah, we look different with clothes on." It was a common hospital joke, but one Derning hadn't heard before.

Then Derning noticed Kumar's bandaged thumb and finger. "What happened to your hand?" He listened intently as Kumar explained about cutting his finger and being relegated to the office for a while. Derning decided to hold off on the breaking news for the time being. After all, it had been Kumar who requested the meeting. "Do you want a coffee or anything?"

Kumar declined. "Do you remember asking me whether I knew anything about the finances of our practice?"

Derning studied Kumar's face as he asked the question. "Yes, I do."

"You wondered if Gary had borrowed money from our account."

"I recall the conversation. You seemed surprised at the time," Derning said.

"Well, I thought about it and had the opportunity to check the finances on the office computer." Kumar paused, pulled something out of his pants pocket, and handed it to Derning.

Derning took the USB flash drive and waited for Kumar to explain further. "I copied the files to this drive and also created a backup on my computer at home. You can check it out yourself, but basically it shows a subfile titled Expenses, and it lists $10,000 withdrawn on a weekly basis for six months. The cumulative amount totaled $250,000, with no explanation beside it."

Derning asked Kumar whether Tamarino had ever mentioned this money to him, and Kumar shook his head. "I can't figure out any purchase that would account for this money. He must have been skimming it from our accounts receivable payments. And the latest entry occurred this past week, so it seems this is an ongoing activity. He's been stealing from the practice—from me." Derning saw anger in his eyes.

"What do you plan to do about it?" he asked Kumar.

"I've given him the benefit of the doubt. I've been nice to him. I've covered for his sloppy ways in the OR. This is it. I'm done. I'm going to confront him and demand he return my half of the money. If he refuses, I'll leave the practice and go on my own. I've been considering it anyway."

"I think he left you no choice. And going it alone may be your best bet. If you don't get anywhere after you confront him, we can pressure him from Critical Cover-Up, threaten to expose him. You can press charges too, you know. Embezzlement is a crime. You have lots of options." Kumar nodded but said nothing.

Derning knew he had to tell him about the latest lawsuit, and no time would be a good time. "I hate to pour gasoline on the flames, but I take it you haven't seen this yet?" He pulled up the news story again and slid his phone across the table. Kumar read the article in silence.

"I expected this, and Gary did too. He may think he dodged a bullet, but the army's coming for him."

"Listen, Kumar. There's more coming too, from my investigation. Do what you need to do to protect your interests. We have good people working on this."

Kumar got up to leave and thanked Derning for his concern and his help. "You hang on to the thumb drive. I have the files at home. I'll stay in touch."

"Okay. Hang in there, Kumar." Derning knew a showdown between the two doctors loomed just around the corner. Too bad he wouldn't be there to witness it.

~ Chapter 62 ~

Saturdays held no special significance for Allison, because she normally worked plenty of weekends — until now. Uncertain about her future, she focused on her business, which operated seven days a week. She decided to make time to get together with her team in person and scheduled a Saturday lunch meeting for today at twelve thirty with Sherry and Christy to discuss the recent cases they were working on and the pending lawsuit. Critical Cover-Up needed no brick-and-mortar office, since most communication happened online or through texts and phone calls. So, a restaurant or coffeehouse became the obvious location to meet.

Allison arrived early and secured a table for three inside the Mission Beach Café, a casual, friendly eatery in the Mission District. Many young, native Californians like Sherry and Christy appreciated organic, healthy food, and Allison thought they'd enjoy the menu. The pear and apple kale salad offered reason enough for Allison to choose this restaurant.

Allison, seated at a corner table in the back of the restaurant, spotted the two young women as they arrived together ten minutes later. Their youthful appearance masked their business expertise and professionalism, two traits Allison respected. "It's so good to see both of you again," Allison said as she stood to hug both women. "Thanks so much for coming on such short notice."

The women seated themselves, and Sherry spoke first. "I'm so glad you've recovered, Allison. You look fantastic." After some small talk, they looked over the menus and gave the server their orders.

Allison steered the conversation to business. "I realize it's Saturday, so we won't make this a long lunch meeting. I'd like to focus on three topics. First, I want to talk about the lawsuit Dr. Tamarino filed against us this week. Sherry, I assume you'll be able to fill us in regarding that situation. I'm not wasting too much time worrying about it. The bigger issues I'd like to discuss relate to Gary Tamarino and Ed Manning, the CEO, or shall I say former CEO now, of San Francisco Bay Hospital. Christy, I know you've been working on these cases with Mark Derning."

"I do have some news on both of those, Allison. But first, maybe Sherry would like to speak about the lawsuit," Christy said, deferring to her supervisor.

"Yes, I've consulted with Ron Farley, our attorney, and he assured me we have nothing to worry about. He has already filed a motion to dismiss. He believes the lawsuit is frivolous and has no merit and will likely be thrown out as such. He thinks Tamarino's just trying to intimidate you."

"I'm sure of it too, Sherry. I haven't had a chance to tell you, but my travel nurse contract got cancelled this week, and I'm almost certain he instigated the action against me. He heard that I reported him to Critical Cover-Up."

"He must have something to hide and is afraid of what we can do to him. And he should be. Between Mark and Christy, they've uncovered information that could be damaging to Tamarino. Christy, let Allison know what you've found and where you and Mark are in the investigation."

"Sure. I know Mark has been updating you," Christy said, "but I've been able to discover some connections Mark doesn't know about yet. I've been delving into the ICU nurse who had the abortion. Her name is Nicole Santorum. It seems that ever since she filed a lawsuit, after which she lost her job, she's been retaliating by blasting Manning and the hospital on her Facebook page. She's not hiding anything."

"Mark mentioned he saw some comments on a Facebook ICU nurses group page," Allison said.

Christy continued, "I decided to message her from my personal Facebook profile and sent a friend request. She accepted, and then I told her about Critical Cover-Up and sent her a link to our page. I told her what we do and asked her if she'd be interested in talking to me. She surprised me when she replied and agreed to talk. I didn't expect her to be so cooperative, but I set up an interview, and she had plenty to say."

Allison's jaw dropped. "Christy, that is incredible news. What did you learn?"

Christy detailed the information Nicole had shared related to her relationship with Manning and how he'd used his position as CEO to harass her into having an abortion. "She's incensed and wants people to know what happened. She's already contacted the EEOC to file another complaint against the hospital for firing her."

"Did she indicate how long her relationship with Manning lasted?" Allison asked.

"Surprisingly, not that long. Once she found out she was pregnant, that was the beginning of the end, from what I understand. But she shared something else that I found even more revealing. It involved Gary Tamarino."

Finally! The connection I've been waiting for, Allison thought as she waited for Christy to share the details.

"This ICU nurse, Nicole, gushed with information. I could hardly believe it, but hey, paybacks are hell, right? She told me that Manning liked to drink, and sometimes he had one too many, and that's when he started to talk. He bragged about the role he played in falsifying records as director of patient financial services. She said he considered it one of his greatest accomplishments, especially not getting caught and being rewarded with a promotion."

"Her story corroborates something Mark uncovered when he talked to a nurse who used to work there during the Medicare fraud," Allison remarked. "She told him that almost everyone in the hospital knew about Manning's involvement. And she said Tamarino played a role."

Christy nodded. "You'll see where he fits in here too. Nicole told me Manning explained that Dr. Tamarino's role with the other physicians proved an invaluable asset. He showed them how to upcode their reports, and then they were compensated with bonuses off the books. They essentially received kickbacks for their cooperation in the fraud scheme. And he received an even bigger bonus for making that happen."

Sherry spoke up. "What we're uncovering is huge, but due to the agreement the government made not to prosecute when the hospital settled, I'm not sure where this leaves us, with the exception of the knowledge that both of these men are scumbags. I'll have Ron Farley double-check that."

Christy smiled and directed her attention to Allison, as though she'd saved the best for last. "There is one additional thing. Nicole told me that before she got involved with Manning, she had an affair with Gary Tamarino. He was married at the time, and their relationship proved a key factor in his wife's filing for divorce."

Allison could hardly believe what she heard. "How did I not know this? I never heard any rumors about Dr. T having an affair when I worked with him."

Christy continued. "This probably happened before you started there. Nicole also said Tamarino introduced her to Manning. They went to a wine bar one evening, and Manning happened to be there, just a casual meeting. After Tamarino's wife learned about his cheating and filed for divorce, he stopped seeing Nicole."

"And then Manning stepped in?"

"That's what I understood from Nicole."

"This whole saga gives an entirely new meaning to friendship. So much drama," Allison said.

"Nicole also told me that Tamarino paid her $10,000 to keep quiet about their affair. She agreed to not post anything about it on social media. From what she said, they had more of a fling, a sexual relationship. She wasn't in love with him."

"Well, now we know why Tamarino and Manning were so tight, and for more than one reason. Did she say whether Tamarino knew about the abortion?"

"She didn't, but she indicated that those two were pretty intertwined in each other's lives, so I would assume so."

"I have a thought," Allison said. "If the lawsuit isn't dismissed, we can confront Tamarino and pressure him with significant criminal exposure, based on these allegations. Mark scheduled a meeting with someone else today who supposedly had dirt on Manning. Since he's already been ousted, I'm not as concerned about him as I am about Tamarino."

Allison's mind wandered to her own contract cancellation nightmare, probably orchestrated by Gary Tamarino. Now, more than ever, Allison's way forward became crystal clear to her. Armed with evidence of Tamarino's unscrupulous intentions, and with the support from Critical Cover-Up, she prepared for her own personal confrontation with him. Filing a complaint with the ethics board of the hospital added another option.

Allison paid the bill and thanked her colleagues. "I think we accomplished a lot. I hope we hear something this week about the lawsuit, Sherry."

As she stood to leave, her phone alerted her to a text. "Wait a second. This is from Mark." She read the brief message before updating Sherry and Christy. "The news just broke. Mrs. Brock's family filed a medical negligence lawsuit against the hospital, naming Dr. Tamarino." Allison's eyes met Sherry's, and they both nodded. "Did we see this coming or what?"

"I'll stay in touch, Allison. I think we're going to have a busy week."

"Thanks, Sherry. Mark may have additional information from his meeting today. I'll keep you posted. Thanks again to you both."

After Christy and Sherry left the restaurant, Allison stayed behind to text Mark. "Wow. Big news. I want to hear all about your meeting. I have information too."

Mark replied back, "Can you meet me in the lobby of my hotel?"

"Okay. I can be there by 3:30."

Energized and motivated by the direction the investigation had taken, Allison hurried outside and called an Uber. Eager to share information with Mark, excitement raced through her. As she anticipated seeing him, she was unable to deny the strong emotional attraction.

~ Chapter 63 ~

Curiosity drove Mark Derning's next move. He returned to his hotel room to view the contents of the flash drive he'd received from Dr. Chanrami. Allison would be downstairs in half an hour, so he had plenty of time. Exactly as Kumar attested, the evidence seemed clear that Tamarino had been embezzling money from the practice, half of which Kumar owned. Mark copied the file from the flash drive to his computer and put the drive back into his pocket.

Allison arrived on time, and Mark greeted her inside the lobby of the Grand Hyatt. With throngs of hotel guests coming and going, the place was a zoo. "Let's go into the lounge where it's a lot less chaotic," Mark suggested.

As they strolled inside the stylish OneUP lounge, Allison peered around the room. "It seems like I've been here before, almost like déjà vu."

"Allison, your mind isn't playing tricks on you. You're right. You have been here before." She turned her head to stare at Mark, her eyes pleading for an explanation. "You and I met for drinks and appetizers here when I first came to town. You spoke in Berkeley that day, the same fateful day as the earthquake."

She shook her head. "It's like fleeting visions zoom by in split-second frames. I only recall bits and pieces, like I'm trying to recall a dream, and then it's gone. I wish I remembered more." She glanced at him with soulful eyes.

"It's okay, Allison. Maybe more of your recollection with come back. Perhaps it's best you don't have memories of the crash. That night could only be described as a nightmare, and I'm thankful you're alive."

The hostess seated them and handed them menus. "I know you just had lunch. Do you want anything?" Mark asked Allison.

"Maybe a cup of tea. I'm definitely not hungry."

"Well, we have a lot to talk about. Update me on your meeting with Sherry and Christy first."

Allison needed no persuasion to bring Mark up to speed on the latest developments and drama. When he learned that Christy had connected with Nicole Santorum and all that she had to say, he couldn't hide his surprise. "I'm impressed she got all that information from Nicole. And now with the family suing the hospital, Tamarino's really going to get hit hard."

"I'm planning to confront him myself about the contract cancellation, but I have to think it through. There may be a better way, and I'd like your input."

"Good idea. We can discuss it in more detail whenever you like. I also have news from Dr. Kumar. I just met with him." Derning shared the gist of their conversation with Allison, and both agreed the pressure was building on Tamarino.

"Allison, I need to tell you something unrelated to these cases."

"What is it, Mark?"

His tone took on a more serious quality. "I have to leave San Francisco tomorrow morning. I need to be in court in Orlando to testify about a homicide I investigated." Allison's mouth fell open, and he could tell that she hadn't expected this sudden news. "I'm sorry, but I have no choice. They didn't give me much advance notice."

"Are you checking out of your hotel in the morning? How early do you have to leave?"

"Early. My flight leaves at 9:00 a.m." He could see the disappointment in her eyes. "I thought we could spend the rest of the afternoon together and then have dinner later in the evening, if you'd like." She nodded.

The server brought Allison's tea and a coffee for Mark. "I guess I've gotten used to you being here," Allison said, "and I'm sad to see you leave. We'll have to make the most of the time we have."

"Hey, you didn't think you could get rid of me that easily, did you?" Mark laughed and so did Allison. "I'm not going away forever. We have lots to talk about." His smile spoke volumes.

~ Chapter 64 ~

Dr. Kumar Chanrami never regretted his decision. He had met with his lawyer to be sure all his ducks were in a row. He knew the time had come to make the big move, yet he felt somewhat nervous. The last concern was Annette, and he arranged to meet her at a restaurant to discuss his plans with her, away from work.

"Hi, Kumar. Nice to meet you at a real restaurant instead of the surgeons' cafeteria."

"Likewise, Annette, and good to see you in real clothes for a change too. Thanks for meeting me. Are you hungry?" Kumar hadn't eaten all day. "I'm starving."

"I can eat. This looks like an interesting place," Annette said. "I've never been here."

Kumar asked for some menus, and they made their selections. Finn Town Tavern in San Francisco's Castro neighborhood served traditional American food in a cozy, casual atmosphere and included a full bar. "I don't have to worry about being on call with this bum hand, so I'm ordering a cocktail," Kumar said with a smirk. He knew Annette couldn't drink, since she had to pull surgery call this weekend.

"Rub it in, big boy. You'll get yours one day." These two shared a rare camaraderie and got along better than most married couples. Kumar's wife liked Annette as well.

He wasted no time sharing his plan with her. "I'll get straight to the point, Annette. I've made my last excuse for Gary, and I'm done for good. If the lawsuit by the Brock family didn't provide enough reason to part ways, I discovered that he's been stealing from me."

"What? Are you kidding me?"

Kumar's deep brown eyes widened, and he shook his head. "No lie, Annette. I had time to check the office accounting files. He's been embezzling money for months, to the tune of $250,000. Just withdrawing it from accounts receivable for his own personal use."

"You have proof then?"

"I do, and I called my lawyer. I'm getting out of the practice and going on my own. I want nothing more to do with him. My attorney is already preparing the documents. It will be up to you whether you want to continue to work with Gary."

"Well, I'm employed by the hospital, like you. So I have no option but to assist him in surgery. But as far as the office goes, I do have a choice. You're going to need a nurse practitioner in your office, and I'd rather work with you than him. I don't need him either. He's become a real liability."

"Before I confront him, I want you to know about another decision I've made. I'm giving him a choice. He can repay me half of what he withdrew from the account, or I'm filing a lawsuit against him. But I'm still leaving the practice."

"Good for you. He's not going to know what hit him, Kumar, but he deserves everything that's coming his way. It's been percolating for some time. When do you plan to talk to him?"

"Tomorrow." A sense of relief washed over him once he verbalized his decision to Annette. This entire state of affairs had taken a toll on Kumar, but now he could smile, knowing the hard decisions were behind him.

Annette's phone interrupted their lunch with a loud notification alert. "Anything urgent?" Kumar asked.

She rolled her eyes, and that was all Kumar needed to know. She replied to the text before she answered Kumar. "Yes, it's Gary. He's doing an emergency surgery, an open heart. I need to go now. Thank you for lunch, Kumar. And good luck tomorrow. You know I'm in your corner."

He watched Annette walk out of the restaurant, grateful to have her as his ally.

~ Chapter 65 ~

Allison wanted nothing more than to spend as much time with Mark as she could before he left for Orlando. "I hate that you have to go, and I'd love to just enjoy our time with no agenda." She gazed into Mark's eyes and wished things could be different, that he could stay with her tonight, but it was not to be.

Allison switched gears and directed her attention to business matters, as she allowed her emotions to fade into the background for now. "Why don't we spend part of our time focusing on these cases? Let's get all the facts nailed down and develop a strategic plan. It's good the two of us can do that together. After that, I'll feel more comfortable, and we can relax and enjoy each other until you have to pack. How does that sound?"

"So, you mean we should put business before pleasure?" He smiled at Allison with those soulful eyes, and she laughed.

"You know me pretty well." Once Mark left, it would be much more difficult to accomplish what had already been set into motion.

"Since we're here, why don't we conduct our business strategy meeting now, in this lounge, however long it takes?" Mark proposed. "When we're done, we can go upstairs to my room and spend some time together, any way you want. We'll go somewhere nice for our last dinner too."

Allison's eyes sparkled and she grinned. "Okay, let's get to work."

For the next two hours they focused all of their energies on business. They reviewed the latest details they'd learned about the issues involving Tamarino, Manning, the lawsuits, and the recent embezzlement story. "We've gathered a lot of information, and some of it has already been publicized by the news organizations. I'd like to tie up all the loose ends from our Critical Cover-Up investigation and make some decisions going forward. Until now, everything has seemed like just a lot of interesting stuff, but nothing has been organized."

Derning retrieved a laptop computer from his briefcase, and together they got to work and crafted a list and a plan. "Do we have permission from Nicole Santorum to go public with what she revealed to Christy?" he asked. "I know Angelina Rodrigues told me we could quote her. She's already posted comments on social media."

"I think we do. Christy took care of that when she interviewed her. If I recall correctly, she indicated that Nicole wanted the story out there for all to see," Allison said. "The *San Francisco Examiner* already published the story about the lawsuit filed by Nicole Santorum's lawyers. Sherry can contact them with added news about the new EEOC complaint for retaliation. She'll also take care of spreading the word on Twitter."

"One down. What's next?" Derning said, eager to keep the pace going.

"Let's contact the Medical Board of California and file a complaint against Tamarino for paying Nicole $10,000 to keep quiet about their affair. It may fall into an ethics violation or sexual misconduct, but once the complaint is filed, they'll be compelled to look into it. And while we're at it, let's call the Hospital Ethics Hotline and submit a complaint on the same issue."

"Tamarino's going to have more problems soon, especially if Kumar presses charges against him for stealing funds from their practice."

Allison's eyes lit up. "We can file a complaint with the medical board about that too. And also have them investigate his role in the kickback scheme from the Medicare case. We might as well send them the whole ball of wax."

"What else?" Derning asked.

"Since the news just broke about the lawsuit filed against the hospital regarding the death of Mrs. Brock, I'll have Sherry publicize it even more and blast it on social media."

"Is that everything?"

"I think so, yes."

Derning reviewed the plan they'd created and the list of items they'd compiled in a Word document. "Look this over, Allison. If everything seems right, I'll save it and send you a copy right now. That way you can email Sherry and move the process along without further delay."

Allison scanned the document. "It's all there. Send it to me, please. We do make a great team."

Allison remembered something else to tell Mark, but she hesitated. She wasn't sure how she wanted to handle this topic, but Derning's opinion mattered to her, so she broached the subject. "I've been toying with the idea of confronting Tamarino in person about my contract. Any thoughts?"

"Well, for one thing, you don't have any clear evidence to prove he initiated it. And do you really want to return to work there? Once all this goes public, the hospital may not be so keen on your return. Allison, you have so much going for you, between your business and speaking commitments. You certainly are making a difference and influencing thousands, if not hundreds of thousands, of people. Tamarino's in enough hot water. Why not leave it alone for now and revisit it later?"

He paused, but maintained intense eye contact. Then he added another thought for her to mull over. "Besides, if you didn't have to work three nights a week, you'd have time to travel. Maybe you'd let me whisk you away to Italy for a month. Think about it."

Italy? Did he say he wants to take me to Italy? Blown away by this thought, she tried to respond but couldn't say a thing. For a moment, time seemed to stand still. *What's happening here?* Happier than ever, she beamed.

Mark took her hand, and they walked to the elevator. Once inside, he pushed the button for the thirty-second floor.

~ Chapter 66 ~

"This must be pretty important, for you to want to meet me on a Sunday, especially when you're not on call." Gary poured himself a cup of coffee in the surgeons' lounge while Kumar sat on a couch near the door.

"So what's up, Kumar? Couldn't stay away from the hospital?"

Ignoring his partner's sarcastic comments, Kumar said, "This is business. It has nothing to do with wanting to be at the hospital." His jaw set, Kumar eyed Gary like a puma staring down his prey. Gary sipped his coffee in silence and waited for Kumar to continue.

"You have to admit things have been rocky between us for a long time, and whether you realize it or not, I gave you the benefit of the doubt and cut you plenty of slack. All the times you screwed up in the operating room, I never said anything. Instead, I made excuses for you to Annette. I knew you had personal problems and financial problems. And all the while I stayed loyal and did my job. I saved patients' lives, and you took the credit."

He paused, and Gary said nothing. "So now we're being sued for the death of Mrs. Brock. I expected that."

Tamarino shot back. "We both knew that family would probably sue. I'm sure the hospital will want to settle out of court as soon as possible. Besides, I have an excuse—my eyesight. And now I've fixed that problem."

He expected nothing less than this type of response from Tamarino. *He's always making excuses and never accepts any responsibility. He doesn't seem to know how to be accountable for anything.*

"Gary, I could deal with all of that, but you've crossed the line this time, and I have no more patience."

Kumar predicted his partner's reaction would be one of total astonishment, and Gary proved him correct. "What the hell are you talking about?" Gary yelled. His face flushed, and a bead of sweat glistened on his brow as he attacked Kumar. "Crossed the line? Explain. Now!"

Kumar maintained his composure while fixating on Gary's beleaguered face. "You really did me a favor assigning me to the office, so I need to thank you. By the way, I found the computer records you created while you were quietly stealing money, $250,000 to date. The way I see it, you've been skimming funds from the practice in secret. Half of that money is mine. Were you just never going to tell me and continue doing it as long as you could get away with it, Gary?"

"I can explain. I—"

Kumar cut him off. "I'm no longer interested in any of your explanations. Here's what's going to happen. You're either going to pay me $125,000 by the end of business tomorrow, or I'm suing you. What you're doing is a crime. Have you heard of embezzlement?"

As Kumar anticipated, he caught Gary totally off guard and, for once, without a snappy comeback.

"Furthermore, I'm leaving the practice, effective the end of this week. You and I will go our separate ways, and you can manage the office all by yourself. Annette is coming with me. I've lost all respect for you."

Gary's usual holier-than-thou attitude disappeared. "Kumar, please, give me a chance to make things good," Gary said, his voice barely audible. "I'll get you the money, but I don't want to lose you as a partner. You're too valuable."

Unfazed, Kumar stared into Gary's eyes, his face set in stone. "It's too late for another chance. I'm done. You created this fiasco, not me. Now you can reap the consequences. My attorney will send over the documents to dissolve the partnership in a day or two. I have nothing more to say to you." Kumar stood up and left a stunned Tamarino staring into space.

~ Chapter 67 ~

Gary didn't sleep all night. No signs of light peeked through his curtain, as he rolled over to look at the clock. He could just barely make out the time: 4:55 a.m. Luckily, the only surgery on the schedule today was at 1:00 p.m., but he had to make rounds this morning. Besides that, he had a 9:00 a.m. meeting with the hospital's risk manager about the Brock lawsuit.

Kumar's imposing threat to file a lawsuit against him today loomed larger than everything else. Since he had no concrete plan for repaying Kumar, he was screwed for sure. An unrelenting, pounding headache exacerbated his misery. Alone, without any allies and unable to see a way out of this, a pervasive fear of the unknown enveloped him. His sheets were drenched in sweat, and he couldn't think straight.

Not a spiritual man by any stretch of the imagination, he prayed silently in the only way he knew. *Just kill me now, God, and take me away from this.* Of course, this wishful thinking had no basis in reality, so his agony perpetuated. He racked his brain to try to come up with a solution to the money situation, and he stumbled upon nothing but a deep void. How ironic that he skimmed profits from the practice because he needed money, and now he found himself in the same basic circumstance, needing money to repay Kumar for what he stole from him. *It's like a goddamn hamster on a wheel.*

Disgusted with everything, including himself, he finally got out of bed at six o'clock to face the inevitable dreaded events of the day. He couldn't stand the stench of his own skin and trudged into the bathroom. He swallowed two extra-strength Tylenol capsules for his throbbing head and turned on the shower. The steaming hot spray pelted his body as he scrubbed it with a loofah. His head still hurt, but the longer he kept it beneath the rainfall showerhead, the less he noticed it. He stayed in that spot until the water cooled—a sure sign he had gone through the entire sixty gallons from the hot water heater.

After toweling off and shaving, he dressed for work in a starched white shirt and tan suit, no tie. He slipped on his Bruno Magli penny loafers and walked into the kitchen to make coffee and a strawberry protein smoothie. Once the caffeine kicked in, his headache started to dissipate, and he sat down to drink his liquid breakfast and check his phone. *No messages? That's a weird stroke of luck.* When he scrolled through his email, two of them seemed to jump off the screen, capturing his attention.

The first message identified the sender as the Director of Ethics and Compliance. The subject line read, "Urgent. Read immediately." *What is this about? Probably some shit about a mandatory class.* He opened the email and read, "Attention: Doctor Gary Tamarino. This is to inform you that we are reviewing an ethics complaint made against you. It relates to an allegation that you paid one of our employees a large sum of money in exchange for her silence about a relationship. We will contact you soon to set up an appointment to discuss this issue. Jodi Rentellier, Ethics and Compliance Director."

"What the . . . ?" Gary muttered, stunned by what he was reading and clueless to where the allegation had originated. He scanned it a second time.

I might as well see what other disasters await me today, he thought as he opened the second worrisome-sounding email. This one came from the Medical Board of California, and the subject line read, "Gary Tamarino, M.D. Urgent." What followed was short, vague, and troubling. "We are notifying you about a complaint filed against you for possible violations. We will contact you in the near future once our investigation begins."

Before he read these messages, Gary Tamarino thought his day couldn't get any worse—a failure of judgment to the highest degree.

~ Chapter 68 ~

Twenty-five-hundred miles separated them, and Allison missed Mark already. Although he'd just left for Orlando yesterday, to her it was a lifetime ago. Their last evening together seemed like a distant, magical fairy tale. She had grown quite close to him, and now that he was gone, she realized how much he meant to her. She knew he'd be back but didn't know when.

Snowball curled up next to Allison on the couch, purring as she relished the one-on-one time with her owner. It might be enough for her beloved cat, but Allison felt the void Mark's absence created.

After spending much of the remainder of the weekend grocery shopping, doing laundry, cleaning, and organizing her apartment, Allison decided to make good use of her time, beginning early Monday. No longer working in CSU, she needed to stay busy. By seven in the morning, just as the sun came up, she exited her apartment to go for a brisk walk. The California sky started to light up with glorious hues of orange along the horizon as the city began to awaken. Allison smelled the sea air as she hoofed up the inclined streets leading toward Lombard Street.

Wondering if Rosa worked last night, she chanced it and texted her friend. "Good morning, Rosa. I'm out for a walk. Want to meet for breakfast after work?" They hadn't spoken in a while, and Allison missed the companionship of her coworker.

She was surprised to get a quick reply. "Great to her from you, Allison. Breakfast sounds good. Let's meet at that breakfast and brunch restaurant on Columbus. I think it's called Eight AM. I'll try to be there around 7:45."

Thrilled, Allison replied back, "Great. See you then." Since she had some extra time, she walked down Beach Street toward San Francisco Maritime National Historic Park, just to be near the bay. She never tired of these nautical locations, and the proximity of the water always affected her mood in a positive way.

By quarter to eight, she had arrived at the restaurant, and the hostess seated her at a table for two. Rosa texted her a few minutes later to tell her she'd arrive soon. Life was good.

Rosa showed up before eight o'clock, wearing a spotless white lab coat over blue scrubs. "You don't look like you just finished a twelve-hour shift," Allison said as she stood up to hug her friend.

Rosa returned the gesture, and then the two of them took a seat. "Believe me, I feel like it. We got bombarded with admissions last night. The place was a zoo. Be glad you're not there."

"Well, if things are as bad as you say, I suppose I should be, but I have mixed feelings about it, as you can imagine. Leaving never crossed my mind," Allison said.

"I know that, and I feel terrible about what happened," Rosa said, trying her best not to cry. "If I hadn't told Tamarino about the investigation by your company, this wouldn't have happened. I'm sorry, Allison. I feel so guilty."

Allison's crystal-blue eyes welled with tears. "I just knew he was behind it, Rosa. Don't blame yourself. He's a prick, and we all know it. He has no morals and stops at nothing to get what he wants. It's always about him."

"I should have known better, Allison. He treats everyone like shit until he needs them for something."

"Let's order. My treat. I'm famished."

After they placed their orders, they continued the conversation about Tamarino. "I'm glad you started the investigation, Allison. He bragged about how he planned to make sure you got fired. I know he pressured Manning before he got canned."

"Our investigation has come up with a lot more stuff. By now it should be on Twitter and Facebook. He's so much worse than we even thought. Did you know about that affair he had with the ICU nurse, the same one who's suing Manning?"

"No, what about it?"

Allison revealed the dirty saga of Tamarino paying off the nurse so she wouldn't talk about their relationship. Rosa listened to every word, her mouth wide open. "Don't worry, Rosa. He's going to get his just punishment soon."

Rosa weighed Allison's words before she spoke. "Allison, why don't you fight him? Come back to the unit. Manning is gone. You can go to the chief nursing officer and explain, and I'll back you up. Maybe you can get your contract back through your travel agency. I miss you at work."

"Thank you, Rosa. You are a true friend. I'll give it some thought."

Although Rosa's proposal flattered Allison, the option of returning to CSU no longer existed. After she exposed corrupt practices by an administrator and a physician, the hospital would never entertain the notion of her return. Even if Allison wanted to come back, she knew it was an impossibility.

~ Chapter 69 ~

After a rare Sunday away from the hospital and leisure time spent with her teenage sons, Annette showed up midmorning Monday to round on the post-op CSU patients. She knew Kumar would be at the office and didn't expect to see Dr. T until just before the scheduled 1:00 p.m. surgery. So, when he came out of one of their patients' rooms, she paused before greeting him. "Dr. T, I'm surprised to find you here so early," she said.

He looked at Annette with a fierce glare that could kill. "I had to be here anyway," he mumbled. "I have a 9:00 meeting with the risk manager about the Brock lawsuit. Not looking forward to it." With none of the usual bravado and bluster on display, tension boiled close to the surface.

He glanced at his inpatient list and told Annette which patients he had seen. "Why don't you make rounds on these others and then go upstairs to see the patients on Stepdown?"

"That's fine," she said. "I guess I'll see you in the OR just before one o' clock then?" Without giving her an answer, he walked out of the unit.

Annette shook her head. *So rude. Too bad no one ever taught him any social skills.* But she had gotten used to his obnoxious behavior, which never shocked her. She could only imagine how much his angst level had ratcheted up since yesterday. Kumar told her he had given Tamarino an ultimatum. And a few minutes from now, Dr. T faced the stressful conference with the risk manager.

In addition, social media had exploded since yesterday, with negative accusations about other damning circumstances. She doubted that he had seen these, since he didn't care about Facebook and didn't even have a Twitter account. Conversations with the nurses confirmed that the entire hospital staff had discussed the condemning tweets. Allison's company was most likely behind the social media denigration campaign. Some of the stuff was even news to her. Tamarino would hear about it soon enough.

Maybe even the risk manager had gotten wind of it by now, and their conference would be that much more unnerving for Dr. T. Annette stifled a smirk. *Karma's such a bitch.* She felt no sympathy for him, especially after how he treated Kumar. The belittling and cruel remarks Kumar endured from Tamarino made her want to scream.

Almost positive Tamarino had precipitated whatever caused Allison to get the axe, she didn't know how long she'd be able to work with him in surgery. For now, though, she had no choice. She'd take it one day at a time.

Annette didn't rush with the other post-op CSU patients, and they expressed appreciation for her kind bedside manner. Two of them were ready for transfer, so she wrote their orders and made notes on the others before she headed to the third floor.

On the Stepdown unit, she had eight patients to visit. She'd always maintained a good relationship with these nurses. The camaraderie they shared paid off. She knew they didn't hesitate to call her about a problem because, unlike Dr. Tamarino, Annette encouraged questions and never said anything that made them feel small. Tamarino would eat them for lunch if they dared asked him such questions. He showed the Stepdown nurses no respect and got away with it, because he was the mighty cardiac surgeon. Soon that would change.

Before she got started with rounds, the charge nurse cornered her. This time, her question didn't refer to a patient issue. Instead, she focused on the Tamarino scuttlebutt. "Annette, what's going to happen to Dr. T now that all this dirt about him is all over Facebook and Twitter?"

Annette didn't want to get too involved but gave her honest opinion. "I don't know, but I think it's safe to say he's going to have to face some stiff consequences. He's gotten away with things for too long. I'm pretty sure we'll know something soon."

~ Chapter 70 ~

To say the meeting with the risk manager did not go well would be an understatement. From Gary's perspective, the experience was a fucking disaster. He'd expected the meeting to be a preliminary conference, where he'd be given some information related to a possible deposition date and a time to meet with the hospital lawyer. He scored A-plus on that aspect, but the situation careened downhill afterward.

The first agita came when he learned that Allison Jamison would also have to give a deposition, since she recovered the patient in CSU immediately after surgery and also after the takeback operation. He had hoped he'd never have to see her again or hear anything about her, but now he learned the unfortunate truth.

And he certainly hadn't counted on being questioned about an affair he had with an ICU nurse. *How did these people find out about that anyway?* During the meeting he realized the power of social media and how it strips an individual of their so-called privacy. Humiliated and aggravated at the same time, he could not wait for the meeting to end. In the back of his mind, though, he sensed this might only be the beginning of worse things to come.

When he left the appointment, he remembered the deadline for Kumar's threat. Stressed and without a plan, he called Kumar at the office. The receptionist put him on hold, adding to his irritation. He had no choice but to wait for Kumar to finish with a patient. Three minutes later, a voice he recognized answered the call.

"Kumar, it's Gary. Listen, man, I'm in deep shit here at the hospital. My life is falling apart. I just left a godawful meeting with the risk manager. And I have to tell you, there's no way I'm going to be able to get that money to you today, but I swear I'll have it by the end of the week." In utter desperation, he begged Kumar for an extension, promising to find a way to repay him. "I can't handle another lawsuit, Kumar."

Kumar's initial inclination to stand firm and stick to his word changed. He couldn't bring himself to be that callous. "Friday. I'll give you until Friday, Gary. But that's it. I'm ready to go through with it, and so is my attorney."

Tamarino heaved a sigh of relief. "I'll have it by then, no question about it. Thank you, man." He had no clue how he'd come up with the money, but he'd bought himself some time.

He still had an hour and a half before surgery. He walked out of the hospital to the parking garage, got into his car, and left the campus. As he drove, all sorts of schemes whirled in his mind, as he struggled to find a way to pay his debt to Kumar. He even entertained the idea of contacting a loan shark, but it was more a figment of his imagination than anything, since he didn't know any. One choice alone seemed feasible to him.

Once he reached home, he went straight to his office and turned on the computer. He remembered he had a second online brokerage account, one that he hadn't used in years. He had converted half of his long-term mutual funds into cash at that time and forgot about the money, until now. After spending twenty minutes researching the stock market, he confidently submitted three large options trades on undervalued and underpriced stocks. His expectation that they would take off within the next two or three days triggered his exit strategy. He executed a sell to close limit order that would essentially guarantee him a one hundred percent profit. Then he'd be able to pay back his debt to Kumar, and that problem would be solved.

Satisfied, he microwaved a frozen meal for lunch and checked email on his phone. Alarmed to find another email from the ethics compliance director, he opened it and read the contents. "Dr. Tamarino, we need to schedule an appointment as soon as possible. Can you come in Tuesday at noon? In addition to the complaint already filed against you related to your relationship with an employee, other issues we need to discuss have come to light. Please advise if this time is suitable and, if not, when you can meet this week. Sincerely, Jodi Rentellier, Ethics and Compliance Director."

Disgusted, Tamarino shut off his phone, finished eating, and grabbed his keys. He put his car in gear and sped out of his driveway to return to the hospital, the one place where he possessed some semblance of control. At least in surgery he knew exactly what to do, maintained a handle on things, and felt good about himself. Now, he couldn't even enjoy the accomplishment of devising a plan to end to his financial nightmare with Kumar. *Why does life have to be so damn hard?* Distracted by thoughts of the email, he failed to notice a black Range Rover accelerating in the lane beside him. An instant later, the luxury SUV collided into the driver's side of Gary's sports car.

~ Chapter 71 ~

As Allison walked back to her apartment, she reflected on Rosa's suggestion that she return to CSU. Though flattered to be missed at work by a colleague, she didn't seriously consider the proposal, despite the fact that part of her wanted to return. She suspected that once the hospital administrators identified her as the upstart behind the Critical Cover-Up investigation, she would acquire the dreaded "do not rehire" label.

Allison lacked the enthusiasm to pursue that idea. Something inside her urged her to wait, almost like a premonition. Did this mean a better option might make an appearance in the near future? Allison trusted her gut, so she delayed making a decision regarding the job at the hospital. Plus, the current situation effectively ended any chance of a confrontation with Gary Tamarino, at least for now.

Back at her apartment, she spent some time on the internet, scrolling through the Critical Cover-Up accounts on Twitter and Facebook in search of new posts or comments and browsing other related profiles. She hadn't seen anything firsthand since she discussed the investigations with Sherry and Christy yesterday morning.

Bingo. Staring at her in black and white were three tweets from @Criticalcoverup that would not be music to the ears of Manning or Tamarino.

> Abuse of power revealed due to cozy business relationship between CEO @SFBayHosp and a cardiothoracic surgeon #CriticalCoverUp

> CEO @SFBayHosp sued by nurse employee for sexual harassment. Hospital fires CEO in scandal #CriticalCoverup #Sexualharassment

> New evidence implicates cardiac surgeon and CEO @SFBayHosp in kickback scheme from former Medicare fraud case #CriticalCoverUp #MedicareFraud #Didn'tgetcaught

And they were just getting started. She knew her company's capabilities and approved of their initial tweets. By now, the major news outlets had published stories about the firing of the hospital's CEO. Allison directed her attention to the comments beneath the stories, searching for anything from disgruntled employees. She knew Christy would be on top of this, so she didn't spend too much time, but one statement in particular caught her attention. "Talk about abuse of power. If you found yourself on the wrong side of this almighty surgeon, you could count on losing your job. He and the CEO were joined at the hip. Now I understand why. Is it too late to indict them?"

Stunned, she noticed the signature: "A critical care nurse." *Interesting. Maybe I'm not the first nurse Tamarino got rid of.* She made a mental note to have Christy see if she could uncover the identity of this person.

Late that afternoon, Mark called her. Seeing his name on the caller ID made her heart skip a beat, like a teenager with her first crush. Her mood lightened as she answered the phone. "Hi, stranger. I've been thinking about you." She made herself comfortable on the couch so she could enjoy the conversation.

"I'm so happy to hear your voice, Allison. It seems like it's been a long time. I've been in court most of the day, and they just wrapped up." Mark and Allison talked for an hour and a half, laughing and updating each other. Allison told Mark about her breakfast conversation with Rosa. "Although I had been weighing the pros and cons of pursuing another contract in CSU, I'm pretty much leaning toward the cons."

"I'm glad you mentioned it, and I agree that nothing would be gained by confronting Tamarino. Allison, you can do anything you choose. You've proven that over and over. You can shape your career to your liking. I guess the main point to consider would be to do what makes you happy."

Leaving work behind for a while sounded appealing. Memories of Saturday evening swirled in Allison's mind, as she recalled Mark's heartfelt offer to take her away to Italy with him. All of a sudden, visions of romantic gondola rides in Venice surfaced. If she heeded Mark's advice and considered what would make her happy, she had no doubts. When they were together, happiness followed.

She didn't have to think much about it, except for that nagging voice in her head, the one telling her that work should be paramount to everything else. What she wouldn't do to squash that demon. Maybe her current circumstance was the spark she needed to live life to the fullest. This moment might not exist again, so it was time to be happy.

Motivated, driven, and responsible, Allison had always made her career the priority, and she'd succeeded at accomplishing her goals. In her heart, though, she knew something was missing. Now, she seemed to have found it. "I'm pretty sure I know what would make me happy, Mark."

"I should be finished here tomorrow morning. I'll try to get a flight back to San Francisco sometime in the afternoon. But I'm not coming back for work, Allison. I could do that remotely. I miss you, and I want to be with you. I think we feel the same way about each other."

Spontaneous tears of happiness welled in Allison's eyes. "Yes, we do, Mark, and I want to be with you too. It seems like you've been gone for so long. If a small living space doesn't bother you, just plan on staying here with me instead of booking a hotel."

"I'd like that. I'll see you soon. I can't wait to hold you in my arms again." Mark paused before he added a hint of what the future might hold. "And then we'll have to talk about us."

"That sounds wonderful, Mark. By the way, I've always wanted to go to Italy."

~ Chapter 72 ~

"Dr. T hasn't replied to my texts," Annette told the anesthesiologist. "I don't understand. He's always here by now or at least would respond to me."

"We'll just have to wait a little longer," he said. He glanced at the large, black-and-white office clock on the wall in the surgery pre-op area. "It's twelve thirty. We still have half an hour, but that's cutting it close. Have you tried calling him?"

"Yes. No answer," she grumbled. She decided to try Kumar in the office to see whether he had heard from Gary. Once he picked up the call, she explained the situation.

Kumar said he had no clue why Gary wasn't there by now. "In fact, he called me an hour ago from the hospital after his meeting with risk management. I'll admit, though, he sounded pretty upset. He seemed desperate and begged me to give him more time to pay back the money he stole from me."

"If you hear from him, please let me know. Surgery's scheduled for 1:00 p.m. The patient's in pre-op, and anesthesia's inserting lines. If he doesn't show up, we'll be forced to cancel the surgery."

The entire surgical staff busied themselves setting up the instrument trays and, by now, had most everything they needed ready to go. The perfusionist double-checked the heart-lung machine. Surgeries normally began on time, and when they didn't, the reasons were usually explainable. Sometimes the previous case in that operating room took longer than expected, or the surgeon needed to wait for clearance of the patient after some last-minute unexpected lab finding. The surgeon coming late or not showing up at all never met criteria as an acceptable reason.

By one, Dr. Tamarino remained in absentia, and there had been no word to suggest he might be on his way, despite two additional phone calls Annette made to his cell phone. While nobody questioned Annette's surgical expertise, she was a nurse practitioner, not a cardiothoracic surgeon. Open-heart surgery required a heart surgeon. With Kumar out of commission and the other cardiothoracic group operating in another room, no one else was available. Annette contacted the director of surgery, who made the decision to cancel the case for today. Annette inherited the task of informing the patient and his family of the unfortunate and disappointing change of plans.

Still emotionally drained half an hour later, Annette reluctantly answered a call from the director of surgery. "Get down to the ER. Paramedics just brought in a trauma. It's Dr. Tamarino."

Shocked beyond words, Annette needed three or four seconds to process the catastrophic news. "What happened?"

"Motor vehicle accident. The other driver came in DOA. I don't know much more. I'll meet you down there."

She raced down the hall to the stairwell and took the steps two at a time to the first floor. The anger reserved for Tamarino converted to fear and worry; she imagined the worst, but hoped she'd be proven wrong. She didn't wish him harm. They had been colleagues for five years, and you couldn't just erase that. *Please, God, let him be alive. And God, please let his injuries be fixable.*

When she arrived in the ER, she ran straight to the trauma bay. From the flurry of activity and the number of people in blue gowns around Tamarino's bed, Annette knew in her gut that the situation was dire. CPR was in progress, and the ER physician leading the code directed IV epinephrine to be given. Annette watched the transfusion of O-negative blood pouring in though a large-bore IV. The code team seemed to have things under control, so she didn't interfere, although she made her presence known. Tamarino's chances looked grim.

~ Chapter 73 ~

Kumar's attention wandered to the OR, and he was unable to stay focused on his office patients. He wondered whether Gary had shown up in time for surgery. His thoughts gnawed at him, and he hoped his partner hadn't gone off the deep end. Midafternoon, the office manager alerted him to an urgent call from Annette.

"Annette, what's going on? What time did Gary finally get to the OR?"

"Kumar, I have bad news. We had to cancel surgery. Gary came in through the ER as a trauma. He coded, and they were able to resuscitate him, but they admitted him to CSU in critical condition. They put him in there as a courtesy, rather than in Trauma ICU. He's on a vent and multiple drips."

"Jesus! What is the extent of his injuries?"

"They're serious, Kumar. He was involved in a car accident on his way to the hospital, and the driver of the other vehicle died. Gary has multiple injuries, including fractured vertebrae and possible spinal cord injury. He had abdominal injuries too, and also sustained fractured ribs, a pneumothorax, and a cardiac contusion. He's a mess, but he's alive. He's in surgery now. Prognosis is guarded."

"Wow. That's awful, Annette. Where are you now?"

"I'm at the hospital, catching up on my charts. I guess his ex-wife is listed as next of kin, and they're trying to get in touch with her. I'm not sure he's going to make it, Kumar," she said, her voice thick with unshed tears. "I understand he was down for some time."

"I'm coming straight to CSU as soon as I'm through here at the office. Can you make rounds on the inpatients? I hope Gary can recover from this, but even if he does, he won't be able to work for a long time. We'll have to figure out a plan going forward, Annette."

"I know. Text me when you get here. I'll take care of rounds, and we'll talk later."

The call ended, and Kumar suddenly became nauseated and dizzy. He lowered his head between his knees and closed his eyes. After a minute, the lightheadedness dissipated, but his stomach remained coiled in a tight knot. A wave of guilt washed over him as he remembered his last conversation with Gary just a few short hours ago. Wishing he hadn't sounded so mean, so uncaring and businesslike, he now regretted his words.

The idea of his patients waiting in the cold examining rooms motivated Kumar to snap into action. The sooner he finished here, the faster he could get to the hospital. He needed to see Gary, to be there in person. He knew some type of intense bond existed between them as business partners, though he wasn't sure exactly what that meant now, given their recent issues. He had read about the special bond between twins, where one's identity is tied to the other's. He wondered if maybe he and Gary had a connection similar to that. As weird as it might sound to someone else, Kumar felt like a piece of himself lay traumatized and broken in that CSU bed. And if any part of his threat to sue Gary had caused this catastrophic turn of events, he'd never be able to forgive himself.

***

Kumar arrived in CSU at shift change, a typically hectic time of day. The unit swarmed with nurses exchanging report on their patients. He noticed Rosa at the desk, clipboard in hand, receiving an update from the day shift charge nurse. Just before he arrived, Kumar had texted Rosa, who told him he could see Gary in Room 1.

As he entered the room, two CSU nurses acknowledged him as they continued with their one-on-one report next to Gary's bedside. Kumar noticed the rhythmic sound of the ventilator and the quieter, continuous beat from the cardiac monitor as he walked closer to the bedside. What he saw startled him, and as a surgeon who has seen thousands of critically ill patients up close, he didn't expect to react the way he did.

The patient—pale, bruised, swollen, and hooked to IVs and machines—appeared lifeless, more like a mannequin than a human being. Seeing Gary like this hit Kumar like a line drive, fast and hard.

He noticed the Diprivan drip infusing, so he expected Gary to remain sedated. Considering his critical condition and the short time out of surgery, no decrease in the Diprivan dose would likely be considered until later. "Sorry to interrupt your report," he said to the nurses. "How long has he been out of surgery?"

"Less than an hour, Dr. Chanrami," the day shift nurse replied. "So far, he's holding his own. His vitals are fairly stable, considering everything."

He thanked her and noted the name of the trauma surgeon on the whiteboard in the room. *At least he's got a decent blood pressure and heart rhythm*, he thought.

Kumar made his way to the nurses' station and hung out there, listening to the shift report for a few minutes. When they finished, he spoke with Rosa. "Terrible about Dr. T," she said. "How are you holding up?"

Kumar expressed shock and asked if she could page Dr. Iammetti, the trauma surgeon. Three minutes later, the two surgeons conversed by phone. Dr. Kumar learned that Gary had sustained internal bleeding due to a liver laceration, a serious abdominal injury. "He coded because he was in hemorrhagic shock. Due to the massive bleeding and resultant hemodynamic instability, I had to do an exploratory lap and repair the liver. Luckily, I got the bleeding under control by ligating the blood vessel and using an omental patch to fill in the gap."

Kumar thanked him. He understood the gravity of Gary's injuries and knew he was lucky to have Dr. Iammetti as his trauma surgeon. Gary should recover from the internal injuries, but his prognosis was far from positive, considering his other injuries and post-code status. Time would tell. Kumar would have to wait and see.

He retraced his steps to Gary's room and spoke more with his night shift nurse. "I'll check back with you in a few hours. If he starts to wake up before then, can you page me?" She assured him she would do so, and he left.

On his way to the surgeons' cafeteria, he texted Annette, asking her to meet him there.

~ Chapter 74 ~

Surprised to see Annette's name appear on caller ID on a Monday evening, Allison answered her phone. She listened while Annette relayed the devastating news about Dr. T. "I wanted you to know Gary is critical. Hopefully he'll make it through this, but it's going to be a long, uphill road. The negative publicity might backfire on you and your business."

Allison, horrified by the news, broke out in a cold sweat. She swallowed back the bile that rose in her throat and prayed she wouldn't throw up. "Allison, are you there? Did you hear what I said?" Annette's urgent voice prompted Allison to speak.

"I'm sorry, Annette. Hearing you describe the awful details about Gary's condition made me sick. When did this happen?"

"Early this afternoon. He didn't show up for the 1:00 p.m. surgery, so we had to cancel the case. Then we heard he came in through the ER as a trauma. It's all so surreal, Allison. Kumar is beside himself with guilt, because he gave Gary an ultimatum to repay a large sum of money by today."

Allison's emotions flitted all over the place. Earlier today, when she read Critical Cover-Up's social media posts, she assured herself that she'd done the right thing in exposing Dr. T's unethical behaviors. Now, she recalled the times when she used to enjoy working with him and felt sympathetic about his circumstance. She had second thoughts about the negative publicity campaign she'd already approved.

"I feel terrible, Annette. I'd never want to see anyone endure this kind of trauma. Even though Gary's been so difficult, he didn't deserve this. I don't know what I can do, though. The posts about allegations against him have been published on social media, and everything has been set in motion. I don't think there's any turning back."

"I sort of suspected that. Well, whatever the consequences, little does he know his priorities have shifted to staying alive. And the world keeps turning, so my fingers are crossed that Kumar can return to surgery next week. All the cases for this week have been postponed, and the other cardiothoracic group will have to take any emergencies."

"I'll see what I can do as far as halting any future Facebook posts or tweets for now, Annette. You're right. They won't do any good, and we don't need to come off as mean-spirited. I'll alert my staff. Please stay in touch."

After the phone call, Allison texted Sherry and Christy and explained the situation. She directed them to pause the campaign related to Dr. Tamarino until further notice. Sherry replied to the group text. "Okay, but what about the stuff on Manning?"

Allison texted back to continue with their efforts related to everything except Tamarino, at least for now. Insecurity crept into her thoughts, and she questioned whether exposing corruption in healthcare justified the cost. When she started the company, she believed she was doing something good and making the world a little better. The business developed into a profitable company, with many healthcare watchdog groups and facilities now contracting with Critical Cover-Up the moment allegations of corrupt practices surfaced.

But this unexpected tragedy hit close to home, and she hadn't expected to react this way. She looked forward to sharing her feelings with Mark, not over the phone but in person, once he came back from Orlando tomorrow.

An hour after she finished her communications with Sherry and Christy, Mark texted her. Eager to get her mind off the awful events of the past couple of hours, she welcomed his message. "Hi, Allison. It's getting late here, and I'm going to call it a night. I have to be up early tomorrow for a meeting with the chief. Wanted to let you know I booked a nonstop flight and should get in to SFO at 8:00 p.m. I'll text you when I land. Can't wait to see you. Good night, my dear Allison." The message ended with a little heart.

Allison texted back without delay. "Can't wait to see you too, Mark. Get some sleep, and safe travels." She added an emoji of a smiley face with hearts for eyes.

~ Chapter 75 ~

Exhausted from the emotional toll of the day, Annette waited for Kumar in the surgeons' cafeteria. Good thing they served food late into the evening, because she was famished. When Kumar walked in, she motioned for him to join her at a table in the back of the room. "I couldn't wait, Kumar. I had to eat something."

"No worries, Annette. That soup looks good. But I need more than that. I'll be right back." Few people were in the lunchroom, and Kumar returned soon with a bowl of vegetable soup and a grilled cheese sandwich.

The two sat in silence while they ate, and then Kumar initiated the conversation. "This whole situation sucks, for Gary and for both of us."

"I know, and the worst part is, we have no idea what's going to happen. What did you think when you saw him?"

He shook his head. "Man, nobody could have prepared me for that. It's so different when the person lying in that bed is someone close to you."

"It's like we're all family, Kumar. No matter the arguments, we spend more time working together in life-and-death situations than most couples spend with each other on a daily basis. We know each other so well."

"You're right. I see my wife and kids much less than I see you and Gary, and that's a sad fact."

"That's part of being a surgeon, and for my part, I'm there right along with both of you."

"Yes, you might as well be a surgeon. You know how it is."

"I do, and you and I need to figure out a plan. I think it's safe to assume Gary won't be returning to work for a long time. Have you come up with any ideas?"

"The shock hasn't worn off yet, but I'm up for hearing any suggestions, if you have some."

"Well, first things first, I guess. I did speak with Allison and told her what happened. I advised her to back off any of the negative publicity exposing Dr. T. You told me you gave Gary a deadline before you were going to sue him. You haven't filed anything yet, have you?"

"No, thank God. In fact, during our last conversation, earlier today, he asked me for an extension." Annette looked into Kumar's dark eyes and could see him fighting back tears. "I feel so bad about the way I spoke to him."

Annette comforted him as best she could. "Kumar, he owed you that money, and he created the scenario by stealing from you. Don't blame yourself." She knew it did nothing to assuage the guilt he felt. "You didn't know that would be the last conversation between the two of you. And let's not even go there. Gary is tough. We have to believe he will wake up and recover. Maybe he won't be able to perform surgery, but I have faith you'll have another chance at a conversation with him."

Kumar finished his sandwich and, with some food in his belly, could concentrate better now. "You're right, and life moves on. I have to think about the practice, and so do you. My hand has improved, and I think I'll be able to operate by next Monday. So for the remainder of this week, let's work together to see patients in the office and round on the ones still here. I can do consults, and you can do H&Ps. If anyone needs surgery prior to next week, we'll turn them over to Dr. Welzer's group. I'll speak with him tomorrow."

"What about asking the hospital to hire a locum tenens cardiac surgeon for a six-month contract? You're going to need another surgeon. It can't just be you, with me assisting," Annette said. "And if surgeries have to be sent to other hospitals, they'll lose money. They won't want that." Kumar and Annette both knew the reality of the situation. One surgeon and a nurse practitioner in the operating room did not make an ideal situation. The best scenario involved two cardiothoracic surgeons and a nurse practitioner.

"I think that's what we'll do, Annette. I'll consult with the chief of surgery and administration tomorrow. I don't even know who's in charge now that Manning's gone. And I guess they're going to have to deal with the Brock lawsuit without Dr. T too."

"Yeah, but we'll have to testify, since we were there," Annette said. "But we know we didn't do anything wrong."

"I'm not looking forward to any of this," Kumar said. "Let's just hope for the best for Gary." They tried to put a positive spin on the situation for each other, but the prognosis didn't bode well.

~ Chapter 76 ~

He woke with a jolt in a pitch-black room. At two in the morning, Kumar's phone alerted him to a page from CSU. "Dr. Chanrami," he mumbled, half-asleep.

"It's Rosa, Dr. Chanrami. You wanted us to page you when Dr. T started to wake up."

"Yes, thank you, Rosa. How is he?"

"He's still on the vent, but he has spontaneous respirations. He might be able to be weaned off in the morning."

Kumar cringed as he asked the next question, but he had to know. "What about his neuro status? Is he able to move his extremities?"

"He's following commands, yes."

"That's great news," Kumar muttered. "Okay, Rosa. Thanks a lot for the update. Everyone else okay?" When she acknowledged that his patients were fine, he hung up and went back to sleep.

At six thirty, he woke up for the second time and decided he'd had enough sleep. He and Annette had worked out their schedules and switched roles. She'd see patients today in the office, and he'd make rounds and do consults at the hospital. He needed to arrange for surgery coverage, as they'd discussed the day before, and also check into the possibility of finding a locum tenens surgeon. With his family still asleep, he made quick work of showering and dressing before heading to the hospital. Orange hues of the rising sun began to emerge over the horizon, lighting up the dark sky just enough for Kumar to see the light traffic at this hour of the morning. Mindful of Tamarino's accident yesterday, he made it a point to drive defensively and took his time getting to the hospital.

He entered CSU and headed straight to Room 1 to see Dr. T. Arriving during shift report once again, he anticipated finding nurses in the room. Instead, he found Gary alone, positioned on his side with his face away from the door. "Gary, it's me. Kumar. Are you awake?" He moved closer to the bed to position himself in Gary's line of vision and reached out to touch his hand. "Gary, wake up."

As Gary turned his head toward the sound of his voice, Kumar observed some slight eyelid movement. A cough set off a momentary alarm on the vent, and Kumar noted the Diprivan had been decreased. The lowered medication dosage confirmed an attempt to wean Gary off mechanical ventilation—a positive shift in the right direction.

"Gary, squeeze my hand. Can you open your eyes?" Kumar stimulated Gary in the hopes he'd awaken more. He also prayed he'd see movement in Gary's extremities. The major concern with a possible spinal cord injury centered on paralysis, and he hoped Gary didn't have to suffer that fate.

After a few more minutes, he left the room to locate Gary's nurse so he could obtain more answers. Kumar always appreciated the opportunity to communicate with the CSU nurse assigned to the patient, since that nurse usually knew the latest and most accurate information. He located Matt, who proved to be a wealth of information. "I know you've been with Dr. T all night and are getting ready to go off shift. Do you think he has a good chance to get off the vent this morning?"

"No problem, Dr. Chanrami. Hopefully we'll be able to get him extubated soon, since he's breathing on his own and his blood gases look good. We'll turn the Diprivan completely off, and Respiratory Therapy will run the weaning parameters when they make their first rounds."

"That's good to hear, Matt. Thanks. Has the neurologist been in? I'm concerned about any injury to his spinal cord."

"I understand. In fact, yes, Neuro saw him around one in the morning. You know those guys. They're like vampires. They always like to make rounds in the middle of the night. He scheduled an MRI for today, once he's off the vent, of course. But I did see some slight movement of his extremities. He wiggled his toes on command just before I gave report, so that's a good sign."

Reassured by what he heard, Kumar closed his eyes and said a silent prayer of gratitude. "Oh, and did they ever make contact with his ex-wife? I believe she's his healthcare surrogate."

"I'm not sure on that one, Dr. Chanrami. I think they might have contacted her yesterday. Do you want me to look in his chart?"

"No need for that. I'll find out later. Thank you for everything you've done. Go home and get some well-deserved sleep."

Encouraged by Matt's report, Kumar rounded on his patients in CSU, wrote orders, and reviewed his list of the other inpatients he needed to see on Stepdown and in the rest of the hospital. Before he left the unit, he looked in on Gary one more time. "Hey, man, you got this. You're going to be okay." Kumar squeezed Gary's hand, and just before he let go, Gary offered a weak squeeze in return.

~ Chapter 77 ~

Alone in her apartment Tuesday afternoon, with no concrete schedule, Allison reflected on the past ten days. So much had happened, in both good ways and bad. She found it difficult to focus. Anxiety's far-reaching tentacles extended themselves in her vulnerable mind. She faced a choice.

Having traveled down this path before, she didn't relish doing it again. She opened an app on her phone and turned on some white noise, the kind that mimicked the sounds of ocean waves. She lay down in her bedroom with the blinds drawn and shut her eyes. By now she had learned to immerse herself into a space of tranquility as a way to remain focused and energized.

When Sean was killed two years ago, she'd lost her best friend and one true love. The overwhelming depression had left an emptiness she couldn't control. During the ensuing leave of absence, she had turned to meditation, a practice that encouraged her to clear her mind, control her breathing, and stay present. She took part in a meditation class taught by a spiritual master, who told her that practicing gratitude was the key to healing. She remembered his words. "Choose three things in your life for which you are most grateful." At first when she endured the depths of grief, she could find no reason to be thankful. But after repeated attempts and gentle nudging in a calm environment, she succeeded.

Today, after taking in three or four deep breaths and holding them before gently exhaling, she visualized what she appreciated most in her life. Her health came to mind as number one. She'd already come close to dying twice in her lifetime. The first time occurred when she was in her twenties and was involved in a high-speed collision in Florida. That experience provided the impetus for her choosing nursing as a career. The car accident during the recent earthquake was the second instance. Due to access to good medical treatment in both disasters, she'd survived and recovered.

Her career and lifestyle were the second reason to be grateful today. She liked her job, which also afforded her the means to live comfortably. And the third aspect of life that made her grateful, and perhaps the most significant, had to be her relationships with others — those people she considered friends . . . and more. She realized Mark meant more to her than anyone else, and for that, she was especially thankful.

Emphasizing gratitude for only three parts of her life clarified where her priorities needed to be. Suddenly, as if a light switch activated her brain, everything seemed clear, and she felt less stressed and overwhelmed. Whatever she couldn't control faded into the background, like some type of gestalt figure-ground image.

Her company's investigations into Manning would continue, and what had already been initiated regarding Tamarino's actions would likely continue through lawsuits and ethics probes. She'd set the processes in motion, but now she could let go of some of it.

Refreshed and invigorated, she left her apartment, opting for some exercise and fresh sea air. Her future may be in flux, but she knew things would work out. Her new mindset brought with it nurturing benefits.

Allison returned home just after 2:00, revitalized and optimistic. She looked forward to Mark's arrival later that evening and wanted to do some light housecleaning to get everything ready. When she heard her phone ping somewhere in the distance, she realized that she'd left home without it that morning. Surprisingly, she hadn't even missed it until that moment.

After a few minutes of searching, she located her phone in the bedroom. A pop-up notification informed her of a terrifying situation, and she froze. The AP News app announced breaking news: "Two dead after Alaska Airlines plane bursts into flames in emergency landing at Orlando International Airport." Panicked, Allison only got the headline, since the pop-up alert disappeared. *Oh no! Mark should be on board his flight by now. I hope to God this wasn't his plane.* With no communication from Mark, she searched AP News for the story and freaked as she read the details.

~ Chapter 78 ~

His throat burned every time he swallowed, and the mask covering his nose and mouth smelled like cheap plastic. The distinctive, harsh, chemical odor impeded his efforts to breathe, and he ripped off the mask. As his oxygen saturation dropped, he became even more restless and disoriented. The nursing staff, alerted by the alarms triggered on his bedside monitor, raced into his room and found an agitated Gary Tamarino.

"Dr. Tamarino, calm down. It's okay. You're in CSU, but you need to keep your oxygen mask on." Andre, Gary's primary nurse, tried to calm his patient as he reapplied the oxygen mask. "Good. Your oxygen saturation is back to ninety-seven percent now.

"Can you get me a nasal cannula, Josh? I'd like to see if he can do without the mask. He might tolerate that better." The PCT hurried off to comply with the instructions.

Gary's success in removing his own oxygen mask validated strength in his upper extremities. Once he settled down, he complied with his nurse's directions, and Andre evaluated his neurological status. "Dr. T, my name is Andre, and I'm your nurse today. Can you understand me?" Gary nodded his head. "Okay, Dr. T, I want you to squeeze my hands." Strength and movement seemed equal. "Wiggle your toes for me." Andre had to repeat this command but saw slight movement in both feet.

Josh returned with the nasal cannula, and Andre applied it after removing the mask. He dialed the flow to five liters per minute, while he explained why he replaced the mask with a more comfortable oxygen delivery method. Dr. T nodded. "Your throat's going to be sore for a day or so because of the tube, but it will get better. Can you tell me your name?"

In a weakened, raspy voice, he replied, "Gary. Gary Tamarino."

Andre smiled. "That's great, Dr. T. You're going to be okay, but it will be slow going for a while. You have a lot of injuries. Right now I just want you to relax and concentrate on your breathing."

Gary watched as Andre studied the cardiac monitor. "All your vital signs are within normal levels, so that's good." Andre updated the respiratory therapist on the oxygen changes, and she brought an incentive spirometer for Dr. T to begin deep breathing exercises to expand his lungs and prevent pneumonia.

The grogginess slowly waned, and Gary followed instructions. Until now, he'd never grasped the level of difficulty a patient experienced trying to breathe after surgery and trauma. The pain shot through his entire body like an arrow. It would have been much easier to give up and not have to try so hard. He'd never been in this position before, dependent on others to help him turn in his bed or try to sit up. He had to do whatever the nurses told him in order to get better. One thing for certain, he had no desire to cash it in yet.

"Hey, look at you, man," Kumar said as he walked into the room with a big smile on his face. "What a difference a few hours make. You were barely awake when I saw you earlier."

Gary attempted a weak smile and moved his hand in Kumar's direction. He didn't try to speak. "Your nurse gave me an update, and I'm happy to see you're alert and moving everything, Gary. It's great you're breathing on your own too."

Kumar stayed with him for fifteen minutes, filling the void with updates on their patients. "I'm going to let you get some rest, man, but I'll be back later. I'm in the hospital today, and Annette's taking care of the office." Before Kumar left, Gary made a gesture with his right hand, indicating he wanted to write something.

Kumar saw a piece of paper and a pencil on the bedside table and gave them to Gary. He watched his partner construct the letters in slow motion to spell one word: money. Gary pushed the paper toward Kumar and pointed to him.

"Money?" Kumar inquired. Gary nodded and pointed again, first to himself and then to Kumar. Kumar moved closer and looked into Gary's eyes. "Is this about the money we discussed?" Gary nodded. "Hey, man, don't worry about it. When you get better, we can talk about the money. It will wait."

Gary let out a sigh and extended his hand. With tears in his eyes, he looked up at Kumar and mouthed the words, "Thank you," while he squeezed his partner's hand.

Kumar squeezed back and said goodbye. "I'll be back, I promise."

~ Chapter 79 ~

Frantic to find out more about the airline disaster, Allison read every word from the brief AP News article.

> Two passengers are dead in an emergency landing in Orlando. Alaska Airlines flight 1305 from Orlando to San Francisco declared an emergency ten minutes after takeoff at 5:30 p.m. The aircraft blew an engine in midair, forcing a return to the airport for an emergency landing. On landing, the jetliner caught fire, and emergency vehicles responded immediately. All 149 passengers and eight crew were evacuated. 30 passengers were taken to local hospitals for evaluation and treatment of injuries. Two of them died from their injuries. Names have not been released, pending notification of next of kin.

Oh my God. She continued reading and then texted Mark again. A few minutes later, and still without replies, her fears escalated. She needed to find out if this airplane was, in fact, Mark's scheduled flight. She searched Google for nonstop flights from Orlando to San

Francisco. What she found confirmed her worst fears. Only one airline had a flight scheduled for an 8:00 p.m. arrival in San Francisco: Alaska Airlines.

With no word from Mark and helpless to do anything more, she attempted to calm herself down through meditation. She wanted to call him but opted against it, hoping he'd see the texts soon and contact her.

She glanced at the time. Four o'clock. 7 p.m. in Orlando. *Why haven't I heard from him?*

All of a sudden, her phone buzzed with a text message from Mark. *Thank God.* "Allison, I'm OK. First chance to contact you. Plane had engine failure. Returned to Orlando airport. Made emergency landing just before the plane caught fire. Scary. Evacuated. Nothing but chaos here. Trying to rebook. Lots of cancellations and passengers trying to do the same thing as me. I might not be back until tomorrow. I'll call you once I've managed to schedule a flight."

Allison stared at the message, rereading it over and over. In shock and only mildly relieved, she texted him back. "I've been so worried ever since I heard the news. I'm so glad you're all right. I'll be waiting for your call." Her stress level on the decline, but not alleviated, she allowed herself to relax a little. *What are the odds? First an earthquake and now a plane crash? And in a matter of weeks.* She calmed herself with the knowledge that Mark had survived.

To avoid obsessing more about him, Allison turned her attention to her business. Before Mark left for Orlando, they'd made a list of loose ends related to Manning and Tamarino. She pulled up the document on her phone and reviewed the details. Because she had personally cared for the CSU patients involved in these situations, she had allocated much more of her energy than normal toward overseeing the investigations. She knew she didn't need to stay so involved, and she had been mulling over her options. Not maintaining such a hands-on approach might be best.

With a clear mind, she made a decision and texted Sherry. She explained her intent to step away for a while and offered Sherry a more expansive role. "Just consider it. I'd be honored if you'd take over as president of Critical Cover-Up, and I'd remain as a consultant. We can discuss the details later, if you agree."

Now her thoughts wandered toward Dr. T, and she struggled with mixed emotions. A desire to speak with him and confront him in person continued to burn inside her, and she texted Annette to ask her opinion "Hi. Can you talk for five minutes?"

Annette didn't reply immediately, and the delay gave her time to evaluate her reasons for wanting to visit Tamarino.

Five minutes later, Allison's phone rang. "Thanks for calling, Annette. I know you're busy."

"Yes, I was seeing patients, but I have a little time now."

"I wondered about Dr. T. Do you have an update?"

"I haven't spoken with Kumar since earlier in the day. Gary's off the vent and is awake, but still a bit groggy. He's following commands and moving everything. I was holding my breath, worrying he might be paralyzed, so I'm relieved he's moving all extremities. That's a huge plus, but he has a long way to go."

"I had considered coming to the hospital to see him, but under these circumstances there probably isn't much point."

"Well, he's barely aware of his surroundings. In fact, Kumar and I are making arrangements for another surgeon, because we know Gary will be out for an extended period of time. At least six months. And who knows how his recovery will go? He may not ever be able to operate again. It's too soon to make that assumption, but it's definitely a possible outcome. I agree, Allison. Now is not the time for a visit from you." Allison ended the call with a lump in her throat and close to tears. The information Annette shared finally ended her wavering on a confrontation with Dr. Tamarino.

~ Chapter 80 ~

Grateful his injured hand appeared to be healing, Dr. Chanrami hoped to be back in the operating room by the first of next week. On Wednesdays the office didn't open until the afternoon, so Kumar utilized the time to check on Gary.

He waltzed into Room 1 to find his partner much more awake and lucid and sitting almost upright in bed. "Hey, look at you," Kumar said, grinning from ear to ear. "They say you can't keep a good man down, and I guess you're proof of that. How's it going?"

Gary responded with a half smile. "I'm told I'm doing better than expected, but what do I know? I'm just the patient."

Thrilled to find him in such good spirits, Kumar pulled a chair close to the bedside so he could sit with Gary. "You almost look normal, dude," he said with a laugh. "It's good to see you alert and talking. Annette and I were really worried about you."

Gary's smile disappeared. In a low, monotone voice, he admitted a revealing truth. "I'm glad somebody cared enough to be worried. My ex never even showed up."

"Really? What happened?"

"Rosa told me they informed her as soon as they could get in touch. She thanked them for the update and hung up. After that, they never heard from her."

"Oh wow, Gary, that's brutal. You always told me how mean she could be." Kumar shook his head. "But look on the bright side. She's not here trying to run your life. Instead, you've got me." They both laughed.

"Kumar, I appreciate what you've done, really I do. I didn't treat you well, and you did nothing to deserve the brunt of my wrath. I apologize. And oh, by the way, I have good news."

"I'm all for good news. What is it?"

Gary reached for his cell phone on the bedside table. "I'm amazed this still works. It got banged up quite a bit in the crash." Then he looked intensely into Kumar's eyes. "You know, the police were here to question me early this morning. I don't remember anything about the accident, but they told me the driver of the other car, an SUV, died at the hospital. I guess he merged into my lane, causing the collision. I never saw him."

"Then I assume you weren't cited?" Kumar asked.

"Not as far as I know. They said I'm not at fault."

"Thank goodness for that. You've had enough problems lately, Gary. So, tell me about that good news you were about to share."

"I'll show you in a minute." Gary opened an app on his phone. "Okay, are you ready for this?" He directed Kumar's attention to an online brokerage account and, specifically, to the transactions screen. "See these, Kumar? This is your money. I made these option trades the day of the accident, and I programmed them to sell once they reached a certain level. I had a feeling they were going to run up quickly, and I made a good call. I made enough money to pay you back." Kumar stared at the screen in silence.

"I'm going to deposit these funds back into the practice's account as soon as the transactions clear. You can take your half out anytime, if you wish."

Kumar scratched his head as he studied the figures on the screen. "Do you mean to tell me this example of financial wizardry is what put you in financial hell in the first place?"

"Sad to say, yes. This time I got lucky."

"But isn't this just like gambling? You could have lost it all again."

"You could say that. Listen, Kumar. I know I'm up shit creek. I've got ethics inquiries and a lawsuit, maybe more than one. Who knows? And the medical board is on my case. Believe me when I say I've not been an angel. I deserve whatever is coming. But all I want to do now is get better, and I want everything between you and me to be okay." He looked into Kumar's sensitive eyes and continued in an earnest tone. "My hope is to be able to operate again. I don't know how realistic that thought may be. It might never happen, but if it does, it's going to take a long time. I know I almost died, and I know I owe my life to the first responders and the trauma team in the ER. This hit me like a Mack truck, no pun intended. It's a wake-up call for sure."

"Gary, you're one of the most determined individuals I've ever known. Some people may call it stubborn, but if anyone can recover from this, you can." He apprised Gary of the plans to hire a locum tenens physician so he and Annette could continue to perform surgeries and manage the practice.

"You're a good person, Kumar."

Kumar reached for Gary's hand and squeezed it. "We're good, man."

~ Chapter 81 ~

It was just before seven o'clock when Mark finally called, and Allison answered on the first ring. "How are you? I haven't been able to stop thinking about you. Where are you?"

"I know. Just to talk to you again is like a dream come true. I'm okay now, except for all the smoke exposure in the cabin and the scare when they announced the pilot had to make an emergency landing. Believe me, I never want to experience that scenario again."

"It must have been awful. I heard two people died. I'm just thankful you're okay."

"Everything happened so fast. We evacuated down those emergency exit chutes, and then there was a mad scramble to figure out how to get our flights rescheduled. I knew you weren't expecting me until later in the evening, so I just waited until I had some concrete answers. Eventually, the airline provided me with a room at the Hyatt inside the main terminal and a voucher for a meal. I just now checked in. I feel lucky I got booked for an early flight tomorrow morning. I can't wait to see you."

"I can't even imagine, Mark. I'm thrilled you'll be home soon. I'll be waiting for you."

When Mark asked Allison how she'd been, she updated him about Tamarino's accident and subsequent surgery and hospitalization. She shared the gist of her conversation with Sherry and her decision to relinquish control of her business. "I'm really having second thoughts about what's important in life, and I need to talk more about it with you in person. A phone conversation isn't sufficient, but I wanted to give you a heads-up."

"I get it, Allison. It's crazy how quickly things can change. Maybe it's a good thing. Listen, when we're together, just the two of us, we'll talk about everything, and I know we'll work it all out. Anyhow, it's been an exhausting day, and it's already late here, so I'm going to say good night. I have a 7:00 a.m. nonstop flight on Frontier, and I'm scheduled to arrive in San Francisco at 9:40. I'll call you when I land."

"Good night, Mark. See you soon." She smiled as she ended the call, and a calm settled on her. She knew everything was going to be all right.

Allison decided to give Sherry a call to confirm the changes at Critical Cover-Up one more time. "I'm so happy you accepted my proposal, Sherry. You know I have full confidence in your leadership abilities, and I have no need to play micromanager."

"Your encouragement means so much to me, Allison. You built this company, and I won't let you down."

"I'll have Ron Farley draw up the appropriate documents to make everything official, including a salary adjustment to match your new title. Just to satisfy my need to know, can you summarize the current status of the investigations one last time, Sherry?"

Sherry told her Critical Cover-Up continued the campaign against Ed Manning, ramping up the social media posts related to the whistleblower role in the Medicare fraud case. She added they were blasting out news about the sexual harassment scandal and subsequent lawsuit involving Nicole Santorum. "Both Nicole and Angela Rodrigues continue to keep this issue alive on their Facebook profiles."

"And what about Tamarino?"

Sherry hesitated before answering. "As much as we tried, the news had already been out, so there's plenty of trash talk about him on Twitter and Facebook. The relationship between Manning and Tamarino connected the two at the hip, and the news organizations have been running with Tamarino's questionable ethics violations. The abuse of power within the hospital got to be too big a story to quash. You could say it became the gift that kept on giving."

"Okay, Sherry, fair enough. Thank you for everything. You're doing the right thing." They talked by phone for twenty minutes, and Allison knew her decision to take a back seat in the business was the right one.

With mixed emotions, Allison concluded that Tamarino deserved the negative news. He created these problems for himself, and although his current situation initially garnered sympathy from Allison, she knew there were consequences for his actions. As she pondered Sherry's last words, a peacefulness surrounded Allison in a way she hadn't experienced in a long time.

~ Chapter 82 ~

She awoke to a dark room. The only hint of light emanated from a dim streetlamp below her window. Thoughts of Mark and his flight preoccupied her mind as she wondered about the time. She groped around in the dark for her phone on the nightstand. Six o'clock. Allison opened the Flightradar24 flight tracker app to check the status of the Frontier flight out of Orlando.

Good news. His flight took off on time, scheduled to land in San Francisco at 9:55 a.m., fifteen minutes late. Although this information pleased her, she wouldn't let go of her worry until the plane landed safely and she heard from Mark.

No longer sleepy, she got up and shuffled toward the kitchen. A few minutes later, she heard a loud meow and saw Snowball stretching her legs. "Snowball, you must have smelled the coffee. Are you hungry, little one?" In answer to her question, the cat meowed and rubbed up against Allison's leg in a plea for some early morning attention. Arching her back and turning around repeatedly, as if asking for more petting, Snowball seemed content, but Allison knew the next expectation involved food. Once she filled the cat bowl with wet food and gave her some fresh water, she knew Snowball would be content. Cats were such a source of joy, even though they were a bit mischievous sometimes. Their good traits definitely outweighed the bad.

***

At ten o'clock on the dot, Allison received a text from Mark. "Just landed. Still on the plane. I'll text you when I'm in an Uber. I'm excited to see you."

Elated, she replied, "Great to hear you made it. Let me know when you're on your way. Can't wait till you get here." She added a heart emoji. The anticipation of being with him again sparked immense joy.

Her phone pinged again with a text from Mark. He was in the Uber and on his way. Allison texted back three thumbs-up and a heart emoji. Earlier, she had walked to the green market to pick up some fresh fruit and cured meats and cheeses. She selected a bottle of California pinot noir and prepared an appetizing charcuterie board for the two of them. She guessed Mark could use a meal at home after his long trip, especially with all the complicating factors from the previous evening. She fantasized spending the rest of the day together inside the cozy studio apartment.

When Allison opened her apartment door and found Mark standing there, she had to fight back the tears that blurred her vision.

"I'm so happy you're home."

He surprised her with a bouquet of long-stemmed red roses carefully wrapped in pink tissue paper. He handed them to Allison as he walked inside. "You don't know how many times I wished I was here."

"They're beautiful. Thank you," she said. She put the flowers down, and they embraced like two lovers who hadn't seen each other in a long time. "I can't say it enough. I'm so glad you're here."

"I am too, Allison. So many things have happened in a short time. It's almost been too much to process."

"Make yourself comfortable. I know you must be tired. Give me a minute to find a vase for the flowers." He sat down on the sofa and asked about Snowball. "You know how cats are. She's probably hiding and will come out later. Are you hungry? I have food here for a light lunch."

"Maybe a bit later. I ate something on the flight, but I'll take some water, please."

She brought him a glass of water with lemon and ice, and he motioned for her to sit next to him. "First things first." He pulled her close to him and kissed her slowly. His tender kiss lingered, and time stood still. She closed her eyes and relinquished any need for control.

For the next two hours they talked almost nonstop, catching up on the details they'd missed over the past few days. Allison admitted to Mark that her life had reached a turning point. "I know I can't go back to the hospital here, and, frankly, I'm okay with it. I can afford not to work for a while. Between my business and book royalties, I have enough income to live on." She laughed and added, "Probably not in San Francisco though."

Mark told her his consulting work could continue on his own terms and timetable. "I'm at a critical juncture in my life too, Allison. I've even toyed with the thought of writing a book." The way he looked at her suggested he had something important to share. "I could live anywhere, Allison. You know I came out here just to be closer to you, to be with you. And now that we're together, I don't want to be apart again."

Her heart melted and her eyes moistened as she listened to his words. She wanted to be with Mark too, but needed direction in how to move forward. She had no commitments here and knew she could pick up and move. She didn't have to live in the same city in which her business was located. She looked up at him with love in her eyes. "When I'm with you, Mark, I feel so good, so happy. Nothing else matters. I'm not sure where we go from here."

"I'll tell you what," he said with a twinkle in his eyes. "I've devised a plan, and I think you're going to like it." He stood up and offered his hand to Allison. "But as I said before, first things first."

She made no effort to hide the grin on her face as he led her to the bedroom.

~ **Chapter 83** ~

Mark detected a sense of contentment and happiness, based on the glow radiating from Allison's face. "There's nowhere I'd rather be than right here with you, Allison."

Allison smiled and closed her eyes once more, enjoying this moment. "I love the way you make me feel." They lay together another fifteen minutes without uttering a word.

"I hate to spoil this, but I'm starving," Mark said as he rolled away from her.

Allison laughed. "I'm hungry too," she said. "You can help me in the kitchen."

They set the table, and Allison brought out the tray of meats and cheeses from the fridge. She handed Mark the bowl of cut fruit and a relish tray. He whistled in approval. "Very nice."

He poured two glasses of wine, and they toasted each other. Allison went first. "To the future."

Mark clinked his glass against hers and winked at her. With a flirtatious look, he said, "To *our* future." For the next hour, they satisfied their appetites while laughing and joking about silly, insignificant things.

"Okay, all kidding aside, you said you had a plan. I'm curious."

The moment he'd waited for had finally arrived. He'd played this story in his mind so many times. "Allison, what do you think about going to Italy together? I don't mean for ten days or two weeks. I'm thinking more like three months."

Allison's eyes brightened and words eluded her at first. She covered her mouth with her left hand, as she emitted a muffled gasp. With her right hand, she reached for Mark's arm. "Italy? I'd love it! But three months? How?"

Pleased she didn't say no, Mark explained. "US citizens can travel to Italy for up to ninety days without a visa. I thought we could fly into Florence and rent a villa in Tuscany. With that as our home base, we can explore the rolling hills of the wine country by car. And we can also take the train or fly anywhere else in Italy you'd like to visit."

Excited, Allison said, "It sounds like a once-in-a-lifetime trip, Mark. When did you want to go?"

"Well, we need a little time to plan the trip, but maybe in the spring. I was thinking April, May, and June."

Allison closed her eyes and didn't answer immediately. He envisioned her deciphering things out in her head. "Well, first, I'd have to figure out what to do with Snowball. My lease isn't up until August, so maybe I can sublet this place to someone who likes cats."

"I'm sure you'll be able to work it out, Allison, but I kind of like that idea. You know, I've already been to Italy, but it would be so much better to go with you." He looked into her eyes, hoping to find an answer.

Her smile widened. "You've made me an offer almost too good to believe. My answer is yes." She got up and walked over to his chair so she could wrap her arms around him and kiss him. She didn't hold back her enthusiasm. "Yes, yes, yes! We're going to Italy! I am thrilled beyond imagination. How can I ever thank you for this?"

Mark's face lit up with joy. "You just did, my dear Allison. And you never know, maybe we'll want to move there permanently."

"Anything is possible," she said, her eyes gleaming.

***

Four months later, Mark and Allison were finalizing the details of their travel plans for their upcoming Italy trip. They were both in the living room researching excursions and small tours on their laptops. "Hey, did I tell you the news?" Allison said. "Sherry said she'd keep Snowball while we're in Italy. It's great not having to leave her with a stranger."

"You mean the person you sublet the apartment to?"

"Right. I feel much more comfortable knowing Snowball will be in loving hands. And speaking of the apartment, I'm glad I found a person willing to commit with a good-sized deposit."

"Just one less thing to worry about," Mark said. Then he shut down his laptop and asked Allison to sit by him on the sofa. Once she got close to him, he reached for her hands and held them. If she had any doubts whether their relationship meant the same to Mark as it did to her, she soon found reassurance. He peered into the depths of her eyes. "Allison, I've fallen in love with you. I've wanted to tell you so many times, but I never had the courage."

She squeezed his hands and gazed at him, smiling through tears of joy. "I love you too, Mark. I didn't know if I could ever fall in love again, but now I believe it." She let her tears flow freely and held his hands even tighter. "I feel so close to you."

Mark shed a tear too. "It's like we belong together, Allison. I feel it deep inside. I didn't expect to find love again either. We both know what it's like to lose someone who loved us. I know what we have is real, and I can't imagine the rest of my life without you by my side. Will you marry me?"

Blinking back tears, Allison whispered, "Yes, yes, I've been hoping you would ask. I love you more than anything, and I'd be honored to be your wife." Mark took her into his arms and kissed her. This was the best day of his life.

~ Chapter 84 ~

Almost five months had passed since Allison initiated the investigation that exposed corruption at San Francisco Bay Hospital. Those days seemed like a lifetime ago. Still embroiled in lawsuits, the hospital no longer maintained its prestigious reputation as a top-level cardiovascular center.

She hadn't given much thought to Ed Manning, the former CEO who had been fired in the wake of a sexual harassment lawsuit. Sherry told her that he had dropped out of sight, and rumors swirled that he'd left his family and moved out of state. Speculation abounded as to whether he went alone or with another woman. Allison found it odd how the onetime powerful administrator had faded into the woodwork.

Some time ago, she had heard the hospital settled the discrimination lawsuit filed by an attorney for Nicole Santorum. Because wrongful termination was tacked onto the original suit, her settlement skyrocketed to $1.2 million. *Good for her. I'm glad my company played a part in that.*

With Sherry Dolan at the helm, Critical Cover-Up continued to enjoy financial success and growth, doubling its number of employees to twenty. Allison took great pleasure in this accomplishment. She never realized, until now, the value of being a silent partner in a flourishing business, while allowing the focus of her life to shift elsewhere.

She didn't see her friend Rosa Perez so often anymore. The CSU night shift charge nurse became disillusioned with the corruptive practices at the hospital and resigned. She didn't know whether it was a coincidence or not, but Rosa accepted a similar position at UCSF Medical Center, in the same ICU where Angelina Rodrigues was employed. Allison made a mental note to call her friend one day.

The last time she spoke with Kumar he informed her that he and Gary had dissolved their cardiothoracic surgery practice and split the remaining proceeds. He joined Dr. Welzer's group as an associate, and Annette continued as an employee of the hospital, assisting the surgeons in the operating room and also at Dr. Welzer's practice. It all worked out okay.

From time to time, she had wondered about Dr. T and how he was recovering after the horrible accident. She heard he never fully recovered from his life-threatening injuries and had to give up any thought of operating again. Aside from his physical incapacities, the medical board disciplined him and suspended his license for various ethical violations. These included bribing Nicole Santorum for her silence about their relationship, not disclosing his visual impairments to the detriment of his patients, and his involvement related to kickbacks and falsification of records in the Medicare fraud scheme. She guessed these consequences were inevitable.

A few days earlier, while Allison was packing for Italy, a letter arrived for her with no return address. Her name and mailing address were handwritten on a plain, white, business envelope. Curious, she opened it. The note inside, handwritten as well, consisted of just four lines:

> Allison, I didn't get the chance to talk to you in person. I owe you an apology. I'm the reason your contract wasn't renewed. I'm sorry for whatever stress I caused you.
> Gary Tamarino

She stared at the note and read it again. She was stunned to hear from him, but what shocked her even more was the apology and unexpected admission of guilt. This was the last thing she ever would have expected from Dr. T. *Maybe a leopard can change its spots.* With mixed emotions, she took some comfort in reading the note.

***

Today Allison's thoughts were far removed from San Francisco Bay Hospital and the people who worked there. Settled in her seat next to Mark on a Lufthansa flight headed to Rome, she inched closer to him. As she admired the sparkling solitaire engagement ring on her left hand, Mark leaned close and kissed her cheek.

"I just can't stop looking at this ring," she whispered. "I can't believe—"

"You have a lifetime to look at it, my love, so believe. Just believe."

About the Author

An award-winning author, Margie Miklas is a recently retired critical care nurse, social media manager, and travel blogger. As a career critical care nurse with a specialty in cardiovascular nursing, Margie has experienced a wide range of changes in the world of healthcare. When she's not writing, she enjoys traveling to Italy, spending time with her family, and relaxing at the beach. She makes her home in Florida and is a member of the Florida Writers Association.

Contact Margie at margieeee49@gmail.com
Facebook
https://www.facebook.com/MargieMiklasAuthor
Twitter https://twitter.com/MargieMiklas
Instagram www.instagram.com/margiemiklas/
Follow her blog, *Margie in Italy*
https://margieinitaly.com

Thank you for reading *A Cure for Deceit*. If you enjoyed it and have the inclination, please consider writing a review for the author on Amazon.com, Goodreads and Barnes and Noble. It really does make a difference.

Also by Margie Miklas

Critical Cover-Up

My Amalfi Coast Love Affair

Colors of Naples and the Amalfi Coast

My Love Affair with Sicily

Memoirs of a Solo Traveler – My Love Affair with Italy

Made in the USA
Lexington, KY
29 October 2019